ALMOST PERFECT

Judi Curtin lives in Limerick with her husband and three children. A former primary-school teacher, she now writes full time and is the bestselling author of *Sorry, Walter* and *From Claire to Here*. Her first children's book, *Alice Next Door*, was published by O'Brien Press in 2005.

GW00418119

Also by Judi Curtin

Sorry, Walter
From Claire to Here
Alice Next Door

ALMOST PERFECT

JUDI CURTIN

TiVOLi

Tivoli
An imprint of Gill & Macmillan Ltd
Hume Avenue
Park West
Dublin 12
with associated companies throughout the world

www.gillmacmillan.ie

© Judi Curtin 2006
ISBN-13: 978 0 7171 4036 7
ISBN-10: 0 7171 4036 9

Print origination by Carole Lynch
Printed and bound by Nørhaven Paperback A/S, Denmark

*The paper used in this book is made from the wood pulp
of managed forests. For every tree felled, at least one tree
is planted, thereby renewing natural resources.*

A catalogue record is available for this book
from the British Library.

3 5 4 2 1

For Dan, Brian, Ellen and Annie

Warmest thanks to:
Mum, Dad, Mary, Derek, Declan, Eileen, Caroline, Martin, Kieran, David, Sarah, Eoin and Alison.

Dan's family (too numerous to name individually).

My agent Faith O'Grady.

Everyone at Tivoli and Gill & Macmillan, who gave me my first publishing opportunity, and then worked so hard on my three books. Special thanks to Alison, Aoileann, Tana, Dearbhaile and Chris. Apologies and thanks to anyone slaving away in the background, whom I never got to meet.

Kim for the title suggestions.

Ann for the red-cabbage story (we'll never know if it's true).

Michael for the soccer story (attentive readers may notice that this story was actually used in *Sorry, Walter* – I forgot to thank him then).

The booksellers who promoted my books so well, especially O'Mahony's, for the launches and the window displays.

Thanks too to Easons in Limerick for your continuing goodwill.

All my friends for your help, support and babysitting.

Chapter One

I have never really approved of First Holy Communion parties. First Holy Communion shouldn't be an occasion for hordes of opportunist friends to gather and engage in hideous excesses of eating and drinking.

First Holy Communion should be a religious occasion, I always used to think. And even though I've never been particularly religious, I found that sentiment to be a useful cop-out when my first child, Luke, donned a smart navy blazer and a pair of shoes that weren't runners for his first trek up the aisle of our local church. And later, when it came to the post-church celebrations, he was quite happy with his trip to the local bistro for pizza and chips, followed by an hour's bowling in the company of lots of other little boys in unsuitable outfits with shiny white rosettes on their lapels.

Things were slightly different when my little girl, Julie, was preparing for her big day. The parenting manuals suggest that prudent parents carefully choose exactly which battles they propose fighting with their sweet darlings. Unfortunately, no manual could prepare me for the guerrilla warfare that was the chosen method of attack by my astute little girl.

She picked her moment carefully. It was late on a Wednesday evening in March, after I had served up a particularly tasty boeuf bourgignon. I had a few glasses of good red wine on board, and my beloved husband Cormac was watching a 'crucially important' Champions League match. (I should mention, at this stage, that every match Cormac ever watched was 'crucially important', so perhaps this wasn't hugely significant.) Anyway, the end result was that neither of us was competent to make a decision. And Julie was probably banking on that fact when she smiled her best gap-toothed smile at us and said, 'Can I have a big party for my Communion?'

'Hmm?'

'What's that, love?'

She smiled at us again – a particularly sweet smile that she'd surely been practising in front of the mirror; a smile almost as bright as the one Orphan Annie wore when she was persuading Daddy Warbucks to adopt about a thousand grubby children from the orphanage. She repeated herself patiently. 'I said, can I have a party for my Communion?'

Just then, the team in red scored, prompting shrieks of delight from my supposedly grown-up husband. Julie nimbly stepped between him and the television, blocking his view of the slow-motion replay. Cormac shrieked one more time. I thought I could detect a touch of desperation in his voice, almost as if he wouldn't get a chance to see the goal five more times during the post-match analysis. He leapt from his seat and, clutching Julie by the shoulders (rather gently, I thought, considering the circumstances), lifted her aside.

The brave girl tried again. She was wasting her time with the smile this time, since it was clear that her father had eyes only for the handsome young men who were prancing around the Italian turf in fetching short pants. 'Dad, can I...?'

He kept his eyes firmly on the television screen. 'Yes, yes, whatever you want. Just go away, please. This goal could be crucially important.'

Julie looked at me, still sporting the smile, which by now was looking rather fixed and unnatural. I shrugged. The wine and the rich food had made me mellow, I was tired from the game of tennis I'd played earlier, and I didn't really care. After all, Communion was months away, so why worry about it now?

'Whatever.'

'Yay!'

Julie jumped up, punched the air, and raced out of the room. I poured myself another glass of wine, Cormac howled in anger at a player with a mop of blond hair tied up in a ponytail, and neither of us paid much attention to the busy sounds coming from the playroom.

Twenty minutes later, Julie reappeared with an alarmingly long list of names carefully printed onto an A4 sheet. Cormac and I spared each other an 'Isn't she so sweet?' smile and ignored her again, happy in the misguided thought that it would all be forgotten by the morning.

After dinner the next evening, Julie arrived into the kitchen with a bundle of party invitations fresh from the printer. When I saw that, as well as sporting appropriately tacky illustrations of bright yellow crosses and chalices and loaves of bread, they contained no misspellings, I knew she'd had help. (But what I didn't learn until much later was that big brother Luke had helped her in return for a promise of ten per cent of the Holy Communion

3

loot. Capitalism was alive and well and hiding under my own roof.) Resistance would have been futile.

And things sort of proceeded from there.

I smiled indulgently when Julie rummaged in my cookery books and pulled out the recipes for my failsafe sticky toffee pudding and the chicken dish with asparagus that I'd been cooking for about a hundred years.

When she produced the Golden Pages, conveniently opened at the bouncy-castle page, during half-time in another 'crucially important' match, Cormac obediently dialled the number indicated by his daughter's less-than-clean finger. Minutes later, as he read the line of digits from the credit card that Julie had obligingly placed in his hand, he found himself committing to pay for a huge, bloated, red-and-yellow monstrosity that was rather too big for our small suburban garden.

There was to be no going back.

So, despite our singular lack of enthusiasm, when the third Saturday in May rolled around, Cormac and I found ourselves presiding over a garden full of screeching children and drunken adults, all fighting for their turns on the biggest and bounciest castle Limerick had ever seen.

Julie's pretty white Communion dress was in a dirty heap on her bedroom floor. It had been removed hours earlier, to be replaced by a ragged old polyester tracksuit. I tried not to dwell on the fact that the dress, which she'd worn for about ninety minutes, had cost more than any item of clothing I myself had ever owned (including my wedding dress). Her little white silk-covered shoes stood outside the back door, hastily abandoned in her rush to be first onto the bouncy castle. The delicate silk ribbon that had been carefully plaited through her hair that morning now hung from the highest branch of our only apple tree, swaying in the gentle breeze.

Cormac's eighty-year-old Uncle Tom was swaying too, as he leaned against the apple tree and sang rebel songs at the top of his very bad voice.

The failsafe chicken dish had failed for the first time ever, because some idiot had turned up the oven in an effort to get the food served quicker, leading the sauce to first separate and then dry up before the chicken turned a nasty dark brown, not unlike the colour of Uncle Tom's badly dyed hair.

At around seven o'clock, I took a moment to look around my trashed house. How could I have allowed this to happen? It was like the closing scenes of a cheap disaster movie. All we needed was a strong-jawed man called Jack, in an artfully ripped snow-white shirt, to come and tell us that we should be glad we had survived, and that we could rebuild a newer and better place for our children.

Luke was sitting on the floor in the middle of the family room, with his knee-length black leather coat spread out around him like a puddle of tar. He was holding his electric guitar in his arms as if it were an oversized, shiny, red baby, and he was determinedly plucking at the same string, over and over and over again.

Cormac was watching him from the other side of the room. Cormac hated Luke's guitar with a passion, and if he had had his way, both of them would have been banished to the garage. It was one of the many sources of ongoing conflict between my husband and son. I went over to Luke and crouched by his side. He could be touchy at the best of times, and I didn't want to prompt a scene, but I had to do something. Before Cormac waded in.

I put on my best non-confrontational voice. 'Er, Luke, love…maybe that's not the most considerate thing you've ever done.'

He kept playing. 'What isn't?'

I nodded towards the guitar. 'That. You know, maybe it's not polite to inflict that on oldies like us.'

He gave me a slow smile, revealing his teeth in all their hideously expensive metal-clad glory. '*I'm* not polite? It's not me, Mum. Wake up and smell the alcohol.'

I looked around the room. Uncle Tom was by now asleep on the couch, snoring loudly. His shirt was unbuttoned, revealing a huge, hairy stomach the colour of white cheddar cheese. He'd kicked off his shoes, and the smell of aged feet and mothballs drifted around the room. His socks needed darning, and I felt a moment's pity, because his recently deceased wife would never have allowed that situation to arise.

My mum was sitting in the corner, knitting busily, as if she were at home in front of her own fire. Maybe I should persuade her to remove Uncle Tom's socks and darn them for him.

I didn't dare to think where my dad had got to. He didn't get out much, and he tended to lose the run of himself when he did. Last time I'd seen him, he had been in the garden, doing the tango with my friend Rita.

Two of my elderly aunties were shakily refilling their glasses yet again, leaving deep purple stains on my best (OK, my only) white linen tablecloth. I could hear a child throwing a loud, shrieking tantrum in the hallway. I looked through the open door to the utility room and saw someone's granny vomiting into the sink. An old man I didn't recognise was rubbing her back gently and murmuring, 'That's it, love. Let it go. Better out than in.'

Through the kitchen window I could see one of my supposedly respectable neighbours swaying gently as he urinated at length on my bergenias.

I looked at Cormac again. He took a step towards us, but just then he was distracted by the sound of breaking glass coming from the kitchen. Luke gave me an almost sympathetic smile and moved one finger half an inch to the left, to begin a lengthy strumming of a slightly different chord.

The only good part was that, by eleven o'clock, everyone had gone home, the drunk ones protesting loudly as they were dragged towards the door by the rather-less-drunk ones.

I went into the garden for a last look around. I checked the bouncy castle for sleeping grannies and pulled the plug on it, smiling as it deflated slowly. I knew how it felt. It had been a long day for both of us.

I found Julie in the playroom, clutching a giant-sized bottle of Coke in one hand and her Communion bag, stuffed with money, in the other. She was watching a most unsuitable movie on the television.

'Come on, young lady, bedtime.'

She clung tighter to her treasures. 'No, it's my Communion. I can stay up as late as I like. You said.'

I smiled to disarm her. 'Well, OK. Maybe I did say that. But you'll have to pay me to let you stay up. Ten euro an hour.'

She scrambled to her feet. 'No way. I need all my money to buy a picture phone.' She was only getting a picture phone if I died during the night, but I felt that argument was best left for the morning. (Just in case I did die – I wouldn't like to think the fight would be wasted.)

I bundled her towards her bed, warned Luke not to stay up too late, and made my way slowly upstairs.

The light in the boxroom was on. I pushed the door open and slipped inside. My sister Deirdre was tucked up in bed, with a glass and a half-empty bottle of wine on the table next to her.

She grinned at me, and I could see that she too was a little the worse for wear. She patted the bed beside her. 'Come on, Sis. Sit down and let's empty our souls. Let's do some sisterly bonding.'

I sighed. Clearly she was more drunk than I had imagined. She'd never in all her life called me 'Sis', and she hadn't confided in me since she was about six years of age, when she told me she loved the skinny, swotty boy who lived down the road. Still, we hardly ever saw each other these days, and a chat, even a drunken one, would be nice. I sat beside her and took a sip of her wine.

She grinned again. 'Great party, Sis. Well done.'

I smiled before she continued, 'No thanks to Cormac, of course.'

My smile faded. Deirdre had never been overly fond of my husband. I had to defend him. 'Cormac helped too.'

Deirdre sat up. Drink always made her argumentative. 'Tell me, then, Sis: what exactly did he do? How did your precious Cormac help with the preparations?'

I sighed again. 'OK, I'll tell you, but only if you promise to stop calling me "Sis".'

Deirdre nodded and swigged her wine.

I tried to think what exactly Cormac had done to help for the party. Suddenly, inspiration came to me. 'Oh, I know – he booked the bouncy castle.'

Deirdre swigged again. 'Oh, big deal. And what else did he do?'

I thought long and hard. I drank some wine and thought some more – to no avail.

'Ha. I knew it,' Deirdre said. 'You did everything, as usual, didn't you?'

I couldn't argue, because she was right.

She continued, 'Cormac sat in his fancy office and sold a few typewriters, and you did all the real work here.'

I had to laugh. Deirdre delighted in calling Cormac's prosperous office-supplies centre a typewriter shop.

'Well…' I began.

'Well, what? I'm telling you, Jill, you've married Neanderthal Man. He's been selling machines for so long that now he's become one.'

Deirdre giggled happily at her own wit. She was now on her favourite topic, but I was too tired to try to deflect her.

'He works, and he watches football, and that's it. What kind of a life is that?'

'But he loves us.' It was a weak reply, but the best I could manage.

'So? He works a twelve-hour day, and shows up for an hour or two in the evening. He barks at Luke, pats Julie on the head and graciously allows you to serve him his dinner and wash up afterwards. What a man!'

'But he's a good provider.' Another weak reply. It was received with a huge, scornful laugh.

'Ha. A good provider. I love it. Tell me, sister dear, which century exactly is it you're living in? You don't need a provider. You're a bright girl. If necessary, you could provide perfectly well for yourself. Come on, Jill. Surely you want more from life than this?'

I couldn't disagree. What she said was kind of true. But things weren't as bad as that. Or were they? Had I become a desperate housewife without even noticing?

Deirdre saw my face. She put her hand over her mouth. 'Oops. I've said too much again, haven't I?'

I couldn't be cross. She looked just like a bold child. It was time to change the subject.

'Anyway, enough about my almost-perfect marriage. How are things with you?'

'Fine.' Her tone of voice implied exactly the opposite.

'Deirdre?'

She put down her glass. She gave a huge, very false yawn. Then she raised her arm and looked at an imaginary wristwatch. 'Oh, is that the time? I should be asleep by now. Turn off the light on your way out, won't you?' She snuggled under the covers and closed her eyes.

I shook my head impatiently. If there was an issue, Deirdre would only talk about it when she was good and ready. There was no point in trying to force her. Years of experience had taught me that.

I patted her shoulder. 'You can always talk to me, you know.'

She opened her eyes for a second. 'I know, Jill, thanks. Some other time, maybe.'

I knew that was the best I was going to get.

She grinned again. 'Now go. Surely your caveman needs his wench.'

It was the end of the conversation. I put out her light and left the room.

I went to the marital bedroom. The marital bed was already occupied by my beloved husband, who was snoring gently. He was still in his clothes, but I didn't dare to try removing them. Even in his sleepy state, I knew he'd get ideas if he woke up to find me fumbling with his trouser zip. And even though I wouldn't have minded a bit of a romp, I suspected that, in his condition, Cormac would fall asleep halfway through, and I had a fair idea that it would end up being a less-than-fulfilling experience for all concerned. So I pushed him to his side of the bed, as gently as I could, and slipped in beside him. I wriggled until I was comfy and closed my eyes. Peace at last.

But, tired as I was, sleep wouldn't oblige by casting its happy spell over me. I wriggled another bit and stretched my legs, but my mind was still too active to allow me to rest. Deirdre's words had hurt. OK, so my marriage wasn't perfect, but when was anyone ever promised perfection? And who was Deirdre to criticise, anyway? As far as I knew, she'd never been in a relationship that had lasted longer than a few weeks.

I gave a deep sigh and leaned towards my bedside radio. I checked that the volume was set to its lowest and switched on the power. I was rewarded with the sound of a male voice, speaking with an air of bored authority. How exciting – I'd tuned in just in time for the business news. I was stretching over to change the channel when my arm stopped in mid-air.

'...Dudley Adamson, who lived in Ireland for some time in the 80s, has been leading the Co-Rite corporation since 1994. Speaking from his home in Texas, Mr Adamson said he's very much looking forward to moving to Limerick and taking over the reins of Well Electronics. Next week he will be making a preliminary visit to the city, where it is expected he will address the employers' conference in the South Court Hotel. Meanwhile, in other business news...'

I flicked off the radio impatiently. Had I heard right? Had he said Dudley Adamson? Could there be another Dudley Adamson? Hardly likely; it wasn't a common name, especially in Cork, where it had stood out like a beacon of originality amongst all the Murphys and O'Sullivans and McCarthys. The first time we met, I actually thought he'd made it up, for a joke. Later, he showed me his passport, so I knew he wasn't joking. I used to tease him about it anyway. I said it was more like the name of a hero in a trashy romantic novel, or the star of a B-movie. He always laughed and said I was just jealous.

Even now, all these years later, it didn't sound like a name that could possibly belong to a real, live person.

More importantly, though, why did the mention of that name bother me so much? I was a mature woman, a fairly happily married mother of two, with my own house, car and cellulite. Dudley Adamson was just a distant memory from many, many years earlier. He was only a small part of my past, and I hadn't thought of him in years. So he was moving to Limerick? Big deal. What was that to me?

I turned over and tried in vain to settle down. I tried to think of how sweet Julie had looked in her pretty white dress, as she walked up the aisle of the church with her school-friends. I tried to think of Luke, and how desperately he wanted to be cool and grown-up. I tried to think of Cormac, and how he had loved welcoming half the country into our house that day, and how he had chatted easily with all, making everyone feel for a moment that they were special and important guests at our gathering.

But, no matter what I did, the happy pictures of my family kept tiptoeing treacherously from my consciousness, to be replaced by faded images of the handsome young man who had breezed in and out of my life twenty years earlier.

Because of Dudley, I hid in my room for months singing along to 'Without You' until my throat was raw, until the neighbours were threatening to call the Guards, until my poor, long-suffering parents were contemplating checking into a home for the bewildered.

Because of Dudley, everything changed.

Chapter Two

Much, much later, I managed to fall asleep, and I dreamed strange, old dreams in which I was a student again. Next morning I slept until after eleven, and woke feeling tired and strangely disorientated. My restless tossing soon disturbed Cormac. He turned towards me and sleepily wrapped his arms around me. I cuddled into him, wondering why I had a vaguely guilty feeling, as if I had somehow betrayed him in my dreams of long ago.

After a while, I became aware of something hard pressing against my groin. I looked down. It was the large metal buckle of Cormac's belt.

He noticed it too. He gave a small groan. 'Oh, no. I'm still in my clothes. I haven't fallen asleep in my clothes since I was a student. Why didn't you wake me when you came up? Or you could at least have taken my trousers off.'

I giggled. 'I didn't want to be giving you ideas.'

He sighed. 'Well, thanks for your faith in me, but even I couldn't perform after all that drink. I must have put away gallons of that beer.'

I grinned. 'Maybe just a few.'

He looked towards the clock. 'Look at the time. Where are the kiddies? Are your folks up yet? Is Deirdre still here?'

'Well, the folks planned to go to eleven o'clock Mass, so I suppose they've left already. Judging by the sorry state of Deirdre last night, I'd say she's still in bed. And the kiddies are probably parked in front of the television watching something entirely suitable like *Pimp My Ride*.'

Cormac leapt from the bed with energy that was admirable, considering the state he'd been in when he'd first made contact with it.

He surveyed his filthy, wrinkled clothes. 'Hmm. Suppose I'd better change.'

I nodded. 'Might be a good idea. You don't want to frighten the children.'

He showered, dressed in cleaner clothes and set off for the shop, returning with rashers and sausages and eggs and newspapers. As he cremated the food, I half-heartedly stacked the dishwasher. This was an entirely unpleasant experience, as I first had to empty countless soggy cigarette butts from glasses and scrape mountains of sodden, half-eaten food from every plate. Crumpled serviettes were squashed into piles of uneaten desserts, and the sweet-stale smell of alcohol lingered over everything.

When breakfast had been burned almost beyond recognition, and I had filled a large bin-bag with soggy debris from the night before, I extricated the children from the television room, and the four of us sat at the kitchen table for a happy family breakfast.

Luke sat in the corner and looked as cool as he could. He picked at his food and then pushed it aside. Cormac eyed him angrily. 'Something wrong with your breakfast?'

We all knew there was something very seriously wrong with the breakfast. In fact, calling the greasy black scraps 'breakfast' was something of a misrepresentation. Luke, though, was the only one likely to mention this to his father.

I put a restraining hand on his arm. 'Luke ate earlier, didn't you, love?'

He looked at me coolly. I knew he was wondering whether he should go along with my lie or start yet another row. I smiled at him encouragingly. He smiled back. 'Sure. I had two huge bowls of cereal already. Otherwise I'd really be tucking in to this delicious food.'

I looked at Cormac. He had to know he was being wound up. He was out of touch with his son, but he wasn't stupid. Luckily he'd lost interest in the conversation after his own contribution, and was deep in the sports page of the newspaper. Another crisis averted.

Julie ignored her food and was busy counting out her hoard. She had almost five hundred euro, an obscene amount for an eight-year-old girl. She also had a phone catalogue, and she flicked happily through this, humming to herself as she mulled over the many choices.

After a while, I could take no more. I grabbed the catalogue from her, ran into the family room and rummaged until I found a battered and ancient toy catalogue. This I plonked on the table in front of my surprised-looking daughter.

'Here, Julie. Look at all the lovely toys.'

She gave me a withering look. 'Toys?'

'Yes, toys. You're eight years old. You're supposed to like toys.'

She looked at me carefully. Her birthday wasn't too far away, and she didn't want to cut off all of her options.

'Well, I do like toys, but I want a phone. Luke has a phone.'

Luke gave her a supercilious smile. 'Yeah, I have, but I didn't get it until I was thirteen.'

She shrugged. 'Well, times change. I'm getting mine this week.'

I thought for a moment of diving in and telling her exactly what I felt about her getting a phone. Then I got sense. I caught a glimpse of Cormac's peaky face as he turned the page of his newspaper, and it was hard to miss Luke's eager grin as he anticipated the unusual prospect of a row that didn't involve him. I spoke softly to Julie. 'Why don't we talk about that later? In the meantime, eat up your breakfast and look at the nice scooters.'

Clearly Julie wasn't able for a row either, so – to Luke's evident disappointment – she began to turn the pages of the toy catalogue, and breakfast continued in relative peace.

When we'd finished eating, I dragged myself from my seat to survey the rest of the damage. Every room in the house was trashed, and a glance out the window confirmed that the garden wasn't much better. I went outside to see just how bad it was. The bouncy castle was gone, with only a patch of flattened grass to suggest that it had ever been there. I sincerely hoped that the castle's owners had slipped in and reclaimed it while we were still in bed. The day before, I'd signed a hefty form without even pretending to read it. No doubt if the castle had been stolen by a gang of opportunistic yobbos, I'd be liable to pay for a replacement.

I cast my tired eyes around the rest of the garden. Everywhere I looked I could see bottles and cans and glasses. A single scarlet stiletto-heeled shoe was half-submerged in a flowerbed. One of the china plates my mother had given me for a wedding present rested precariously on the rim of a beer glass. At the back door there was a mound of cigarette butts, just next to a stash of empty wine bottles. I went to pick a bottle up, and pulled back in horror. Someone had found their way into the garage and helped themselves to the bottle of 1986 vintage wine that Cormac was saving for a mega-special occasion. (My funeral, hopefully, so I wouldn't be there when he discovered it was gone.) I looked around in a panic. There were a number of glasses, several of them with traces of red wine in the bottom, scattered on windowsills and pathways. Cormac would absolutely lose his reason if he found out what had happened.

Just then Luke came out with a black plastic bag.

'Here, Mum, chuck that in here. Dad's going to the bottle bank in a few minutes.'

I clung tighter to the bottle.

'Mum, what's the prob...?' I could see his eyes resting on the label of the bottle in my hand.

He whistled. 'Now that's a problem. I haven't heard any screaming this morning, so I suppose Dad doesn't know.'

'Of course he doesn't,' I hissed at him. 'He'll have a fit when he finds out.'

Luke nodded wisely. 'You're right. He will. I wonder how many typewriters he'd have to sell to buy another bottle like that.'

I gave him a cross look. 'Hey, no need for that kind of talk. I can see you've been chatting to your Auntie Deirdre.' Luke and Deirdre had always been the best of buddies. Sometimes I felt they enjoyed having a common enemy in Cormac.

Luke grinned at me. 'Maybe we have had a small chat. But anyway, leave Deirdre out of this. Let's get back to Dad. He's going to lose it completely. It'll be worse than the time Julie threw the remote control down the toilet. It'll be worse than the time I scraped his precious new car with my bike. It'll be worse than that awful time when...'

This really wasn't making me feel any better. 'I know, I know, I get the message. It'll be the worst thing ever. Now what are we going to do?'

I heard the front door open, and then Cormac's voice from the front garden. 'Hurry up with those bottles, Luke, I want to be back in time for the Arsenal match.'

Another minute and I knew he'd be out to see what was delaying us. Luke stepped into action. He took the bottle from me and threw it into the bottom of the bag. He winked at me. 'Don't worry, Mum. I'll make sure he doesn't see it.' Then he raced around the garden, gathering all the innocent bottles and flinging them into his bag, before rushing through the side gate to join his very impatient dad.

I sat down for a moment and put my head in my hands. I always seemed to be protecting Luke from Cormac. Now Luke was protecting me in return. Were all these silent conspiracies normal? I could remember a time when Cormac would have laughed at the idea of some drunken reveller getting into the garage and liberating a special bottle of wine. He'd have laughed and said, 'Easy come, easy go,' and promptly forgotten all about it.

How and when had he become so serious? When did his life become ruled by fancy cars and fine wine? When did he become someone who could feel real affection for a green glass bottle full of dark-red liquid?

Once, many years earlier, I had been the centre of Cormac's universe. Now I had been pushed aside. His business seemed to take most of his time and his energy, and I was no longer sure where exactly I fitted in. Had I become an accessory to his lifestyle, fitted in somewhere along with his soccer matches and his expensive aftershaves?

18

I got up and began to tidy up the garden. It was easier than thinking.

An hour later, when the men were back from the bottle bank, and the house was almost returned to its usual not-too-untidy state, and I was relaxing in the living room with a nice cup of tea, the doorbell rang. It was my mum and dad, who'd left the house long before anyone else was up. I knew their routine, though. They'd have gone to Mass, then they'd have gone for a long walk, followed by a pint in the local.

I grabbed Julie by the shoulders and spoke with as much authority as I could muster. 'Don't tell Granny and Granddad how much money you got, OK?'

She looked at me with innocent eyes. 'I can't tell a lie.'

I fixed her with a hard stare. 'Well, you know what? Lies aren't always bad. Did your teacher ever tell you about white lies?'

Julie put on her most pious face. It didn't suit her at all. 'She just said that lies will put a huge big black stain on my clean white soul. So I'm not telling any coloured lie at all – not even a white one. Not on the day after my Communion. I'd only have to go to confession again, and everyone would see me and they'd all think I was a very bad girl.'

I smiled at her. 'No, I suppose you can't tell a lie, but make sure you don't tell the truth either. You're a clever little girl. I know you'll think of something. And they're going back to Cork soon, so you'll manage fine.'

Mum and Dad came into the room and settled themselves on the sofa. Mum slipped off her left shoe and rubbed her big toe. I wondered how old you had to be before that kind of thing changed from being complete bad manners to being almost acceptable.

'Well, Jill, Dad and I came home to help you tidy up, but I see we're too late. We'll just have to help you eat the leftovers instead.'

'Sorry, Mum. Remember the chicken was so burnt yesterday? Well, this morning it was so awful-looking that Cormac threw it into the bin.'

Mum nodded. 'Well, now you mention it, it was a bit over-done, wasn't it? We'll have a cup of tea instead. Flick on the kettle, there's a love.'

I dragged myself up and went to put on the kettle. When I returned, Julie was sitting next to my dad, all innocent-looking. Well, Dad was innocent-looking, Julie was her usual inscrutable self.

He smiled at her. 'Tell me, Julie. Did you get a lot of money for your Communion?'

Mum tutted at him, but it was only a token tutting – the kind you could always expect from a granny. I could see she was dying to know too.

Julie looked to me for guidance. I gave her the fiercest look I could manage. Even though it wasn't my fault, my mum would somehow find a way to blame me for the riches that had been bestowed on my daughter the day before.

Julie took a deep breath. 'Well, I did get quite a bit of money, but I don't want to say how much. My teacher said Communion isn't about the money, so I don't want to talk about it. Oh, and thank you for the lovely prayer-book.'

Mum smiled at her, and I was glad she hadn't witnessed the way Julie had flicked through the pages in a vain search for a nice crisp blue banknote. 'Will I help you to read it later?'

Julie smiled and nodded, but as soon as my mother looked away, Julie flashed me a look that said, *You owe me – so get me out of this one.*

Just then, Cormac arrived in with a pot of tea and a lemon tart that I'd forgotten to serve the day before.

Mum sat back with her tea and tart. 'Any sign of Deirdre?'

I shook my head. 'I think she's still in bed.'

'Poor lamb. She's not used to late nights.'

Or to drinking gallons of red wine. I couldn't say this to Mum, of course. In her eyes, Deirdre was still a baby and always would be.

Deirdre is my only sibling, a year younger than me. When I was born, my parents thought I was the brightest creature who'd ever lived. Then Deirdre appeared and knocked that notion on the head. She was the most precocious toddler in the history of the world. And that was only the beginning.

She achieved the best Leaving Cert in the history of our school, and went on to collect a string of university degrees. Eventually, just when it was beginning to look as if she'd be a student forever, she was head-hunted by a huge multinational company based in London. I've no idea what she actually does for a living, but it's very high-powered and exceedingly well-paid. Still, though, no matter how hard I try, I can't feel jealous of Deirdre. For all her success at work, she's a disaster at personal relationships and never seems to be particularly happy. I wouldn't want her life.

Recently her employers had sent her back to Cork, to study for yet another degree. Mum and Dad figured it was because they were afraid she was getting too stressed and was in danger of burning out. (Clearly they watch too much American TV.) I figured they sent Deirdre home because, valuable though she must be to their company, she probably had them driven crazy with her sharp wit and her endless enthusiasm for her work. Everyone else probably just needed a break for a while. Anyway, after last night, I had a funny feeling that Deirdre was even more unhappy than usual. But if she wouldn't confide in me, what could I do?

After the tea and cake, Mum, having decided she'd exhausted all the food possibilities of my house, suggested to my dad that it was time to leave. 'We can stop in that little restaurant in Mallow and have their carvery lunch. I fancy a nice bit of beef.'

At the mention of lunch, Dad perked up. 'Now you're talking. Get Deirdre out of bed, and let's get on the road.'

I went upstairs to wake Deirdre. I shook her gently. 'Get up. Mum and Dad are leaving.'

She poked out her head from under the covers. 'Please, Jill, rescue me. My head is pounding. I couldn't face a drive with Mum and Dad. Dad will have some GAA match on the radio at full blast, and Mum will drive me insane by blessing herself any time he goes to overtake anyone.'

I grinned. 'They're stopping for lunch on the way.'

She groaned. 'Even worse. They'll eat every scrap and embarrass me by asking for seconds, and then they'll go on about how they were robbed, and how everything is so expensive, and how when they were first married they used to get grand meals for two and sixpence. Please, Jill, tell them I'll get a train down later.'

I did as she asked, and five minutes later, Mum and Dad were gone.

Shortly afterwards, Deirdre appeared. She had showered, and looked slightly better. Not much, though. Deirdre didn't believe in making a fuss about her appearance. Her hair was cropped short, and was showing signs of grey that she refused to cover up. She was dressed, as usual, in denim jeans and a loose cotton shirt. Perhaps she'd have been pretty if she made an effort. I had a funny feeling I'd never know.

She grabbed a quick breakfast, and then she too was ready to go. I offered to drive her to the station.

'Let's walk. I could do with the exercise.'

I was surprised. Deirdre never bothered with exercise. Still, I needed to get out of the house.

As we went out the front gate, Deirdre took my arm. 'Sorry about last night, Jill. I was way out of line.'

I shrugged. 'It's OK. I know it was the drink talking.'

She gave a sly smile. 'Well, *in vino veritas*. Isn't that what they say? If Cormac wants to let work rule his life, good for him. Just don't let it ruin yours too. You should be having more fun. You're getting old before your time. That's what I wanted to say last night, but I might have made a bit of a mess of it.'

I smiled. 'I'll think about it, OK?'

Luckily a sober Deirdre was a lot less argumentative than the one I'd had to deal with the night before, and she was happy with my half-answer.

We strolled along in silence for a while. Then the big sister in me came to the fore.

'What about you? How are things with you?'

The familiar closed look came over her face. 'I'm fine. I told you.'

I felt like shaking her. 'Deirdre, I'm your sister. If there's some-thing wrong, please tell me. Maybe I can help.'

Part of me wanted her to answer. Part of me wanted her to brush me off, so I wouldn't have to get involved. We walked along in silence. I had a feeling that Deirdre was struggling with herself. After a while, the tension became too much for me.

'Deirdre, just tell me. Please.'

She gave a long sigh. 'There's not really much to tell. It's just that...' She did her best to run her fingers through her shorn hair.

23

'It's just that…I don't know. There's nothing really wrong, and I'm not really unhappy. I'm just not terribly happy either.'

I felt relieved. That didn't sound so bad. I felt like that a lot of the time.

She continued, 'Maybe it's just being back home again, living with Mum and Dad. It's like I never left. It's like I'm a teenager again, and nothing has changed.'

I had to protest. 'But lots has changed. You've got your great job, and heaps of money, and you get to go back to college again.'

She shrugged. 'Big deal. I spend a year here, then I go back to London. Same job, same apartment, same old life.'

'But you love your job.'

'Do I? I'm not sure about that any more. There's no challenge left.'

'So get a new job.'

'That wouldn't help. My job is one of the best around. I just don't want my life to be all about my job. There has to be more.'

'You mean you want to be like me?'

Deirdre gave a sudden laugh. 'Well, maybe not that. But there must be something else. Some middle ground between Career Girl and Desperate Housewife.'

'Deirdre? Is…' It was difficult to know how to put this. 'Is there any romance in your life? Is that the problem?'

'No, there's no romance. But I'm not sure that's the problem anyway. I'm not lonely. Not really. I'm just fed up, I suppose.'

'Maybe you should move out from Mum and Dad's. Get your own place.'

'I'm looking. Maybe I'll just look harder and everything will be OK.'

She put her head down and began to walk faster. The conversation was over. She had told me all I was going to hear, and the matter was officially closed. We got to the station, and we hugged as she boarded the train, and she promised to come and visit again soon.

I walked home. I was tired. It was only afternoon, but already it felt as if I'd had a very long day.

When I got back, Cormac and I went into the family room and threw ourselves in front of the television. I rested my head on his shoulder, like I used to when we were first married. I knew he was really tired, as he wasn't flicking through trade magazines or threatening to go in to 'tie up some loose ends in the office'.

Not long afterwards, Luke and Julie joined us. There were a few low-key rows, but no one had enough energy for anything too serious. We watched two movies in a row, had some sandwiches, and then it was time for bed.

I snuggled next to Cormac, and was pleased with myself for spending the whole day without thinking of Dudley Adamson once.

Then I realised that congratulating myself for that was probably indicative of something.

I just wasn't quite sure what exactly that was.

Chapter Three

Cormac usually left for work at seven-thirty. He said he did this to avoid the traffic and to 'get a head start on the day'. Also, I knew it was a matter of honour for him to be seen to be at work before his main rival in the office-supplies business. Sometimes I suggested that he park his car outside the office overnight, in an effort to really spook the opposition, but for some reason he never took my suggestion seriously.

Lately I had had a funny feeling that his early departures were also motivated by the desire to miss the joys of early mornings in the company of his beloved offspring.

On this particular Monday morning, Cormac left extra early, shortly before seven, perhaps because he considered a whole weekend in the company of his family to be a form of slacking from his real job.

I snoozed for a while after he left, and then got up to face the day. First I called Julie, who did her best to drag me into bed with her. I escaped her clutches and went to beat on Luke's bedroom door, prompting a few sleepy grunts and a lot of aggravated rustling of bedclothes. Then I went downstairs, threw some bread in the toaster and legged it back up for my shower. When I was dressed, I checked on the children, to discover that, as usual, they had both gone back to sleep. Time for the rough stuff. I went into each room in turn and pulled the duvets from their sleepy bodies. Then I ran downstairs so I wouldn't have to listen to their aggrieved threats to phone Childline.

Ten minutes later, Julie arrived in the kitchen in her crumpled, filthy Communion dress. She looked like a child from a horror movie. Since she'd removed the dress almost as soon as we got home from the church on Saturday, I couldn't quite figure out how she'd managed to make such a mess of it.

'Julie, love, that dress is a disaster area. You can't wear it to school.'

'But I have to, Mum. There's photographs today. Remember we got a note?'

Now that she mentioned it, that did have a faint ring of familiarity to it. I sifted through the growth of paper that adorned the fridge. At last, under the takeaway-pizza menu, I found a note that, thankfully, requested that the children wear their Communion outfits to school on the following Monday. I waved it in her face.

'Look, it's next week, and at least I can get your dress cleaned so you'll look pretty.'

She wasn't impressed, and stomped upstairs with a very poor grace, returning three minutes later in her school uniform.

Meanwhile Luke was trying to convince me to spend the morning shopping for a computer.

'Mum, we need one. That old thing's a total dinosaur.'

Everything more than five minutes old was a dinosaur to him.

27

'No, it's not. It's only four years old.'

He gave me one of those irritating looks, managing to imply with one super-cool flick of his eyelashes that I too was a total dinosaur.

I looked back at him and found my eyes drawn to the wall on his left, where there hung one of his baby photographs. In it he's about seven months old, and he's grinning at the camera in all his gummy glory. As I gazed fondly at the photo, I had one of those all-too-brief experiences when, just for the tiniest moment, I could remember what it was like when he was a baby. I could remember how he used to sit on his little bouncing chair, contentedly chewing his fat toes. Whenever I walked into his line of vision, his whole body would go rigid with excitement (the only time I ever had such an effect on a member of the opposite sex). Then his pudgy little arms and legs would flail wildly, and he'd practically bounce himself out of his chair in his effort to get closer to me. He'd gurgle and laugh, and his eyes would shine with a joy that was really rather excessive considering that I'd left the room only seconds earlier.

I love Luke, and he probably loves me in his own adolescent kind of way. And I know I'm a good mother. In about twenty years' time (with enough of the right therapy), Luke might even realise that I was a good mother. But for now, I was the mother from hell, whose very existence was a constant source of embarrassment to my beloved only son.

'Hello? Earth calling Mum. Come in, please.'

I was cruelly dragged back to the present. I tore my eyes from the curly-haired angel in the photograph and settled them on the newer version – the lank-haired, accusatory boy in front of me.

'Sorry, love. What were you saying?'

'I was saying that a four-year-old computer is totally geriatric. It's almost like having no computer at all. Don't you appreciate how fast technology is moving?'

'Apparently not. And anyway, if you want a new computer so badly, why don't you buy a new one? You've still got most of your confirmation money in the bank.'

That quietened him. How had I managed to rear such mercenary children?

Unfortunately, it was only a brief lull. After a few bites of his heavily buttered toast, he bounced back again.

'I have a proposal for you. How about if I pay ten per cent? And I'll set it up, too, so that will save us at least a hundred euro. Those engineers are complete rip-off merchants.'

The one-sided discussion continued for the next ten minutes, until I chased him out of the car at the junction just near his school. He stood on the footpath and gave me his brightest smile, the one he was frugal with, saving it for times like this. 'Surprise me, Mum.'

He gave me a big wave and went to join his friends, slipping into the required slouch as he did so.

Then there was only the North Circular Road and the Shannon Bridge to contend with. Even though I drove my children to school, I felt an irrational anger at all the other doting mummies who did likewise. I sat in the long line of traffic and wondered for the seven billionth time why I hadn't sent Julie to the local national school. Eventually I made it onto the bridge, and it was time for my daily fit of fuming at the insolent drivers who insisted on driving in the left-hand lane, knowing that most of them would then cut across at the roundabout, slowing my lane even further. As I edged along, I spared a few moments to glare at the gas-guzzling drivers who spent their time driving around the well-paved city streets in four-wheel-drive vehicles designed for slightly more rugged terrain.

Still, even after all the drama of a normal school morning, I was back home shortly after nine. I liked that time of the day, especially on Mondays. It was nice to have the house to myself again after the busy weekend. I pottered around the kitchen, tidying and sweeping and listening to the morning chat on the radio. There was a woman on the show who'd just come back from a trek in the Andes. She was the first woman ever to have travelled a particular route, and she was now fundraising for an orphanage there, before returning to her job in Stockholm, researching cures for some rare but fatal childhood illness.

I sighed as I swept cornflakes from under the table. How could one woman achieve so much? I was a stay-at-home wife and mother who hadn't worked outside the home for fourteen years.

Still, I consoled myself, I was a good wife and mother, and surely that counted for something?

I was happy. Well, happy-ish, anyway. So why should I feel inadequate?

I shook those foolish thoughts out of my mind and set up the ironing board in the living room. Cormac had bought me the *Sopranos* boxed set for my birthday, and it was time for my weekly fix.

As I waited for the iron to heat up (rubbing my back, which I'd almost put out, carrying the huge basket of ironing from the utility room), I consoled myself with the thought that, if we all downed tools to go trekking in the Andes, it would become very crowded and about as exciting as a trip to the local Tesco.

Just as I was hanging up the last of Cormac's shirts, there was a ring at the door. I ran down, hoping it wasn't someone horrible. Luckily it was my friend Rita.

'Perfect timing. I've just finished the ironing. Come in and I'll put on the kettle.'

She followed me into the kitchen and sat at the kitchen counter. 'Jill, before you say anything, I have to apologise. Was I really dreadful at the party on Saturday?'

The sad truth was that she had made a complete show of herself. One of my most vivid memories of the night was of Rita trying to do forward rolls on the mucky grass, apparently forgetting that she was wearing a dress. The sight of her black lace knickers had sent one of the older neighbours into a fit of coughing that for a while threatened to floor him.

I lied, of course. 'No, you were fine.'

She looked at me doubtfully. 'I can't remember anything much after I fell out of the bouncy castle. Look what happened me.'

She pulled up her sleeve to reveal an impressive bruise all down one arm.

I flinched. 'Ouch.'

'Well, when it happened, I was so drunk I didn't feel the pain, and in the morning the pain in my head was so bad that it distracted me from everything else.'

I laughed. 'Now that you mention it, I suppose you did put a few drinks away, all right.'

'Please tell me the truth, though. Was I obnoxious? Did I offend anyone? I was completely out of it. Jim says I even went into the garage and helped myself to a bottle of your wine. Like I hadn't had enough of it already.'

So it had been Rita. Poor Rita – a rock of sense when she was sober, an irresponsible idiot when she had drink in. She'd die if she knew she'd taken Cormac's best wine.

Unfortunately, Rita wasn't a stupid woman.

'Er, Jill, I didn't take anything too good, did I? Was it expensive?'

Only about two hundred euros' worth.

I shook my head. 'Nah. It was nothing special.'

'Oh, no. I don't believe you. Please don't tell me. No, do tell me. I have to know. Was it good? The best? Tell me what it was and I'll replace it. Did Cormac get it in Mac's?'

Hardly. Cormac had bought that wine when we were visiting California three years earlier. It was the last of some special vintage in a tiny winery in Sonoma Valley. Only something like five barrels of it had been produced that year. After he paid an arm and a leg for it, he carried it home all wrapped up in cotton wool, like a pampered baby. I didn't mind him buying the wine so much. It just made me cross that he made such a fuss about it. Something in me resented the fact that the easy-going guy I married, the guy who once drank only Blue Nun and unashamedly liked it, had somehow changed into this pretentious wine snob.

Even so, telling Rita the truth would only make her feel bad, and there was nothing she could do to rectify the situation.

She wasn't giving up, though. 'Please tell me, Jill. I'd feel better.'

I looked her in the eye and spoke as sincerely as I could, considering I was telling a complete lie. 'Honestly, Rita, you did us a favour. You found a bottle of old plonk that Cormac was too snobby to serve to our guests. It was dreadful old stuff, and we're glad to be rid of it. It might even have gone off.'

'You're sure?'

I nodded, wondering when I'd got to be such a good liar. 'Yes, I'm sure.'

She looked relieved. 'Anyway, thanks for the party. I quite enjoyed it until I drank myself into oblivion. While I was still relatively sober, I met your sister Deirdre. She's nice. We had a great chat.'

'Lucky you. She drank too much as well, and we had a big row.'

'Oh, I'm sorry. What did you row about?'

'The usual stuff. She started giving me grief about Cormac. She thinks he's stuck in the Dark Ages and is dragging me back there with him. She thinks he's sucking all the joy from our lives.'

Rita leaned forward. 'And what do you think?'

'I don't know, really. Maybe she's not entirely off the mark. He is kind of obsessed with his work.'

Rita looked at me carefully. 'That's putting it mildly.'

Something in her tone made me feel I had to defend Cormac. 'He can't help it. It's his father's fault.'

She raised one eyebrow. 'Didn't his father die years ago?'

I nodded. 'Yeah. I never met him. By all accounts he was a total waster. He drank a lot. And he couldn't hold down a job. The family never had a penny, and they had to move around a lot.'

'I never knew that.'

'Well, Cormac doesn't like to talk about it much. He's very sensitive about it all. He didn't have a very happy childhood. The family probably suffered more than I'll ever know. His older sisters went to America as soon as they were old enough. They rarely come back.'

'And what about his mother?'

'Glenda? Before I met her, I imagined a glamorous, exotic kind of woman. In reality she was a bitter, broken-down old hag. When Cormac and I were first married she used to come and visit us. She was thin, and always kind of sick-looking. She used sit on a chair in the corner and hold on to her purse like someone was going to steal it from her. She used to think I was dreadfully extravagant because I served chicken mid-week, and because I bought soft pink toilet paper instead of that horrible shiny grey stuff.'

'God, the poor thing. She must have been so unhappy.'

33

Typical Rita, feeling sorry for Glenda. The truth was, I always felt more sorry for myself, as I scrambled around frantically, hiding Luke's toys and deliberately dressing him in his shabbiest clothes when Glenda was due to visit.

I decided not to share that with Rita. She was too generous to understand that kind of thing. 'Yeah. She was a pity. Cormac used buy her stuff – you know, like nice clothes and things for her house. She didn't appreciate anything, though; to her it was all a waste. She had no capacity for happiness left.'

'What a way to end up.'

'Mmm. She died just over a year after Luke was born. She'd given him two bananas and an apple for his birthday present. I bitched about her all that day, and two days later she died of a heart attack. I know it sounds awful, but it was a relief to us all in the end. I think even Cormac was glad she was gone. Anyway, what I'm trying to say is, I think that's why Cormac works so hard. He wants to be everything his father wasn't. He wants to provide for us. And since the kids came along, he's even worse. He wants us to be secure.'

'And are you secure?'

'Yeah. We're fine. The business is great, but Cormac can't see it. He always wants to get one more big deal, one more huge order. He can't sit back and say, "I've done well." He always wants more.'

'I suppose it's hard to blame him, in the circumstances.'

I sighed. 'Oh, I know. I don't blame him, exactly. He says he's doing it all for the kids, and he is, I suppose. But he can't see that they suffer too. They have food on the table, and all of life's material luxuries, but they'd like to see more of him. They don't care about his bank balance, they just want a dad who's there when they need him.'

34

Rita patted my arm. 'They have a good mum.'

I shrugged. 'Maybe. I think the problem is that I've kind of slipped into a rut too. Maybe I'm just playing at Happy Families. Cormac is the big wage-earner, and I'm the little wifey who stays home and keeps house.'

Rita laughed. 'Hey, it might not be perfect, but that's how half the world lives. And the other half probably dreams of a life like that.'

'Maybe you're right. But I started out wanting more. I married for love, not security.'

'I've seen you together. Cormac still loves you.'

'You're probably right. I think he still loves me. He says he does. But I'm not sure if he *likes* me that much. Does that make sense?'

She nodded. 'I think so.'

'I don't think I'm special to him any more. I don't excite him like I used to, you know? When he brings me flowers, it's almost like a lifestyle thing, like something he read in a glossy magazine. It's always white lilies. He selects them because they're fashionable and expensive and because they go with the decor in the hall. And I still dream of the days when he used pick me bunches of wild buttercups, and hand them to me like he was giving me the Crown jewels. Or huge bunches of wild poppies that wilted after ten minutes, but it didn't matter, because they were only a trick so he could drag me into a ditch to have his wicked way with me.'

Rita laughed. 'Hey, we all dream of the good old days of our courtship.'

I laughed too. 'I know. It's just that lately I feel I might be missing out on something, that's all. I need some excitement. I need something to make me feel young again. Sometimes I think the most exciting part of my life is my weekly dose of *ER*. Oh, by the way, tell me what happened on *ER* last night; we went to bed early and missed it.'

And so I clumsily steered the conversation back to less contentious issues. Maybe some things were better left unsaid.

Next day, Rita arrived at the front door clutching a bag from the local off-licence. She held it out towards me. 'Here, Jill. No protests. I feel really bad about helping myself to your wine the other night. And even if it was only cheap stuff, I shouldn't have been so rude.'

I took the bag and peeped inside. There were two bottles of very nice French wine. A lovely present, but I couldn't help feeling that the cork from the bottle she had opened had probably cost more than the two bottles she'd just given me. Still, if the gift made Rita feel less guilty, that was something.

I smiled at her. 'You shouldn't have, but thanks.'

I put them on the kitchen counter, so I wouldn't forget to hide them before Cormac came home. He'd want to know why Rita was giving us wine. And, while I should have been brave enough to tell him that my dear friend had accidentally opened and drunk his precious Californian wine, I knew I wouldn't do it.

Not for the first time, I wondered why so much of family life involved hiding the truth from the people I was supposed to love so much.

Chapter Four

On Wednesday night, Rita called at around eight. Most Wednesdays the two of us went for a drink in the Davin Arms, a treat we felt we deserved after getting through half a week in the company of our beloved families.

I got into her car and strapped myself in. I gave a long, deep sigh. It was probably a bit sad that these weekly drinks with Rita seemed to have become the highlight of my life, something I actually found myself looking forward to for a day or two in advance.

'So how are things?'

I could feel Rita's frustration even before she answered. It was fizzing around and filling up all the fake-leather-scented air-space in her brand-new Ka.

'It's Fiona again. She's going to drive me to do something I'll regret.'

Fiona was her twelve-year-old daughter. I smiled. 'It's not that bad, surely?'

Rita nodded grimly. 'Oh, it is. You'll never believe what she's done now.'

'What?' I asked, sure that I'd believe anything of the precocious little strap.

'Without consulting anyone, she's packed up all of her belongings and moved into the spare room. She declared to us all over dinner that she needs her privacy, and that it's a crime against humanity to expect her to share a room with her ten-year-old sister. Jim's fit to kill her, so I have to defend her, even though I'd happily help him. I know exactly what's going to happen. The next time we have visitors there will be a huge scene, and poor Lisa will end up having to move out of her room. And Fiona will have won. Again.'

'Maybe you're misjudging her,' I said. I didn't believe that, but I was trying to think of a way of introducing the next subject without arousing Rita's healthy sense of curiosity. We were already on the North Circular Road, so I had to move quickly. Just as we approached Fort Mary Park, and Rita flicked on her indicator, I spoke quickly.

'Let's not go to the Davin tonight. We're always going there. Let's go somewhere else for a change.'

'OK.' Rita switched off the indicator and kept driving. 'How about the Woodfield? I hear they've done it up.'

I tried to sound casual. 'Nah. Let's go further. How about the South Court?'

Rita turned to look at me in surprise. 'Why the South Court, of all places?'

I shrugged. 'I hear it's lovely. It's been done up too, you know. And we're so boring, always going to the same place. Have we no imagination at all?'

Rita laughed. 'Hey, speak for yourself. I've got a great

38

imagination, and I plan to put it to good use devising wonderful punishments for Fiona. Anyway, I don't mind. The South Court is fine by me. I haven't been there in ages. And next week, when it's your turn to drive, I know a lovely little place just outside Nenagh.'

We both laughed, and we drove across town in an easy silence. I knew I hadn't fooled her for a moment.

When we got to the South Court, it was very busy and it took a while to find a parking space. Still, Rita didn't comment. She saved her attack until we were settled with our drinks in a corner of the lobby.

She took a long drink of her beer and fixed me with her fiercest look. 'OK, old friend. Time to tell me what's going on. Why are we drinking in the lobby of a hotel right at the other side of town from where we live? And don't give me any more of that crap about "we need a change". Just tell me the truth. It'll be easier that way.'

I thought of deflecting her one more time, but decided against it. I knew I'd only be fighting the inevitable. Rita was a great friend, but I often thought she'd learned a few interrogation techniques from the KGB. I always ended up telling her the truth, whether I wanted to or not.

I leaned forward and spoke quietly. 'All right. You've cracked me. But this is just between us, OK?'

She leaned towards me, so our heads were almost touching. I hoped the head-lice I'd caught from Julie the week before were cleared.

She spoke in a dramatic whisper. 'Whatever. Just tell me. I love it when you go all secretive.'

I wasn't sure that telling the truth to Rita was a very good idea, but I couldn't think of a halfway credible lie. I lowered my voice even further. 'Well, there's this guy I used to know in Cork, when I was a student. He's just got a big job in Limerick, and I think he's in this hotel tonight.'

Now I put it into words, it sounded really stupid. I was like a lovesick teenager. I was already sorry for having come.

Rita gave an evil, throaty cackle. 'Ha. I love it. *A guy you used to know.* Tell me, was that in the biblical sense?'

I blushed. 'Actually, it was.'

She laughed again. 'And you want to casually meet up with him, and get to *know* him again?'

'No!' I was horrified. How could Rita think that? 'No, not at all. That's not why we're here. I just thought it would be interesting to see him again. That's all.'

Rita looked at me through narrowed eyes. 'You know what? It's totally ridiculous, but I think I believe you. I think you're so sweet and innocent, that's all you really do want.'

'It is. I'm just curious. I want to see if the years have been kind to him, that's all.'

'Hmm.' Rita looked as if she had a lot more to say on the subject, but, to my relief, she decided to keep it to herself.

So we sat and enjoyed our drinks, and talked about light, noncontentious issues. And all the time I watched every door, wondering why on earth I was, at the age of thirty-nine, hanging around a hotel lobby, hoping for a glimpse of an ex-boyfriend I hadn't seen for almost twenty years.

An hour passed before my vigil was rewarded. There was a flurry of movement, and then a tide of smart-suited men washed into the lobby from the lifts. Everyone looked very businesslike, with their small black briefcases, and their name-tags pinned carefully to their lapels. Rita sat up and surveyed them.

She grabbed my arm. 'Look, is that him?' she hissed, indicating a good-looking man in a well-cut navy suit.

'No.' I was indignant. 'That guy's sixty if he's a day. How old do you think I am?'

'Sorry.' She didn't sound it. 'How about him? The guy wearing his dad's suit?'

The guy she indicated this time looked to be about fifteen years old. Rita was right – he looked as if he'd never worn a suit before, and his face was ravaged with active acne.

I shook my head. 'Give me a break.'

We watched for a while, but there was no sign of Dudley. I felt something that might have been disappointment, but I wasn't sure. I'd skipped dinner, and that always made me feel a bit strange. I picked up my drink. 'We might as well finish up and go home. He mustn't be here.'

Just then, the lift doors opened one more time, and Dudley stepped out. Even though I'd been expecting him to be there, I felt a sudden shock at the sight of him.

Rita saw my reaction. She sat back and folded her arms. 'Ha. So that's him. Not bad, not bad at all. You had good taste when you were a young one.'

She was right. Dudley had always been handsome, and he still was. Apart from the tiniest cluster of small lines around his eyes, and a few token grey hairs, he'd hardly changed at all. He was walking towards a group of men who were standing beside us.

'Quick,' Rita whispered. 'Get up. Talk to him. You said you needed some excitement in your life, and here it is.'

'No way.' I was embarrassed. 'All I wanted to do was see him. And I've done that. I've nothing to say to him.'

To my horror, I noticed that my palms were sweaty and my breath was shallow. I could feel my cheeks glowing in a way that could not possibly have been flattering. This was so pathetic it was beyond belief. If I had to be like a fifteen-year-old again, it

41

wasn't fair that I had to do it with the added inconvenience of cellulite, and stretch-marks, and wrinkles around my mouth.

Dudley was almost beside us, striding along in that confident way I remembered so well. Rita gave a huge false cough, and he looked in our direction. (So did everyone else in the lobby – Rita sounded as if she were dying.)

Dudley's grey eyes met mine for a moment. I smiled a nervous smile, hoping it didn't accentuate my wrinkles too much. What should I say? Should I shake his hand? Or was that too formal? Would a hug be too familiar? That might frighten him a bit – after all, it had been nearly twenty years. Casual would be best – a slow 'Hi, Dudley, what a nice surprise.' I swallowed hard and took a deep breath. I could do this.

Then, without any flicker of recognition, Dudley's eyes left mine and moved on to the group of people standing beside me. He held his hand out, ready to shake the hand of a tall man in a too-small grey suit.

'Shit.' As she said the word, Rita's glass fell to the tiled floor with a huge crash. Once again, all eyes in the lobby turned towards us – we really were turning into the life and soul of the party. I flinched as transparent golden beads of beer splattered my bare legs and dripped down towards my new beige shoes. I wondered if the beer would streak the fake tan I'd spent hours applying that morning. Would it react with the hair remover I'd used, and dissolve my skin? Would this non-encounter turn out to be even worse than it already appeared?

The few drops of beer that managed to miss me splattered the pure-wool-covered legs of the first love of my life. He turned, and didn't quite manage to hide the irritation in his beautiful grey eyes.

'What the...?'

Rita jumped to her feet and handed him a tissue. 'I'm so sorry. It's all my fault. How could I be so careless?'

Dudley looked as if he wondered that too, but he took the tissue and began to dab at his trousers. While he was distracted, Rita bent and whispered in my ear, 'You've got a choice. Either you say something or I will.'

I looked at her desperately. I knew she wasn't bluffing. After all, she'd already hurled her glass to the ground to get Dudley's attention. And I knew for sure that whatever she'd say would be a lot worse than any words I could form. So I stood up straight, smiled my best smile and said, 'Dudley, isn't it?'

Dudley stopped rubbing his trousers. He stood up straight and looked at me. I could see he was ready to smile in recognition, but unfortunately recognition didn't dawn. He furrowed his eyebrows slightly and gave a half-smile. I remembered that smile, and I wasn't sure I liked what it meant. I smiled again. He smiled a broader smile, but behind it I could see his confusion.

He held out his hand towards me. Had he no recollection at all of who I was, and what he had once done to me with that hand? Even the thought of it made me blush.

He spoke with practised charm. He was smoother than I remembered. 'I'm really sorry. I know I've met you somewhere before. Do you work in the Limerick plant? Did I meet you on the fact-finding mission?'

No. I was once the girl you enticed into the bushes in a lay-by in Bandon, and had joyful sex with as articulated lorries rattled past.

I smiled. What could I say to this man who had so successfully wiped me from his memory?

Suddenly he waved his finger at me, as if I were a particularly bold child, as if it were my fault he couldn't remember. 'Oh, I have it. Now I know who you are.'

43

At last. Still, it had been a long time, and no doubt I had changed. I could forgive him this lapse. 'Yes, it's...'

He interrupted me. 'No. You don't have to tell me. I know you. You're the receptionist in my hotel, aren't you?'

I could hear Rita catching her breath. This was too embarrassing for words. I had made a big deal of coming to see this guy, and now he didn't even remember me. This was a guy I had kissed and loved and adored, and now he was confusing me with the girl who handed him his bedroom key each evening and suggested that he have a good night. How sad was that?

I shook my head, unable to speak.

'You're not my receptionist?'

I shook my head again. If I had lost the ability to speak, was this going to deteriorate into a game of Twenty Questions?

Dudley didn't seem bothered by my silence. 'Gee, sorry about that. You look just like her.'

He was still holding out his hand towards me. I took it, because it seemed like the right thing to do. The sweat on my palms met the traces of beer on his. I smiled one more time, glad that the dentist had insisted on whitening my teeth on my last visit. 'It's Jill.'

Still nothing. Why couldn't I have been given a more memorable name, like Petronella, or Jasmine? How could he be expected to remember a boring old name like Jill? He continued to smile. He continued to shake my hand. Perhaps he hoped the repetitive movement would jog his memory and dislodge some recollection of the smiling imbecile in front of him.

'From Cork. UCC,' I added helpfully.

And then he remembered.

A small flush spread across his tanned cheeks, and his smile became rather less broad. He stopped shaking my hand.

'Jill, of course it's you. Forgive me, I've had a long day.'

He'd had a long day? Had he any idea how long it takes to get a streak-free tan on the backs of your legs?

'That's OK. It's been a long time.'

'Yes.' I knew he was calculating in his head. He'd always had a thing about numbers. Numbers weren't usually my thing, but this time I was with him. I knew that it was exactly nineteen years and eight months since I had last held this man's hand.

He continued, 'So, Jill, how've you been? Do you live in Limerick now?'

I nodded. 'Yes. I drink here in the South Court every week. Every Wednesday night, here I am, having a nice quiet drink with my friend.'

I knew Rita was making a face at me, from somewhere behind Dudley's shoulder, but I avoided her eyes and continued. 'Funny meeting you here.'

'Yes, isn't it?'

I've been involved in many inane conversations in my life, but surely this was the worst ever. This was worse than what you'd hear in the *Big Brother* house in the early hours of the morning. I was fervently wishing I were safe in the Davin Arms, where I belonged.

Just then a man hurried over to Dudley. 'Mr Adamson. We need you for a photograph.'

Dudley smiled at me again. 'Sorry, Jill, have to go. You know how it is. We should meet for a drink sometime. Catch up on old times.'

'Yes, we should.'

And then he was gone.

I picked up my bag and took Rita by the arm. 'Come on, let's get out of here.' She didn't argue.

45

When we got to the car, Rita was sympathetic. 'The horrible pig! He was so rude. How dare he not recognise you? His receptionist, indeed. How dare he?'

I pretended not to care. 'It's been a long time. Maybe I've changed.' I tried a small laugh. 'Maybe I'm like one of Cormac's wines, and I've improved with age.'

And then, to my absolute horror, I found I was fighting back tears.

Rita noticed at once, of course. She put her hand on my shoulder and squeezed it gently.

'Jill, what is it? What's going on here?'

I shook my head. 'I don't know, honestly. It's just...'

Rita was firm. 'Just what?'

'Well, you know. All I wanted from tonight was the novelty of meeting Dudley again. I thought perhaps we might have five minutes of shared bittersweet reminiscing. I wanted a bit of fun and excitement, and maybe a bit of a laugh, and all I got was total humiliation.'

Rita gave me a sympathetic smile. 'Come on, Jill. It's not that bad, is it?'

I shrugged. 'Maybe it is. You see, for better or worse, this guy was part of my past.'

'Forget the past. The past is a dangerous place. The only good thing about the past is that it's over.'

'But I can't help it. I've always been a sucker for nostalgia.'

Rita spoke firmly. 'Well, get over it. No smart woman wants to go romping around the remains of her own past. It's not healthy. Forget bloody Dudley. After all, looks like he's managed to forget you. And now you've got Cormac, and the kiddies.'

'I know. And they're great – most of the time. It's just kind of sad, though, when I realise that this guy, who meant so much to me once, has managed to wipe me almost entirely from his memory. And...'

I hesitated again.

Rita gave an exaggerated sigh. 'And what? Is there something else I need to know?'

I spoke softly. I'd never mentioned this to anyone before. 'Well, Dudley was my first real boyfriend. The first guy I really cared for. I was totally and madly in love with him. And when he finished things between us, I thought I was going to die. I made a total fool of myself. I cried and begged him to take me back. I told him I'd change, I told him I'd be anyone he wanted me to be. I told him I'd do anything he wanted me to do. He was kind. He didn't even laugh. But he left me anyway.'

'But we all did that.' Rita's voice was soothing. 'We all made fools of ourselves in the name of love. That's part of growing up. That's why we're so wise now. Because we've learned from our youthful mistakes.'

'I know. I know. It's just I've always regretted being such an eejit. And maybe that's why I wanted him to see me tonight. Maybe I wanted him to see that I've got on with my life. I wanted him to know that I'm all grown up. I can put fake tan on by myself, I'm still thin, I can drive around Limerick without getting lost. That's all. I just wanted him to know I've left him behind. That, despite early indications, he didn't ruin my life.'

Rita started the engine, apparently happy that I wasn't totally losing it. We drove in silence for a while. I was pensive now, no doubt partly because of the three drinks I'd put away so quickly.

'Don't you ever wish you could go back to your youth?' I asked as we arrived back on the North Circular.

Rita shuddered. 'No way. Once was enough for me. But why?' She took her eyes off the road, and we hit a speed ramp too fast.

47

Rita gritted her teeth. 'Well, I wouldn't mind going back ten seconds so I could slow down before hitting that ramp, but in general, no. I prefer the present. But why do you want to go back?' Her voice softened. 'Don't tell me you've got some dreadful skeletons.'

I laughed. 'No. Don't worry. There's nothing major back there. It's just when I was at college, I always felt I was one step behind everyone else. Everyone else seemed sophisticated, and wise, and I always felt I was struggling. I'd love to go back and get a chance to be like everyone else.'

Now Rita sounded seriously concerned. 'But, Jill, look at yourself. You're smart and funny and confident. What more do you want?'

I shrugged. 'I don't know, really. I worked hard to leave my inoffensive past behind. Now I'd love the chance to go back and show off. "Look at me. I've grown up at last."'

Rita laughed. 'I don't know if you're funny or a total saddo. And anyway, didn't you ever know the secret?'

'What secret?'

'Everyone was putting it on. Being young is a huge con job. It's not half it's cracked up to be. Don't you know everyone felt like you, but they were all pretending not to? Underneath the calm exteriors, everyone was shaking inside.'

'Yeah, right. Everyone except my old friend Linda.'

Rita sighed. 'Not her again. Not the perfect, wonderful Linda. I bet you're worth ten of her now. In fact, you probably always were.'

We were at my house. Rita stopped the car.

'Coffee?' I asked her.

She shook her head. 'No, thanks. I need a good night's sleep. I need all my strength to face Fiona in the morning.'

Suddenly I realised that, even though Rita was upset because of her wilful daughter, the whole evening had ended up being about me. 'God, Rita, I'm sorry. I went on a bit this evening, didn't I?'

She laughed. 'No, you're fine. Now just go to bed and dream of how wise and confident you are.'

I got out of the car and watched as she drove off. She was a good friend. Everyone needs lots of friends like Rita. Everyone needs friends who build you up, and encourage you and make you feel good about yourself.

So I'm not really sure why I reacted as I did when, out of the blue, my old friend Linda rang me.

Chapter Five

The phone call came the very next morning.

The rest of the family had gone about their important out-of-home lives, and I was spending part of my precious time on Earth sorting out the family's socks and knickers. (Once, when I was really bored, I tried to work out exactly how many items of clothing my family wore each week. But by the time I'd got to Tuesday it was time to hang out the washing, so I never got the right answer.)

I was at home on my own. On my own and defenceless. And then the phone rang. I was glad of the interruption, even if it was only someone trying to persuade me to sign up for a wonderful new telephone service. I dropped the socks I was holding and picked up the phone.

'Hello?'

'Jill.'

One word, one syllable, but it was enough to make me forget all about Julie's socks and knickers and sit up straight. I knew that voice. It was a voice I'd never forget. It was a voice that brought back all the fears and uncertainties and foolish moments and wild happiness of my distant and half-forgotten youth.

'Jill, are you there? Say something.'

'Yes, Linda, I'm here.'

'Hey. How are you? We haven't met up in ages. What's happening in your life? Tell me what's going on.'

I couldn't help smiling to myself. Linda still had the girlish enthusiasm I'd so loved when I was fourteen. Unfortunately, I wasn't quite so keen now. I'd outgrown Linda's enthusiasm about twenty years ago. Still, I didn't like to offend her, so I carefully matched one of Julie's pink socks with one of a slightly deeper shade, and settled in for a long chat.

Much, much later, the conversation was edging to a close.

Linda was as enthusiastic as ever. 'So you promise you won't change your mind?'

'Yes, honest, I promise.'

'Yeah, but you must keep your promise, even later on when your lovely sensible husband comes home from work and tries to change your mind.'

I hadn't seen her for a very long time, but she still knew me well. Maybe that was what scared me most about her.

'Yes, I promise I won't let Cormac talk me out of it.'

'Great. Just leave all the details to me. I'll get it sorted, and I'll ring you next week. It's going to be fantastic, I promise. And Cormac will love it too, you'll see.'

I was fairly sure he wouldn't, but once again the force of Linda's personality prevailed. 'Yes, I bet he will.'

'OK. Talk soon.'

'Bye.'

And we hung up.

I sat at the kitchen table and put my head in my hands. It was starting again. Once more, Linda was breezing into my life, and once more I wasn't strong enough to resist her.

I could still remember the first day we met. I was only ten years old. It was a sunny day in spring, and I was skipping on the path outside my house, when Linda appeared in the front garden of the house next door. The house had been empty for months, and until then I had thought it still was. It was almost as if Linda had appeared out of nowhere. One minute there was just the wild, overgrown garden, and the next minute she was standing in the middle of the weedy lawn, watching me with a half-smile on her face.

She was taller than me, with exotic-looking features and a wild mane of curly black hair tied up in a huge scarlet ribbon. She was wearing a long dress made up of layer after layer of brightly patterned cotton. Her skin was a deep gold colour and her eyes were almost black. Suddenly I felt dull and dowdy in the denim shorts and blue gingham shirt that I'd begged my mother to buy me only the week before.

I watched her for a moment, not sure what to say or do. If I'd been close enough, I would have reached out and touched her, just to see if she was really there.

She walked towards me. 'I'm Linda. We moved in last night. Won't you come in? My mum is making madeleines. You can have one.'

I smiled as if I knew what she was talking about. This was Cork in the 1970s. The most exotic cake I'd ever eaten was a chocolate slice from Thompson's bakery. I had no idea what madeleines were. If I were to get one, I didn't know if I should wear it, eat it or hang it on the wall. It didn't matter. I could figure it out when the time came.

I spent the afternoon in Linda's house. And though the madeleines were disappointing, a bit like my mum's buns when she was in a hurry and forgot to use baking powder, I convinced myself that they were the most wonderful things I had ever eaten. Because I was hooked. I loved Linda's exotic American mother, and her laid-back artist father, and I loved everything about Linda herself, who was to be my friend and leader for the next ten years. And suddenly all my former friends, who were nice quiet little girls like myself, seemed drab and boring and hardly worth the effort.

When Cormac came home from work that evening, I meant to tell him about Linda's call. Honest, I did. But he looked really tired. He was in the middle of a huge business deal, and it was occupying his every waking moment. (And, judging by the way he thrashed around in bed at night, it was invading a few of his dreams also.)

And Luke was droning on and on about changing the computer.

And Julie was once again proclaiming loudly and often that she was the only child in the Western world without a picture phone.

And so the opportunity passed.

Anyway, it didn't matter. I'd had time to think. I wasn't going to be bullied by Linda any more. I was thirty-nine years old, and it was about time I learned to stand up to her. I'd decided to ring her first thing in the morning and tell her that her fears were perfectly well-founded, and that I'd changed my mind and maybe I'd drop in to see her the next time I was in Cork.

Next morning, I got up full of good intentions, but before I got a chance to pick up the phone, Rita dropped in for coffee. She laughed when I told her about Linda's call. 'Ha. That's what you get for mentioning her the other night. She picked up the vibes and had to call you. You brought it upon yourself. And, anyway, is there any independent evidence of Linda's actual existence?'

'What do you mean?'

'Well, you often talk about her, but I suspect she's only an imaginary friend.'

I had to laugh. 'Of course she exists.'

'How come I've never met her, so?'

'Yes, you have. She was at our wedding.'

No one who was at our wedding could forget Linda. As I stood at the back of the church, ready for my big entrance, Linda entered through a side door – late, as usual. Everyone turned to see who had arrived, and then they kept looking when they saw her. She was wearing a cerise dress that looked as if it had been moulded onto her. She had killer shoes with six-inch heels, and her black curls were piled on her head in a picture of elegant sophistication. The organist had to play the intro to the wedding march twice, to get the crowd's attention back to me. And later on, Linda was the one leading the conga line when my cousin broke her ankle. Linda hadn't been organised enough to book into the hotel, but she spent the night curled up in a corner of the foyer, practically fighting off all the men who wanted to cover her with their jackets.

Rita interrupted my thoughts. 'I wasn't at your wedding, though. I didn't know you then.'

'Oh, yeah. That's right, you didn't. Well, Linda visited here a few years ago. She and her husband and their little girl stayed with us for the night. Remember, we went out to dinner. We ended up in Ted's. I think Linda got barred for dancing on the table and singing "If You Think I'm Sexy". Cormac wasn't impressed.'

Rita giggled. 'I bet he wasn't. I wasn't there, though. You invited me but I was in Kilkee, remember?'

'Oh, yeah. So you were.' I thought for a moment. 'So you've really never met her?'

'Nope.'

It was hard to imagine. Linda had been so much a part of my early life, and Rita was so much a part of my present, it was strange that they'd never overlapped.

Rita looked at me closely. 'Is there something wrong with her? Has she two heads?'

I laughed. 'No, there's nothing wrong with her. She's quite normal, actually. And she's nice, too. You'd like her.'

'So why aren't you friends any more? Did she break into your garage and drink all your expensive wine or something?'

I laughed. 'No, nothing as bad as that. Linda and I are friends. We're just friends who don't see each other any more. That's all.'

Rita laughed too. 'Anyway, if you don't see her any more, why was she ringing you all of a sudden?'

'She often rings me.'

This was true. Linda did ring every few months, and, while I was flattered by the fact that she made an effort to keep up contact, her calls always left me feeling rather tired and dispirited. Like I was missing out on something, but I wasn't quite sure what that was. I very rarely phoned her.

'So had she anything interesting to say for herself, this phantom friend?'

I told her, and she fell around laughing. 'That's a scream. What did you say? I suppose you said no.'

'Well, actually, I said yes. I couldn't resist her. She's very persuasive. She always was. It was part of her charm.'

'So you're going to do it, then?'

'No way. It would be mad. I'm going to ring her in a while and tell her I've changed my mind.'

'I don't suppose she'll be very pleased.'

'Well, no. She won't. But at least she'll be displeased sixty-five miles from here. I won't have to live with it.'

We chatted for a while longer, and then Rita got up to leave. I waved her off and went back inside. For some reason, tackling the kitchen floor seemed a more enticing prospect than making that call to Linda. I filled the bucket with hot, soapy, lemon-scented water. (Who ever decreed that kitchens are supposed to smell of lemon, and bathrooms are only clean if they smell of pine?) I plunged the mop into the bucket, squeezed it and swept it in a large arc across the floor. It was scary how different the clean bit looked. Just as I was squeezing the mop for the second time, the phone rang.

It was Linda.

'Hi, Linda.' I wondered if she could detect the trepidation in my voice. 'I was going to ring you. I—'

She interrupted me. 'Hey, Jill, great news. It's all booked. We were lucky, Max had to pull a few serious strings, but he got it sorted in the end. We got the last places. It's going to be the holiday of a lifetime. Anyway, gotta go. I'm at work. I'll ring you during the week with all the details. Bye.'

'Bye,' I echoed weakly.

I listened to the dial tone for a few minutes while I wondered how exactly I'd got myself into such a mess. Despite my best intentions, Linda had won again. She'd presented me with an idea that I was sure was totally ridiculous, and somehow, one more time, I'd been persuaded to go along with her.

I fished into my huge bank of memories of times when Linda had persuaded me to do something against my will. I remembered the time she wanted me to mitch from school and hitchhike to Crosshaven for the day. It was January, and I knew it was a totally stupid idea, and I refused point-blank. At first. But still, a few hours later I found myself standing on the side of the road in Carrigaline, frozen and totally fed up and trying to ignore Linda, who was dancing around next to me, saying, 'Isn't this such fun?'

One of the funny things about Linda was that she was totally transparent. Even back then, I always knew when she was bullying me. But that knowledge was never a whole lot of use to me. I invariably went along with her anyway.

Linda was the most charming bully in the history of the world.

Chapter Six

In bed that night, I decided it was time I shared the good news with Cormac.

He thought it was funny at first. In fact, he thought it was very funny indeed, until he realised I wasn't joking. Then his sense of humour seemed to fail him rather quickly.

'You what?'

'I agreed that we'd go on holidays with Linda and Max and their daughter.'

'Yeah, I got that bit. And that's bad enough. In fact, that's really very bad indeed. We both know that Linda's as mad as a hatter. I don't suppose that's changed since I saw her last. After being in the Locke with her that time, I didn't dare to go back in there for weeks, I was so ashamed. And that awful scene afterwards in Ted's – it was like something from a horror movie. If any of my customers had been there it could have been very embarrassing. Linda and Max were only here for one night, and afterwards I felt like I needed to check into a rest home.'

I tried to think back to the days when Cormac would have been up for a bit of fun himself, and might actually have joined in with Linda. The days when his only fear would have been of a bad headache in the morning, not that his business would suffer just because he let his hair down for a few hours. The days when he still had hair to let down.

Those days seemed very far away.

I spoke reassuringly. 'OK, so I admit that Linda was a bit out of line that night. But maybe you overreacted. And that was a few years ago. She's probably a bit less manic now.' I didn't believe this for a second.

It didn't matter. Cormac wasn't fooled anyway. 'Ha. Fat chance. That girl will be protesting on the way to her own funeral. I can hear her now: "Can we go to the pub first? I can't be dead, there's this party I want to go to."'

I had to laugh. Cormac didn't join in. He was just warming to his subject. 'And anyway, it's not just that family I object to. It's the holiday.'

'What about the holiday?' I knew exactly what he meant about the holiday, but felt it was prudent to pretend otherwise.

'It's everything about the holiday that I object to. Tell me you're joking about the exact holiday you've planned for your loving family. Just tell me it again. Look me in the eye and say those words without laughing.'

I hesitated.

He spoke triumphantly. 'See, you can't do it. I knew it. You couldn't say those words and keep a straight face.'

'Yes, I could.'

'Go on, so.'

I took a deep breath. 'Er, we're canoeing down the Dordogne.'

He looked at me with a rather glazed expression in his eyes.

'Yeah, that's the bit. That's the joke, isn't it?'

I shook my head. 'No, I'm not joking. I've never been more serious in my life.' No point letting him know that I too thought it a totally crazy idea.

'But you've never been in a canoe. I bet you don't even know what a canoe looks like. And the closest I've been is those pedal-boats in Marbella when I went away with the lads the summer before we got married. I know you're joking. Very funny, I'm sure. Now the joke's over, can we go to sleep?'

He reached for the overhead light, but I pulled his hand back. This had to be sorted, before we went to sleep and I lost my nerve again.

I spoke with a certainty I didn't feel. 'No, I'm not joking. It'll be fun. We stay in a different place every night. They even move our stuff from place to place for us. That's the plan.'

'Well, plans are made to be changed. I'm not spending a week canoeing down the bloody Dordogne with that dysfunctional shower from Cork.'

'Two weeks, actually.'

Then he really lost it. 'No way, Jill. Forget it. That's complete madness. That's not a holiday. There's no way I'm staying in a different hotel every night for two whole weeks.'

I hesitated. 'Er, actually, you won't be staying in a different hotel every night. Some nights you'll be staying in a tent.'

This time he was so excited he actually put down the sports supplement. 'I'm sorry, Jill. I know Linda is your friend, but it ain't going to happen. Don't you know how hard I work?'

Of course I bloody knew. 'Yes.'

'Well, I work like that for forty-eight weeks of the year. And when I take my precious few weeks off, I do *not* want to spend them hud-dled up in a canoe with your mad friends. It's settled. I'm not going.'

'But I've told Linda we'd go.'

'So tell her you've changed your mind.'

'I can't. She's my oldest friend. And she sounded really pleased when I said we'd go.'

'Well, no wonder. She's probably asked everyone else she knows, and been laughed off.'

'Come on, Cormac. That's not fair. It was nice of her to ask us.'

He gave a wry laugh. 'Yeah, I know. Very nice. You should send her a nice card to thank her for her consideration. Maybe even a nice bunch of lilies. With a polite little note. "Thanks, but no, thanks."'

'Please, Cormac, be reasonable.'

This time he laughed out loud. 'You want me to go canoeing for my holidays, and you're implying that I'm the one who's not reasonable? Hello?'

'But this is a great trip. Max knows a guy who knows the guy who organises it. Apparently it's a big deal. It was on the travel show last year. We're very lucky to get a booking. It's usually booked out years in advance.'

Cormac laughed again – yet another cold, mirthless laugh. 'Well, let's not be selfish, then. Let's say no to Linda and give some other family an opportunity to make total eejits of themselves.'

Of course, this was the stage at which I should have given in, agreed with him and backed out of it altogether. But I felt a strange loyalty to my old friend. And, after the whole stupid thing with Dudley, I wanted to feel like I was in charge of my life. (Of course, defying my husband just so I could do what my friend told me to do was hardly the act of someone who was in full charge of her life, but I only thought of that afterwards.) And all of a sudden I wanted to do something crazy.

And maybe canoeing down a French river in the company of two seriously mismatched families wasn't all that crazy in the great scheme of things. But it was quite crazy enough for me.

And maybe there comes a time in everyone's life when, no matter how happy you are, you want to take a small step backwards and remind yourself, if only for a short time, of how wild and wonderful life was when you were young and free and you didn't care about anything. When you lived for the moment, and every moment was filled with endless possibility. When the highlights of your life weren't the daily Sudoku puzzle and a weekly trip to the local pub for two glasses of beer and a packet of peanuts.

Cormac protested for a while, but I had a few trump cards up my sleeve, and I produced them as required.

'Just tell me one more time why we should do this.'

'Because I want to.'

'Fair enough, but what about me? Where do I stand in all of this?'

I grinned. 'Well, you stand in the same place as I did last year when we had to go to Greece on holidays because you wanted to take in the Olympics.'

'Yeah, but that was different. The Olympics are only on every four years. That was a special case.'

I grinned at him again. Cormac had been planning our holidays for years, and he always planned them around his own interests. But he was a fair man at heart. And now that, for the first time ever, I was expressing a strong preference, he had to respect it. I had more than enough ammunition. Arguing is such fun when you know you're going to win.

'Fair enough. But how long ago was it that I got no summer holiday at all, because you spent two weeks in Korea trekking around after Roy Keane and his buddies?'

'Actually, Roy Keane wasn't there, remember? They had this big row, and he walked out. Remember, I didn't sleep for two nights after I heard the news.'

Ha. I knew I had him when he started dragging irrelevancies into the equation. I threw in a few bland comments about how much Julie would love to spend some time with Linda's little girl Lauren, and how the exercise and the fresh air would be so good for all of us, and soon he threw his hands up in defeat.

'OK. OK. You haven't convinced me. You'll never convince me of the wisdom of this trip. But you've beaten me into submission. I think it's one of your crazier ideas, but what the hell? It'll be an experience, if nothing else. And I need to rack up some credits. I'd love to get a few Champions League matches in next year, and before we know it the World Cup will be rolling around again.'

'So we're going?'

He smiled a resigned smile. 'Yes, we're going.'

He leaned across the bed and ran his hand along my thigh. 'Now, any chance of getting my conjugals?'

It didn't seem fair to refuse, under the circumstances.

Chapter Seven

On Monday morning, after I'd dropped the children to school, I called in to Rita's. I had a million jobs to do, but none seemed quite as attractive a prospect as a chat with my friend.

As usual, Rita welcomed me with a huge smile that suggested I'd made her day just by showing up on her doorstep. I didn't mind that she greeted everyone the same way. Once, when we'd been in the middle of a serious heart-to-heart about our sex lives, we'd been interrupted by the arrival of Joan, a gossipy woman from the tennis club. Rita had beamed at her and insisted that she stay for coffee. Instead of the juicy sex talk, we spent the next hour discussing platinum detox treatments – not quite the same at all. Rita apologised afterwards, but how could I object when she'd only been her usual unselfish self?

Now she led the way into the kitchen and reached for the kettle. 'Coffee?'

I shook my head. 'No, thanks. Let's go for a walk. It's a lovely morning and I'm not getting enough exercise.'

Rita looked at me doubtfully. I wasn't usually that keen on exercise, and I hadn't refused a cup of coffee in all the many years she had known me. Still, she said nothing and reached for her fleece, which hung over the back of a chair. I knew she was just biding her time, planning her attack.

We were on the main road before anyone spoke. Then Rita started the interrogation. 'There's something funny going on, isn't there?'

I tried to look innocent. Evidently I failed.

Rita gave me a sly look. 'What are you like these days? Don't tell me another of your childhood sweethearts is lurking around the North Circular Road? Is he going to pop out from behind a bush bearing roses and a passionate declaration of his undying love?'

I poked her gently with my elbow. 'Hey, that's not fair. There's nothing going on. I promise. And, after what happened last week, I'm finished with childhood sweethearts.'

'So why the sudden interest in walking?'

'I just need to get fit for my holidays, that's all. Cormac and I have decided to go on the trip with Linda and Max.'

Rita couldn't hide her surprise. 'But I thought you'd decided against it.'

I shrugged. 'We had. But...'

'But what?'

I was almost embarrassed to admit my weakness. 'But Linda persuaded me it would be great.'

Rita giggled. 'Ha. What are you like?'

I pretended not to understand. 'What do you mean?'

'You know exactly what I mean. That'll be some holiday.'

I sniffed. 'I'm sure it will be great.'

She laughed again. 'I hope you're right. Don't you think,

though, that it might be like one of those reality TV programmes? You know, *Holidays from Hell*. Two mismatched families bickering and fighting from start to finish, rowing over blow-up beds and dinners and whose turn it is to dig the toilet hole each night, that kind of thing. I'd love to be a mosquito on the wall of your tent.' She laughed again, pleased with her own wit.

I stopped walking as the true awfulness of what I'd agreed to dawned on me. 'I shouldn't have said we'd go, should I? I should have said no to Linda. And now it's too late. She has it all booked. I can't back out. And you're right. It is going to be the holiday from hell.'

Rita was instantly contrite. 'Oh, Jill, I'm sorry. I was only having a laugh. I'm sure it will be great fun. And it'll be more exciting than my holidays, that's for sure.'

I grinned. 'Kilkee again?'

She sighed. 'Yes, Kilkee again. Same house. Same beach. Drinks every night with the same people. Only difference is seeing just how many crow's-feet each of the women has acquired since last year, and how far the men's hairlines have receded since we last got together to prop up the counter of the Atlantic Hotel. I'd love a change, but Jim won't hear of it. He's been going to Kilkee since he was a child. His mother went there when she was a child. Holidaying in Kilkee is bred into that family. Jim thinks all holidays begin and end there. He loves it so much, I don't want to insist on something else. Even a trip down a French river would be better than that.'

I laughed. 'Oh, dear. That bad, is it?'

She gave a wry smile. 'Well, maybe not. But still, I'm sorry for mocking your plans. I hope you have a great time.'

We'd started walking again. 'Yeah, me too. It's just...'

'Just what?'

66

'Well, it's Linda.'

Rita laughed. 'I knew it. I was right all the time. You did make her up, didn't you? She's just a figment of your overactive imagination, isn't she? Didn't you get all that imaginary-friend stuff out of your system when you were a child?'

I shook my head. 'Believe me, Linda's not made up. You couldn't make her up.'

'What is it, then? Oh, no. Don't tell me you don't get on. Are you going on the holiday from hell with the friend from hell? I thought you said she was nice.'

'No, it's not that. She is nice. Really. We get on great. I've known her since I was ten and we've never had a row in our lives.'

'Never?'

'Well, except for the time she tore all the coloured squares off my Rubik's cube, and I called her poo-face and we didn't talk for a whole afternoon. Otherwise we've never exchanged a cross word. It's just that...'

'Come on, Jill, get on with it. This is like pulling teeth. It's just what?'

I'd never discussed this with anyone. In fact, I'd never even thought it out fully for myself, until that moment. But all of a sudden I knew exactly what the problem was.

'You see, Linda and I have been friends since national school. We lived on the same road. We practically grew up together. Our childhoods sort of mingled. Almost all of my early memories feature Linda. Sometimes it was like she was more my sister than Deirdre was.'

I stopped talking. I knew where this speech was leading, and I wasn't sure I wanted to go there.

Rita prompted me gently. 'And?'

'Linda is clever and funny, and pretty, and exciting. You'd love her. We had fantastic times together. You couldn't be bored for a single second if Linda was around.'

Rita made a face. 'And the problem is?'

'Well, the problem is, everything I did, she did better. Like one year, when we were still at secondary school, I had this notion of wearing my sweatshirts inside out. It was just a stupid teenage affectation, and no one paid any attention. Then a few weeks later, Linda started doing it, and all of a sudden it was like a new religion. Everyone was doing it.'

'So? You thought of it first.'

'I know. But that didn't matter. Everyone thought they were copying her. No one had noticed when I did it. And that was only a stupid thing, but that's how it always was. Everything was...'

I stopped for a moment. It was hard to describe how I felt without sounding petty and jealous. Maybe all this teenage-angst stuff was best forgotten.

Rita nudged me gently. 'Go on, Jill.'

I took a deep breath. 'Well, maybe this will help you to understand. A few years ago I met this girl I used to know quite well when I was a teenager. For one whole summer I liked to think we were friends. But she didn't recognise me. I thought she was messing at first. I said, "You know, we used to hang out in Douglas together. Remember, we used to go to the discos in Cork Con?" She looked at me blankly, like I was some kind of madwoman; and then, very slowly, recognition dawned. "Yes, of course, I remember now – you were Linda's friend, weren't you?" And that's how it always was. Everyone knew Linda. Everyone loved Linda. And everyone knew me, sort of. I was Linda's friend. That was my identity. My badge of honour.'

Rita spoke softly. 'Was that so bad?'

I shook my head. 'No, not always. Sometimes it was great fun. We did crazy things together. Linda always had mad ideas, and she persuaded me to do things I'd never have done without her. We went on wild camping trips. We had crazy parties in her house when her parents were away. We dossed off school, and went into town and drank coffee and laughed for hours on end. Every funny, crazy thing I did in my life, I did with Linda. But sometimes...'

I stopped. I suspected I was getting seriously carried away.

'Sometimes what?'

'Well, look, I know this is going to sound a bit loopy, but humour me, please, Rita. I need to say this. I've never said it before. In fact, I've never even thought it out before. You see, sometimes it was like in that song – you know the one from *Beaches*? The one about the girl who wasn't Bette Midler? "The Wind Beneath My Wings".'

'That dreadful soppy thing? About the shadows?'

'Yeah, that one. I know it's soppy and stupid, but that was how it felt sometimes. I was always in Linda's bloody shadow, and often it was very cold indeed. When Linda was around, I never got my moment in the sun. I was always stuck in the shade.'

Rita laughed softly. 'Well, look on the bright side. We know now that the sun is very bad for you. Maybe she did you a favour.'

I laughed too. 'I suppose. But still, now that I think of it, maybe it's no accident that you've never met Linda. Since I came to Limerick, I've only been mixing with people who never knew her. And I like it that way. I feel secure here. More like my own person. You know? I don't like the person I was when I was Linda's friend. I did every single thing she said, even when I didn't want to.'

'Like agreeing to go on canoeing holidays with her?'

I nodded. 'Exactly. That's exactly how it's always been. It was like I had no mind, no identity independent of her.'

Rita spoke soothingly. 'Was it really that bad?'

I nodded. 'Yes, it was. And now I feel better when Linda's not around. Sometimes I feel I've shaken off a huge weight that I'd been dragging around for most of my life. Does that sound horrible?'

Rita shook her head. 'No. It doesn't sound awful at all.'

I surprised myself by being angry. 'Well, it is awful. I've just abandoned her. She was my best friend for years, and yet I don't want to be with her.'

'But that was all so long ago,' Rita said softly.

'So what? Linda was always a good friend to me. It's not her fault that she's better and brighter than me. She still rings me, for God's sake. She sends me birthday cards. She still wants me to be her friend. She's asked me to go on holidays with her. She's kind and generous. She's never been deliberately mean to me in her entire life.'

Oops. That was one word too many for my perceptive companion. There was a brief silence. I looked at Rita, and she very slowly raised one eyebrow. 'Deliberately?'

I looked away from her, ignoring her searching look.

Unfortunately, Rita wasn't the type to let a gem like that slip through her fingers. 'How about accidentally? Was Linda ever accidentally mean to you?'

I kept my eyes firmly fixed on the road ahead.

Rita hesitated. 'Are you telling me everything? I feel like I'm doing a jigsaw, and you've kept the last piece hidden in your pocket. Is there something else I should know?'

I began to walk faster. 'No,' I lied. Some things were best forgotten.

Rita gave a relieved laugh. 'Well, then, accept the fact that you've moved on. You don't have to prove anything to Linda or to anyone else. Just go on your road trip – or your river trip, should I say – and enjoy Linda. Have a laugh together. Relive old times and pretend to be fifteen again. And come back here afterwards and we'll laugh about it. Toilet pits and all.'

I began to walk even faster. 'You're right. It's all behind me. I'm as good as her, and we're going to have a ball.'

Chapter Eight

Fate can be a very strange thing. Just when everything is tootling along nicely, fate decides to trip you up, and when you pick yourself up and gather yourself together again, you find that you're facing in a whole new direction, and things you thought you were sure of suddenly seem very vague indeed.

On the next Wednesday evening, I was brushing my hair and getting ready for my usual night out with Rita. I remembered how foolish I'd been the week before, when we'd met Dudley in the South Court. I shook my head firmly and made a face at myself in the mirror. That had been total foolishness, and was best forgotten. This week, Rita and I would just go to the Davin Arms like we usually did. It was for the best.

Still, though, at the back of my mind, I could remember telling Dudley that I went to the South Court every Wednesday night. Maybe he'd remember what I said and go there too.

I made an even fiercer face at myself. What were the chances of him going there in hopes of seeing me? About zero, I figured.

He hadn't even remembered me. Why was I wasting my life hanging around hoping to get a look at a guy like that?

I was only being foolish. I brushed my hair roughly, flung on some lipstick and picked up my car keys.

When I got to Rita's house, I was met with a scene of total chaos. I could hear the shouting before I rang the doorbell.

Rita came to the door, all flushed and agitated-looking. 'Sorry, Jill. It's like World War Three in here. The two girls started a row about a dress they're supposed to own between them, and I'm trying to keep Jim out of it.'

Not very successfully, I thought, as I heard his deep voice mixing with the plaintive, self-pitying tones of his older daughter. It was the same old teenaged-daughter-and-her-dad stuff. I could remember similar scenes from my own youth.

Fiona's strident tones washed over me. 'I'm going out, and there's nothing you can do about it.'

Jim's voice was quieter, but no less dangerous. 'Oh, yes, there is something I can do about it, young lady. And in about a hundred years, when you're not grounded any more, you certainly are not going out in that excuse for a dress. It's even too small for Lisa, and she's only half the size of you.'

'So now you're calling me fat, are you? I hate you!'

This last was followed by the sound of a door slamming. Then there was a deep, rhythmic thumping that might have been the sound of Fiona stamping her foot. Then again, it could have been Jim beating his head against a wall.

Rita looked over her shoulder. 'It's not as bad as it sounds.'

I was glad to hear it, because it sounded very bad indeed. It sounded even worse than one of Luke and Cormac's rows, which was saying a lot.

Rita continued, 'It'll all be fine in a half-hour, but do you mind if we skip tonight's drink? I couldn't relax for fear they'd all be killing each other while I'm gone. Sometimes I think I'm the only one in this house with a scrap of common sense and self-restraint.'

I shook my head. 'I don't mind at all. I could do with an early night anyway. I'll give you a call in the morning, and you can share the casualty list with me.'

She smiled. 'Thanks, Jill.'

Just then there was the sound of another door being slammed. If the windows hadn't been nice new double-glazed ones, I'm sure they'd have rattled right out of their frames. This was followed by a burst of loud, attention-seeking sobbing.

Rita gave a small wave and went inside, closing the door behind her.

I walked back down the drive and got into my car. I put the key in the ignition, but didn't turn it. I sighed and tried to ignore the crazy notion that was lurking at the edges of my brain.

I knew what I should do. I should go home and start on Julie's outfit for her school play. I only had two days to make her a Trojan-soldier outfit, and I didn't even know what that was supposed to look like. And I'd be competing with the mummies who would have spent hours doing research on the internet, and who would have driven to some specialist shop in Cork to get the exact shade of fabric necessary.

And Cormac was working late again, and maybe I should go home to make sure that Luke was studying for his summer exams and not playing guitar or surfing pornography sites on the computer.

I had a heap of ironing to do, and I could do with an early night.

In fact, there was no choice, really. It was very, very clear what I should do.

But all my life I'd watched other people having all the fun, all the excitement. I had always been the sensible one. And now that Linda had bullied her way back into my life, maybe I wanted to assert myself. Maybe for once it was time to be selfish, and to do something just for the hell of it.

And so I made up my mind. I started the car and drove out of Rita's road. I turned left onto the North Circular. I passed the entrance to my own estate, knowing that this was the moment of betrayal. I drove on towards the Shannon Bridge and tried to convince myself that I was acting for the best.

When I got to the front door of the South Court, I felt very foolish indeed. What on earth was I doing there? I was on my own, hoping that someone I had known almost twenty years earlier might remember that I'd said I'd be there and, crazier still, that he might go there himself.

And, even if he did show up, what then? What on earth did I think was going to happen?

What did I want to happen?

I had to be very strict with the sensible part of me, which wanted to run back down the steps to the car park, into my car and home to my wifely chores. The part of me that wanted to be home chatting with Julie about her school play. The part of me that wanted to potter around in the calm, inoffensive life I'd carefully made for myself.

I bought myself a gin and tonic and went to sit in the lobby. There was a discarded newspaper on a table nearby. I picked it up gratefully and began to read. It would occupy me until I finished my drink and set off for home.

I was engrossed in an article on global warming, and he was next to me before I saw him.

'Jill.'

I looked up. He was smiling. He looked glad to see me.

'Dudley. What a surprise.' I was very glad to see him, and I hoped it wasn't written all over my treacherous face.

'May I?' He indicated the couch opposite me.

'Sure.' I tried to look as if I didn't mind whether he sat down or not. Like I hadn't been half-dreaming of this moment for much of the previous week.

He sat down. He was dressed in casual clothes and looked younger than he had the week before – a bit more like the Dudley I remembered from twenty years earlier.

'Where's your friend?'

I could feel my face going red. I hadn't actually thought that far. In fact, I hadn't really thought past Dudley sitting down and smiling at me.

What kind of an eejit was I? How could I explain being there on my own? Would he believe me if I said Rita had gone to the toilet and neglected to come back? Could I pretend she had some rare psychiatric complaint that caused her to rush out of hotels with no warning?

Dudley and I both looked at the single glass on the table between us. I thought quickly. Luckily I'd been lying to my children for years, so I was good at it. 'Oh. Rita and I were to meet here. She just rang, though. She can't come. Her daughter's not well.'

It wasn't really a lie. Fiona was actually psychotically selfish – that was an illness, wasn't it?

Dudley smiled at me. I had a sudden strange notion that the super-white teeth he flashed in my direction weren't quite the same ones I'd licked and sucked on a regular basis twenty years earlier. The ones I remembered were slightly flawed, but real-looking. These ones looked like they'd been moulded from the finest white porcelain and shoved into his mouth about five minutes earlier. These were teeth Donny Osmond would have been proud of.

'Well, isn't that a coincidence? My friend has let me down too. How about I get a drink and join you?'

I nodded, and he went to the bar. I sipped my drink and thought frantically. I knew Dudley hadn't believed my half-lie. And he hadn't even tried to sound convincing when he tossed his own lie carelessly at my feet. I knew that the sensible thing to do would be to get up, walk out and go home to my family. But I'd been sensible for far too long, and Dudley had once meant so much to me, and I felt as if the impatient, discontented feeling that had been stalking me for weeks were going to overwhelm me.

I knew I'd stay. And I knew what was going to happen. And I didn't care.

It was the cheapest and most predictable of seduction scenes. Dudley didn't even have to buy me a drink. I quickly finished the one I'd bought for myself. My hand shook slightly as I held the glass to my lips. Dudley left his drink untouched on the table. I didn't like to see it wasted. I wondered if he'd put it on his expense account.

He suggested going for a walk. I agreed. It was like the walks we'd shared before, back when I was nineteen and still had romantic notions and natural mousy hair and an intact pelvic floor. We were so engrossed in each other, it felt like no time until we were in town. He was staying in a hotel, waiting for his new house to be finished. I presumed there was a wife somewhere, waiting to move into the new house with him. Maybe he had seven kids, a nanny, a dog and a goldfish. I didn't care. I mentioned Cormac and our children once. I knew that Dudley didn't care about them either. I didn't mention them again.

We got to his hotel. He said he needed to get money from his room for a taxi. I knew he didn't. I'd seen his wallet, which was stuffed with fifty-euro notes. He wasn't trying very hard with his lies, but I didn't care. I wasn't trying very hard to believe them.

He hesitated in the lobby, just for one second. His eyes met mine. 'Will you come upstairs with me?'

I nodded. The evil deed was as good as done.

He pushed the button for the lift. I watched as the lighted numbers descended slowly. Soon the number 1 was lit up in bright green, and then the letter G. There was a sudden loud ping (just in case the few people standing around the lobby hadn't seen me). The lift doors slid open. Dudley put a hand on the small of my back and guided me into the lift.

I should have said no. I knew that, of course. But it was as if the ropes of caution and convention that usually kept me tethered firmly to the earth had suddenly, unexpectedly snapped. I was floating, wonderfully and blissfully helpless. It was as if the real, honest, faithful me was sheltering behind my inner slut.

We walked along thick, soft carpet until we got to his bed-room. Number 19 – the age I had been when we met. Surely an omen. Dudley used a small white swipe-card to open the door. The room was warm, tastefully furnished, impersonal.

I sat on the bed and ran my hand over the silky beige covers. I knew that, even then, it wasn't too late to leave. I hadn't done anything really wrong yet.

But I wasn't going anywhere in a hurry.

Dudley sat on the bed beside me. His breathing was deep. I closed my eyes and tried to pretend it was twenty years earlier. As if that would somehow make the whole thing, if not right, then at least not quite as wrong.

The pretence didn't work. Back then, he'd smelt of soap and

cigarettes. Now he smelt of wealth and designer aftershave. I raised my eyes and met his. Even as I leaned towards him, I knew it was probably the most stupid thing I'd ever done.

I didn't care.

If I'd ever pictured such a scenario in advance, I would have thought that afterwards I'd feel cheap, nasty, sordid.

When the time came, I didn't feel any of those things. Of course, I felt guilty. After all, I had sixteen years of faithful and fairly happy marriage behind me, and now I'd just betrayed my husband for the first time.

But the small guilty feeling was overshadowed by the wonderful feeling of liberation that washed over me. I looked at the ceiling with its tasteful recessed lights and wondered if heaven would be anything like this.

Dudley leaned across the bed. He wound a strand of my hair around his fingers and smiled. 'Now you can't escape.'

I caught my breath. Did he remember how he used say that to me before? Or did he say that to all the girls?

He released the strand and kissed the resulting ringlet. I wondered if my hairdresser had managed to replicate the hair colour he would remember.

He seemed rather amused. 'We shouldn't have done that, should we?'

He didn't look one bit guilty. He didn't look like he'd be lying awake that night fretting over what he had done.

I grinned at him. 'No, we shouldn't. But it was kind of nice, wasn't it?'

'Very.' He lay back, stretched his long and still fairly lean limbs and gave a deep, contented sigh. I thought for a moment of a cat purring.

Suddenly I remembered Julie learning the Ten Commandments at school.

'What's adultery?' she'd asked me one evening, a few weeks earlier.

I remembered how I'd tried to fob her off. 'Oh, you don't need to worry about that one. It's just something that very bad grown-ups do.'

Now I'd joined the ranks of very bad, adulterous grown-ups. I shut my eyes and tried not to feel like a sinner.

Soon I checked my watch and decided I'd better leave. Maybe I could get some of the ironing done before going to bed.

I wasn't quite sure what the protocol was. I'd never been in a situation like this before. Should I slink into the bathroom, with a sheet carefully draped around my less-than-perfect body? Could I turn out the light, so Dudley wouldn't see the imperfections he might have ignored earlier?

Dudley decided for me. He threw back the covers. We both stood up. We put on the clothes we'd torn from each other's body shortly before. We straightened the bed. We took a taxi back to the South Court. I didn't feel like walking – I'd had more than enough physical activity for one night.

Dudley walked me to my car. I leaned on it, and we looked at each other in the harsh, unflattering light. Was he going to declare his undying love for me? What would I do if he did?

'I leave for the States tomorrow.'

I knew I shouldn't ask, but I couldn't help myself. 'When will you be back?'

'Next week. I'm back for one night then, for the official opening of the plant. I'll only be in the country for about twelve hours before flying out again.'

I knew what he was saying. He'd be here for twelve hours, and none of those hours had any room in them for me. He was giving me the brush-off once again. I raised my head and tried to look as if I didn't care.

He continued, 'After that I'll be back in about four weeks.'

That wasn't much use to me. I'd be canoeing down the Dordogne by then. Was there any chance that Dudley would shadow us and drag me into the bushes whenever Cormac wasn't looking?

I smiled regretfully. 'I won't be here. I'll be on holidays.'

He looked around cautiously, and then he stroked my cheek with the back of his hand. 'Afterwards, then. Let's meet again when you get back. This could be the beginning of something very special.'

Did he mean an affair? Or was he offering more?

I leaned forward and gave him a brief, daring kiss. 'Yes. Let's meet again.'

There was a flurry of checking pockets until we found a pencil and two scraps of paper. We exchanged phone numbers.

I tried to keep the lascivious, self-satisfied smile from my lips as I climbed into my car. I was useless at so many things in this life – hockey, embroidery, lining cake-tins. Maybe it would turn out that adultery was something I was good at.

As I drove away, I looked in my rear-view mirror. Dudley was standing with his arms folded, watching me leave. Was he sorry to see me go? Or was he just wondering why I'd taken so long about it?

As I drove out of the car park and headed for home, I wondered how exactly I'd turned from a faithful housewife into such a brazen hussy, in the space of one short evening.

Chapter Nine

The following week, it was time for the finishing-up party for the ladies' tennis morning. In a tradition that seemed to go back for about a thousand years, women had been gathering in the tennis club on Thursday mornings for friendly games of doubles followed by coffee and chocolate-chip biscuits. When summer approached, the numbers began to dwindle as the citizens of the north side of Limerick began to pack up their houses in preparation for the annual sojourn in Kilkee. Around the middle of June, there was a finishing-up party, and the group disbanded until September.

I arrived at the tennis club at ten o'clock. It was a special morning, so in honour of the occasion I had ironed my tennis gear and washed my hair. It was rumoured that certain women bought new tracksuits for the occasion, though when this was suggested they always waved their hands as if in horror at the very idea – 'That old thing! That's been gathering dust in the back of my wardrobe since Christmas.' No one was ever fooled for a second.

There was an unusual buzz as I got out of my car and headed for the clubhouse. Groups of women wandered in, fixing their hair and clutching their best Nicholas Mosse bowls full of their special salad, or plates covered with sweet, creamy concoctions that got rolled out twice a year, summer and Christmas.

The tennis was, as usual, pleasant and uneventful. Since it was the end of the year, there was a small competition, with prizes for the winners. The one or two players who took it all a little bit too seriously were shamed into silence by the general air of good-will. And any dodgy line calls were glossed over and forgotten as we enjoyed ourselves in the gentle sunshine.

I'd been partnered with Jacinta, one of the least popular members of the club. She wasn't a particularly bright woman, but she was bossy and opinionated – a dangerous mix. Still, the upside was that she was a great tennis player, and I knew that I'd be guaranteed a nice ornament at the end of the morning's tennis.

After we'd played, everyone showered and changed out of their tennis gear. What to wear on these occasions was always a difficult choice. Some people went totally overboard, donning outfits that would have been suitable if they'd been accepting Oscars. For my part, I always aimed for a sort of middle-of-the-road look, not too scruffy and not too fancy – as if I hadn't really been trying too hard.

Then, all clean and sweet-smelling, we assembled in the bar for our buffet lunch. As usual, it was excellent, and no one seemed to mind that the food was exactly the same as the year before. And the year before that. That was the way we liked it, so why change?

We ate our food, and lingered over the single glass of wine that we each allowed ourselves, and chatted about trivialities. Usually, I loved these days, but this time I found I couldn't concentrate. My mind kept wandering back to the night with Dudley. I kept imagining the cool touch of his hand on my skin, my trembling joy, his sighs of pleasure.

What would these decent, clean-living women think if only they knew what I'd done just a few nights earlier?

And what would they think if they knew how desperately I wanted to do it again?

I was dragged back from my daydreams as Rita was cornered by Sheila, one of the older members of the group. 'That pickled red cabbage you brought was simply delicious. I'd love to make it for my daughter's graduation party. She's a doctor, you know. Can I have the recipe?'

Rita looked rather uncomfortable, and I knew exactly why. 'Er, that might be a bit of a problem. Can I get back to you with it next week?'

Sheila put on a most supercilious look. 'Well, Rita, it's only pickled cabbage. It can't be that complicated. Did you use red wine vinegar or balsamic?'

Rita gave me a 'what the hell?' kind of look and spoke in a rush. 'Well, actually, I'm not sure what kind of vinegar is in it. I'll check the jar when I get home.'

Sheila looked suitably horrified. 'Jar? What jar?'

'The jar I bought the pickled cabbage in. I got it in Lidl, actually – two euro fifty for a half-kilo.'

Sheila flounced off, resplendent in her layered polyester dress, and Rita and I allowed ourselves a few relieved giggles.

Bringing ready-made food to the tennis lunch was one thing – I suspected it happened rather often, in fact – but admitting to it was totally unacceptable. If you had to bring a cheesecake from Ivan's, it was important to take it out of the box and put it on one of your own Stephen Pearse plates. No one would actually be fooled, but conventions had to be followed.

As I was getting ready to leave, I was approached by Norma, a woman I didn't know particularly well. She took my arm, almost knocking my best salad bowl to the floor.

'I saw you last week.'

'Really?' Maybe she had only seen me in the supermarket, or outside Julie's school, but still, I was sure guilt was written all over my face. 'Where?'

She smiled. 'You were a long way from home. In the South Court Hotel.'

She surely heard the horrible gulping sound I made. I fixed my hair and tried to avoid her eyes. What exactly had she seen? Had she seen Dudley? Had she seen me leave with him? Had she seen that stupid, foolhardy kiss in the car park? What had I been thinking of, in a small city like Limerick?

Just then Rita came over. Norma smiled at her. 'I was just saying how I saw Jill in the South Court last week. Wednesday, I think it was. Limerick is such a small town. You can't do anything, can you?'

Was I imagining it, or was she putting more meaning into those words than was strictly necessary?

Rita gave me a funny look. Then she spoke brightly. 'Oh, yes, I was there too. Didn't you see me?'

Norma's smile faded a little. 'Actually, I didn't. Now, must go, time for my personal training session. Darren hates me to be late.'

She hurried off, but before she left the clubhouse she joined a bunch of her buddies in the corner. She said something to them; then they all looked my way and laughed. My heart sank even further. The tennis club, a place I'd always loved, was beginning to close in around me.

Rita walked me out to the car park. 'What was all that about?'

I shrugged. If I was going to continue to be an adulteress, I'd better perfect the false-casual look. 'Seems obvious to me. Norma must have seen us that time we went for a drink in the South Court. What's the big deal?'

Rita looked puzzled. 'But that was two weeks ago, wasn't it? Actually, I know it was, because last week was the week Fiona threw that huge tantrum.'

She looked at me closely. 'Don't tell me. Please don't tell me you went back there again last week. Don't tell me you…'

…met Dudley and went back to his hotel room for glorious, sordid, adulterous sex?

She hadn't finished her question, but it didn't matter. There was no way I was telling her the truth. How could I put it into words? How could I tell my honest, honourable friend what I had done?

I decided to attack. My voice was light, but fear gave it a cold edge. 'What exactly are you implying, Rita? Do you think I…?' I couldn't finish the sentence either.

Rita held her hands up in mock surrender. 'Nothing. I'm implying nothing. Norma must have got her weeks mixed up.'

She gave me another funny look, then got into her car, waved and drove off.

Just then, Norma too drove by. She stopped and wound down her window. 'I often drink on that side of town. I'll keep an eye out for you in the future.'

I smiled weakly. Was that a promise or a threat?

What on earth was I going to do now?

That evening, after dinner, Cormac and Luke did the clear-up, and managed not to have too many rows in the process. I sent Julie upstairs to put on her pyjamas and to clean her teeth.

Instead of going to bed, she doubled back and sneaked into the family room, where I was half-heartedly watching television. She jumped into my arms, and I hugged her warm body, savouring the mingled scents of clean child and fabric conditioner. Cuddle-times with my boisterous daughter were becoming less frequent, making me enjoy them more when they came my way.

Just then, Cormac came into the room and threw himself onto the couch next to us. Fearful of being chased to bed, Julie closed her eyes and feigned sleep. Shortly afterwards, her steady breathing told me that she had in fact dropped off. Every time she fell asleep in my arms, I wondered if it would be the last time.

I stroked her soft brown hair, and Cormac idly rubbed her bare toes. I noticed that she had a small blister on her baby toe, probably from wearing last year's sandals, which were much too small for her. She snuggled closer to me and gave a short sigh. I rested my hand on her chest, feeling its gentle rise and fall. Her little hand lay easily on my thigh. Each of her fingernails was adorned with a different shade of chipped pink nail varnish. Her eyes flickered open and briefly registered my presence. Then they drifted shut again.

A mantle of content slipped around me. All of a sudden I knew how valuable my marriage and my family were. How could I have been so foolish as to get involved with Dudley? How could I have put myself at the mercy of evil gossips like Norma? Whatever could I have been thinking? My marriage wasn't per-fect, but it was too good to throw away on a romantic whim and the faint dream of a distant past.

I turned to Cormac and smiled at him. I was wasting my time, as he was intent on the television screen, which had split in two and was showing two different soccer matches, with an interest-ing multicoloured overlay of teletext.

I tried unsuccessfully to tell myself that watching TV was his form of infidelity, almost as serious as my own, more conventional form.

And so the weeks slipped by. Linda rang me every few days, full of excitement about our upcoming trip. That hardly surprised me, though, as Linda was always able to work up a fizz of excitement about the tiniest thing. (When we were in fifth class, she got a school report that said, 'Linda is a remarkably enthusiastic girl.' Linda boasted about it for months, never suspecting that our poor, tired old teacher might not have meant it as a compliment.) And, even though I still had a deep sense of foreboding about our planned jaunt, sometimes Linda's enthusiasm got to me, and I found myself almost looking forward to it.

Cormac and I didn't discuss the trip very much, but after the first week or two he stopped griping about it, and that was good enough for me. I took that as meaning he didn't mind too much. Or maybe he was just plotting how many soccer trips he could wangle in return for his compliance on the French trip.

And all the time, as I meandered happily enough through my daily life, I thought about Dudley. I tried not to, of course, but I failed miserably. I didn't want to hurt Cormac, and I didn't want to wreck my marriage, but I was helpless. The thrill of that one night with Dudley lingered, and as I stacked the dishwasher and cleaned the cutlery drawer, all I could think of was when I would see him again.

One night, about a month before we were due to travel, Cormac and I were tucked up in bed together, flossing our teeth. He had one eye on the evening paper, and I was reading the style section of the previous Sunday's paper. As I flossed a particularly difficult spot at the back of my mouth, I looked up from my paper and surveyed the room. Two of Julie's huge teddy family were sitting at attention on the chair in the corner. Her dressing-gown hung from the back of the same chair. Luke rarely entered our room any more. Cormac said it was because he was afraid of interrupting us having sex. I knew that wasn't true, though, as even when Cormac was at work, Luke found excuses not to enter our domain. It was as if he wanted to be cut off from any idea of us even sharing a room. Even so, his guitar was propped up against the wardrobe – probably Julie had put it there to annoy him. Cormac's clothes were in a heap at the bottom of the bed, and my paltry few cosmetics were tossed around the dressing-table. It was a scene of almost-perfect family bliss.

I looked at Cormac, intent on the business section of the paper, and I smiled to myself. For the hundredth time, I promised myself I'd forget all about Dudley and concentrate on my marriage. Maybe I should take more interest in Cormac's business. Maybe I could take some of the pressure off him, and he wouldn't have to work too hard. If he didn't work so hard, maybe he'd be less snappy with Luke. Maybe I could persuade Cormac to actually play some sport instead of lying on the couch like a big stranded whale watching it on television. Maybe the solutions to all my niggly problems lay in my own hands.

Cormac interrupted my thoughts. 'Good news. At last they've got their act together and opened that new electronics plant in Raheen. Look, they even got a few ministers down for the formalities. You'd never think there was an election coming up, would you?'

As he spoke he waved the paper in front of me. I left my piece of floss dangling inelegantly from between my two front teeth and looked obediently at the page he was holding out. I knew exactly what I was going to see.

It was a big colour picture, taking up a quarter of the page. There were two government ministers, a few local hangers-on and political wannabes and, of course, Dudley. He was beaming out of the shot, looking all tanned and debonair and powerful. Before I'd quite finished looking, Cormac took the paper back. 'Who's that guy in the middle? Looks like Mr Bloody Universe. That tan has to be fake.'

He read the caption and gave a sudden laugh. 'Dudley Adamson! Did you ever hear such a name? I bet he made it up.'

I tried to sound casual. 'Yeah. Stupid name, isn't it?'

I couldn't think of anything else to say. What exactly are the appropriate words when your husband is looking at a photograph of your lover?

It didn't matter, anyway. Cormac had turned to the sports page. I had escaped – this time.

That was exactly what I'd said, when Dudley first told me his name. 'I bet you made it up.'

He pretended to look insulted. 'Why on earth would I make up a name like that?'

I shrugged. 'How on earth should I know? Maybe to be like the actor?'

He gave a scornful laugh. 'Dudley Moore? Give me a break. In the most unlikely event of me taking an actor's name, don't you think I'd choose an actor with talent, or at least one who was good-looking?'

We both laughed then. I liked his faint American accent. I liked him. I knew that already, even though we'd just met.

It was June. We were in UCC. I'd gone to the travel office there to see if I could get a refund on my ticket to Denmark. I'd been due to travel there to work for the summer, with Linda and a few others. Then, the day before I was due to leave, I'd had a stupid stumble on the stairs at home and sprained my wrist badly. A chambermaid with a sprained wrist was never going to be an asset to the hotel, so I'd had to cancel my trip. The whole thing was a total, depressing disaster. Until that day when I bumped into Dudley, on the steps of the travel office, and all of a sudden my damaged wrist seemed like the best thing that had ever happened to me.

Dudley told me his family had moved to America when he was ten, and had just returned to Cork to live. He'd started college in Texas, but had decided to transfer to Cork for his final year. He was in college that day to catch up on some course reading, to get ready for October.

By the time he'd told me this, we were sipping coffee in the college restaurant. It was funny being there without the usual hubbub of students. There were only a few people around, but I didn't care. I was staring into the most wonderfully deep grey eyes I'd ever seen, and trying not to look like a total simpering idiot.

After I'd had two cups of coffee, I was dying to go to the loo. There was no way I was giving in to that urge, though. I was afraid that, if I stood up and broke the moment, Dudley would remember an appointment elsewhere and head off too. So I sat there with my legs tightly crossed, fiddling with the fraying cuff of my sweatshirt, wondering how to prolong the moment and whether the damage I was doing to my kidneys in the process was likely to be permanent.

In the end, Dudley turned to look at the huge clock over the door. 'Geez. Is that the time? I gotta go. It's been great meeting you, Jill.'

I smiled. 'You too.'

I tried not to look too sad. I'd had my time. I was just your average-looking, rarely noticed girl. Good-looking guys like Dudley didn't usually pay me any attention at all, so twenty minutes in his company was a bonus, more than I deserved, really. After all, if Linda had been there, Dudley wouldn't have given me a second glance.

Dudley got up. He waved cheerfully and walked out the door. I had to wait until the coast was clear. When I stood up, I knew I'd actually need to run to the toilet. I counted to twenty to give him time to leave the building. On fifteen, when my bladder felt like it was going to explode, he was back by my side. 'Hey. How about we do something?'

Like a bit of passionate snogging under a tree in the president's garden? Like getting married and producing ten fat, smiling babies?

I shrugged and tried to look as if I didn't care. My mother had always taught me to play hard to get. (Unfortunately, despite her efforts, the game I really excelled at was 'hard to notice'.)

'Well?'

I shrugged again – a bigger shrug this time, in case he'd missed the first one. 'Sure. I don't mind.'

'Tomorrow night? Will you meet me? Just outside this building? Eight o'clock?'

'Sure. See you there.'

Luckily, he didn't seem to notice that my casual manner was false. What I really wanted to do was to kneel on the faded, dirty tiles and hug his knees and howl, 'Thank you, thank you, thank you,' over and over. Unfortunately, my legs were so tightly crossed, I'd never have balanced on my knees. It could have been very messy.

He sauntered out, and this time I couldn't wait. On the count of four I legged it from the room and threw myself towards the nearest toilet, where I sang happily to myself as I weed.

Three weeks later, my wrist was better, and I could easily have travelled to Copenhagen to join Linda. She phoned every week to tell me what a marvellous time they were having, and how they were missing me and how the housekeeper said there was plenty of work for one more crazy Irish girl.

Wild horses couldn't have dragged me there, though. I was having far too good a time at home. I'd found a job in our local shop, and even though it was the most boring job in the history of the world, I didn't care. I stacked shelves, and dusted ancient cans of fruit cocktail in syrup, and served the occasional grumpy customer, and hummed contentedly to myself as I dreamed of my last, or my next, meeting with Dudley.

We met most evenings. Sometimes we went to the pictures, or for a drink, but mostly we just went for long, leisurely walks. Then, as his parents were away a lot, we usually retired to his house for long, leisurely snogging sessions.

After the first week, though, those sessions were rather less leisurely, and had gone far beyond what anyone could call snogging.

I thought I'd died and gone to a wonderful, secular, sexy heaven.

Chapter Ten

Soon, there were only two weeks to go before the big canoeing trip. Time to start preparing.

Cormac, in his happy aloof male existence, thought that preparing for your holidays begins the evening before you leave, when you put seven pairs of trousers, seven T-shirts, two pairs of shorts and your seven best sets of underwear into a suitcase. On top of these should go a year's supply of *Business and Finance* magazines, which will tip the load just over the airline weight allowance and will of course never be opened.

The reality, of course, was different. I had to weed the garden, run down the supplies in the fridge, try to get on top of the ironing, and make sure the children and I had enough clothes to wear.

Luke had hardly any clothes, but didn't want any either. I decided not to argue. If he wanted to spend his holidays in the same two pairs of revolting baggy denim trousers, and three black T-shirts with pictures of skulls and barbed wire on them, I really didn't care enough to row about it. And maybe, in the warmth of the French sunshine, Cormac would pretend not to care either, and it wouldn't become an issue.

Julie had lots of clothes, but wanted more. I indulged her. We went to town and stocked up on yet more brightly coloured T-shirts and skimpy shorts and skirts. Even so, she wasn't happy, and she threw a total wobbly in the shoe shop because I was ever so slightly reluctant to shell out fifty euro for a pair of glorified flip-flops with glittery straps that she could barely walk in. Instead I shelled out seventy-five euro for a pair of denim sandals that looked as if they had already had three owners, none of whom had been careful.

Next day, I emptied my summer wardrobe onto my bed. It didn't take long, and when I was finished, it was a sorry sight. A few tired pairs of Capri pants, lots of striped tops, two denim skirts that I'd been wearing every summer since Julie was a baby, and an ill-advised flowery dress I'd bought in a street market in Portugal three years earlier. I sat on my bed and put my head in my hands. I felt like Cinderella.

Then my fairy godmother rang the doorbell.

Rita, of course. She headed automatically for the kitchen, but I pulled her back. 'No coffee yet. Today you have to earn it.'

I brought her upstairs and held her back for a moment at my bedroom door. I looked at her carefully. 'Don't go in just yet. You must promise to give me your honest opinion. Even if it hurts.'

What was I saying? I knew it was going to hurt.

Rita held one hand in the air as if taking an oath. 'I so promise.'

I opened the door and led her into the room. I waved my hand over the collection of clothes on the bed. 'What do you think?'

She surveyed the pathetic display for a few moments. She looked at me carefully, and then looked back at the clothes. Then she spoke. 'You want to know if I think this lot should be sent to the charity shop, right?'

I shook my head. 'Wrong.'

She looked back at the sad heap of clothes on the bed. I almost felt sorry for the clothes. It wasn't their fault. I rearranged the denim skirts so they almost hid the flowery dress, and I picked my best strappy sandals off the floor and put them next to the T-shirt pile. It didn't help at all.

After a long while, Rita spoke. 'You're sure you want me to be honest?'

I nodded. 'Sure, I'm sure.' I wasn't sure at all.

She took a deep breath. 'OK. Honest it is. This is the saddest collection of summer clothes I've ever seen. Your bed is like the "before" set in *What Not to Wear*. This is like the stuff no one wanted at the end of the parish jumble sale. It's...'

She stopped, apparently lost for words. For one small moment I thought of crying. What kind of friend was Rita? Honest would have done. I didn't need brutal as well.

Then I looked at the clothes and saw them, for a second, as she must have seen them. And I realised she was right. I began to giggle. Rita looked at me, relieved. Then she began to giggle too. All of a sudden, my pathetic clothes seemed incredibly funny.

Rita grabbed a bundle and threw it into the corner of the bedroom. I followed it with another bundle. The flowery dress seemed to float in the air for a second, hovering in a cloud of pink and violet, prolonging my shame. I picked up a pair of Capri pants that were only two years old, and not that badly faded at all. I held them up, questioningly. Rita shook her head violently, so I tossed them aside. She threw the last few things into the corner, and then we sat together on the empty bed.

'Now what?' I felt rather elated all of a sudden.

'We need a plan. I need to know what exactly you are up against. Firstly, you said before that Linda was good-looking. Exactly how good-looking is she?'

I shrugged. 'Very? And she always looks great – glamorous and sophisticated. She's got a great sense of style, but it's wasted on her. She'd even look good in...' I ran over and picked up the flowery dress. '...in this.'

Rita laughed. 'Wow, she must be something. But be more specific. Score her out of ten.'

'Eleven.'

Rita grimaced. 'Ouch.'

Then she recovered herself. 'When I'm finished with you, you'll be a twelve. Come on, no time to waste.'

In the first shop, it took Julie, Rita and me two trips to carry all of the clothes Rita had selected into the changing rooms. Before drawing the curtain, I protested mildly. 'It's not going to be a dressy-up kind of holiday. We'll be canoeing, and camping. We'll be roughing it.'

Rita was firm. 'You can rough it in style, you know. Think Posh Spice on holidays.'

I grinned at her. 'Do I get Becks too?'

'Only if you're very bold. Now stop prevaricating and get going.'

Rita held the curtain open for a second. 'Hey, what about Linda? If she's Miss Glamour, how is she going to rough it? Canoeing doesn't sound like her kind of thing. She sounds like she should be on a yacht in the Mediterranean.'

I sighed. 'You'd have to meet her to understand. She's glamorous, but she's mad too. She won't be happy unless the river is wild and dangerous. Sitting on a yacht would be far too boring for her. And believe me, Linda doesn't do boring.'

Rita had a funny twinkle in her eye. 'Well, from now on, neither do you. You're going to shake off those cobwebs and knock them all dead.'

She dropped the curtain, and I began my marathon changing session.

Rita had a good eye. She'd selected shorts and casual trousers that were unexpectedly flattering. Then she persuaded me to try a few tops that were a size smaller than I was used to. I protested. 'But I have no chest for these.'

She looked closely, and couldn't disagree. Then she raced off to the lingerie department, returning with a strange-looking bra. 'Look. These are new. They're inflatable. Two puffs and you're irresistible. Three puffs and you can be Dolly Parton.'

I laughed. 'And if I fall out of the canoe, I'll have my own buoyancy aid.'

Julie shook her head at the foolish adults, and went to wait outside.

One shop, and we'd managed three new outfits – not bad for a reluctant shopper like me. I was very pleased. 'Coffee? There's a great new place in Thomas Street.'

Julie looked brighter. 'Yay. Can I get hot chocolate with marshmallows?'

Rita looked at us crossly. 'No way. We're only getting started. What are you going to wear in the evenings?'

I shrugged and held up my shopping bags. 'These?'

Rita didn't even bother to reply as she led me into another shop. Here she enlisted the help of a pretty young shop assistant. 'Jill needs three outfits suitable for evening wear. Casual, but smart. Nothing too fussy.'

The girl took to her task with good spirits, producing outfit after outfit, and within twenty minutes I was kitted out to everyone's satisfaction. At last we were allowed to retire for refreshments.

Half an hour later, as we got up to leave the coffee shop, I asked if we had time to go to the supermarket. Rita looked at me in horror. 'Supermarket? You won't get to be a twelve by buying lamb chops and toilet cleaner. I'm not half-finished with you.'

Julie giggled, amused to see her mother being bullied. She didn't know that was how I had spent half my youth. 'Come on, Mum,' she cajoled. 'Be a good girl and do as you're told.'

Rita led me to the cosmetics counter in Brown Thomas. She presented me to a fierce-looking woman who had more make-up on her face than I'd worn in my life. 'What can you do for my friend?' Rita asked.

The woman leaned towards me. Her false eyelashes almost brushed my cheek. She raised one hand and the stones set in her fingernails glinted in the light. She tilted my chin and turned my face to see it from different angles. She shook her head and tutted loudly. I was afraid she'd say I was beyond help. Apparently I wasn't. The woman began a litany longer than I'd ever heard at a novena. 'Facial scrub. Eye rejuvenator. Lip buff. Concealer. Foundation. Loose powder. Bronzer. Lip plumper. Lip pencil. Lipstick. Lip gloss. Three shades of eyeshadow. Eye pencil. Mascara...'

The list continued. Julie, Rita and I looked on in awe. I almost felt I should say, 'Pray for us,' as the woman solemnly intoned each successive word.

At last she appeared to be finished. There was silence as everyone examined me closely. Two passers-by had even lingered for a pitying look at the person who needed so much work. I could feel my cheeks reddening, even without the addition of any ultra-light bronzing veil.

'I...I'm not sure...' I began.

Then the woman gave a huge, happy laugh, totally at odds with her fierce appearance. 'I'm only having you on. I can see you're not into all of that. How about a nice tinted moisturiser, some concealer for those black circles, a touch of something on the eyes, and a slick of this new summer lip gloss?'

I could have hugged her.

In ten minutes, she was finished. She held a mirror for me to view her handiwork. She'd worked magic. I didn't look like a teenager again, she wasn't all that gifted, but somehow she'd made my eyes look bigger and brighter, and without those dark circles, I almost looked youngish.

Rita was very pleased with herself. As we got back into the car she looked at me again. 'Definitely. Twelve and a half. If not thirteen.'

'Thirteen what? What do you mean?' asked Julie.

Rita ruffled her hair. 'Your mum just looks great, that's what I mean.'

As we drove home, I hummed happily. But then I found myself wondering what Dudley would think of my new appearance. Would he like it? Would he look at me and be able to recapture some of the lost moments of our distant youth?

I stopped humming. It was worrying how all my thoughts seemed to lead to Dudley in the end.

Julie interrupted my thoughts. 'I bet you can't wait to show Daddy your new stuff. He's going to be very happy.'

I turned around and smiled at her. 'Yes, love,' I said. 'I bet he is.'

Chapter Eleven

Julie persuaded me to model my new clothes for Cormac that night, and he appeared to like them. Or, at least, he didn't laugh and ask if I was wearing them for a bet. And he did mumble something like 'Very nice,' before he went into the family room and parked himself in front of the television.

I was exasperated. I had hoped for a better response, a sincere one, even. I had hoped he would look closely, and like what he saw.

And, besides, Cormac had promised me he was going to watch less television and get more exercise.

I bravely went into the family room after him and stood between him and the television screen. He didn't protest too much, but then the ads were on at the time.

I put my hands on my hips and did my frustrated-housewife bit. 'Look at you. I thought you were going to play some sport. I thought you said you were going to exercise some other part of your body than the thumb you use for the remote control. One fine day you're going to keel over from stress and lack of exercise.'

He leaned around me and flicked the screen into darkness. He smiled. 'Actually, I have done what you asked. I am going to play some sport this week.'

I was genuinely pleased. 'That's great. Are you joining an indoor soccer game?'

He shook his head. 'Better than that. I've entered a tennis competition.'

My heart sank. Cormac had been a member of the tennis club for years, but he never actually played. As far as I knew, he hadn't darkened the door of the clubhouse in recent history. And now, of all times, I didn't want him hanging around there, where he might meet Norma and her gossipy friends. For all I knew, my indiscretion with Dudley could be the talk of the place by now.

'That's nice.'

I went into the kitchen, put on an apron to protect my new clothes and started to chop the onions for the dinner.

Cormac followed me. He leaned on the counter and grinned. 'And that's not the best bit. I called in this evening to look at the draw. I'm playing the first round tomorrow evening. And guess who I'm playing against?'

'Who?' I didn't care. I just wanted him to get knocked out quickly, so he'd be less likely to meet Norma.

'That guy. You know the one. The one with the funny name.'

I felt a small stab of fear.

'Which guy?'

'You know, the one in the paper. The one who brought all the TDs running to Limerick. Mr Big-Shot from America.'

The stab of fear became larger and more painful. I kept my eyes on the task in front of me.

Cormac scratched his head and thought. Suddenly he banged his hand down on the counter and exclaimed, 'Dudley! That's it. Dudley Adamson. How could I forget that name? He's the guy I'm playing in the first round.'

I couldn't stop myself. 'You're playing tennis against Dudley Adamson tomorrow night?'

Cormac nodded. 'Yep. And I'm going to whup his fake-tanned ass.'

Actually, I knew that particular part of Dudley's anatomy didn't have a tan at all, fake or otherwise, but it was hard to see how I could slip that little gem casually into the conversation.

I chopped furiously at the onion. Dudley had told me he was going to be in America. Had he just been trying to shake me off? While I had spent the past weeks reliving the wonderful, passionate evening we had spent together, had he already dismissed me from his mind? Was I nothing to him but a casual fling? Easy sex? Was I still the same fool I had been twenty years earlier?

Tears began to sting my eyes. The onions were a convenient alibi. I scraped them into a pot and reached for some carrots. Cormac was doing imaginary tennis swings and making macho whooping noises.

As I scraped the carrots clean, I calmed down a little. Maybe Dudley's plans had changed. Maybe he had expected to be in America, but it hadn't turned out that way.

But, if so, why hadn't he called me? Was the scrap of paper with my number on it scrunched up in a corner of a rubbish bin somewhere? Had he tossed it away even before the taste of me had disappeared from his mouth?

Cormac stopped his jumping around. 'Do you want to come?'

'Where?'

'To watch the big match, of course. To cheer on your loving husband in his big return to the tennis court.'

And then the true horror of the situation began to dawn on me. My husband and my lover were going to meet on the tennis court. This was the kind of thing that happened in Hugh Grant movies. Those movies always had happy endings. Would I be so lucky? This was real life. Anything could happen. It could give a whole new meaning to the term 'love all'. Neither man knew that they had me in common.

Cormac could be all buddy-buddy and invite Dudley over to dinner. Or, between sets, Dudley could tell Cormac about his great conquest. I could picture it. They would stand on either side of the net and try to impress each other. I could hear Dudley's bragging words.

'The craziest thing happened recently. This girl who had a big thing for me when I was a student showed up at my hotel. Threw herself at me. Dying for it, she was. Practically dragged me to my room. Couldn't get her clothes off fast enough.'

Cormac would laugh. 'That's the way to have them. Desperate.'

Dudley would go all macho. 'Sex wasn't great, though. She'd sagged a bit over the years. Still, it was an act of charity. She was exceedingly grateful. Sad, though, really. I'd forgotten Jill even existed.'

'That's funny, my wife's name is Jill...'

I couldn't continue the imaginary conversation. It was too horrible.

Cormac interrupted me. 'Well? Will you come?'

I shook my head. 'Sorry. I'd love to. I can't, though. I'm... Well, I have to finish Julie's outfit for the school play.'

It was a stupid excuse, but the best I could do. Luckily, Cormac didn't know that Julie's play had been on the week before. He hadn't made it, as he had some important business meeting scheduled for the same morning. And when Julie had tried to tell him about it later, he had been watching a 'crucial' darts match on the television and hadn't heard a word.

Next evening, when Cormac came home from the tennis club, his macho fighting talk had dried up. Clearly he had lost.

'I'm sorry.' I put a hand on his arm in what I hoped was a consoling manner. The truth was, I was absolutely delighted. Maybe now he'd stay away from the tennis club. He could take up soccer, where I hoped the main topics of dressing-room conversation would be the Premier League transfer list and the merits of the Bundesliga.

Cormac tossed his head. 'I was robbed. He had a few lucky shots. I'd have taken him, only my old ankle injury started to play up.'

I hid my smile. There was no independent evidence of Cormac ever actually having received an ankle injury, but it flared up whenever it suited him as an excuse.

I spoke as casually as I could. 'What's he like, this Dudley?'

Of course I knew exactly what he was like. I probably knew more about him than his own mother did. In fact, there were certain things I sincerely hoped his mother didn't know about him. But I needed to know how well Cormac had got to know him. I needed to know how much damage had been done.

'Oh, you know the type. Good-looking. Arrogant as anything. Smooth. Thinks he's God's gift to women.'

Sarcasm came easily to me. 'Sounds lovely. Did you chat much?'

Like, did either of you mention me at all?

He shook his head. 'Nah. He was all business during the game, and afterwards he had no time for a drink. Said he had to meet his wife and kids off a plane.'

105

So that was that. My dream was over. Dudley was going to play Happy Families, and he had already forgotten all about me. I'd had my moment in the sun, and now it was time to move on.

But still, as I lay in bed that night, listening to Cormac's steady breathing, I tried to convince myself that Dudley too had felt something special between us, and was just biding his time before he called me.

Chapter Twelve

I shut my eyes and ran through the list in my head.

Plants watered. Neighbourhood extortionist teenager bribed to cut grass. Bread-bin emptied. Milk cancelled. Paper cancelled. Washing machine free of wet sheets (not like last year, when the smell of damp and mildew lingered until Hallowe'en). Clothes packed. Tickets packed. Passports packed. Husband doing something totally irrelevant like rearranging his CDs, or perhaps tidying the garage. Children in car, already fighting about exactly how much of the empty seat between them each should have.

Everything was done. It seemed like we were ready to go on holidays.

I dragged Cormac out from the downstairs toilet, where he was patching the piece of wallpaper that Julie had ripped when she was about two years old. Since he'd managed to ignore it for the past six years, I really couldn't see why he felt a sudden urge to repair it right now.

I switched on the house alarm, shut the front door and climbed into the car. I turned back to face the children. I tried to sound enthusiastic. 'Well, isn't this just great? Off on our holidays again, for two lovely weeks.'

'Two weeks of hell, more like. I'd rather stay at home watching telly. I'd even rather stay at home not watching telly.' Luke's morose voice from the back seat.

'Canoeing – huh. Canoeing is stupid. Zoë can't stop laughing at me. She says canoeing is only for losers. She's going to Disneyland. In Florida. She's staying in a cowboy hotel. And Molly's going to this totally cool place that has three water-slides and a disco every night.' Julie's plaintive wail.

'Actually, this whole trip is child cruelty. There are laws against this kind of thing. Parents have been jailed for less.' Luke again. I wondered if he really believed what he was saying, or if he was just trying to start a row. That would have been a record – the first row before we'd even driven out of our street.

I carefully straightened my new tight top and turned to face them again. 'This holiday is going to be great,' I hissed. 'And you two are going to enjoy it, whether you like it or not. You do not have a choice in the matter. Is that clear?'

Cormac giggled, and I gave him the filthiest look I could manage. I was stressed out enough without him taking Luke and Julie's side. He eyed his children in the rear-view mirror. 'Come on, guys. Lighten up. Give your mother a break. It's going to be an experience. We'll have a ball. I promise.'

I smiled gratefully at him, and he took my hand and squeezed it. 'Don't worry, Jill. I'm looking forward to this trip. If it's great – that's great, we'll all be happy. If it's dreadful, hey, I get to bring you to the finals of the Lithuanian schoolboy league next year, and you don't even get to argue. I can't lose, can I?'

We all laughed at that, and we drove onto the North Circular on the way to our big holiday.

Two hours later, we left the car at Mum and Dad's house, and Dad drove us to Cork airport. He offered to come in and wait with us, but I knew he wanted to watch a match on the telly, so I declined. He shook Cormac's hand, kissed the rest of us and jumped into his car with almost indecent speed.

'Lucky Granddad,' muttered Luke as he watched him drive away.

'Luke!' I hissed. 'This holiday is important to me. So I don't care if you're happy. I just want you to look happy. OK?'

He shrugged and put on a false smile.

Julie danced around with an even falser smile. 'Look at me. Look at me. See how happy I am.'

I couldn't help laughing. 'Come on, guys, everyone take a bag. Let's go check in.'

As we walked in, I couldn't stop myself from rearranging my hair and holding my stomach in. It was foolish, I knew. After all, Linda had seen me in every possible state. I had no secrets from her.

She arrived just as we took our place in the check-in queue.

'Jill. Jilly. Great to see you.' She ran towards me with her arms outstretched, and I felt a funny sad-guilty feeling. She wasn't pretending. I knew she really was glad to see me. She was always glad to see me.

We hugged, and then she stepped back to look at me. 'You look fantastic, Jill. That's a great haircut, and those jeans are fab on you.' I smiled, and mentally thanked Rita.

Linda, of course, looked absolutely sensational. She too had a new hairstyle, one I wouldn't have dared to try. Her hair was short and spiky and the ends were barely tipped with red. It was a hairstyle fit for a pop star, and Linda, of course, was well able to carry it off.

She was wearing ripped denims and a tight top that left nothing to the imagination. I could see all the men in the queue eyeing her. I looked at Cormac and tried to see if he was looking at her face or her cleavage. Unfortunately, he still had his sunglasses on, so I couldn't tell for sure. I decided to give him the benefit of the doubt. It was going to be a long holiday. There'd be plenty of time later for jealous rows.

Linda's husband Max and their daughter Lauren arrived, dragging two huge suitcases behind them. My heart sank when I saw that Lauren was wearing the expensive sparkly flip-flops that Julie had wanted so badly. They looked exotic and beautiful next to Julie's faded denim sandals. Luckily, Julie didn't notice Lauren's footwear. She was too busy eyeing the industrial-sized box of gel pens that Lauren was carrying under her free arm. I thought ruefully of the six mismatched markers that Julie had in her rucksack.

Max hugged me and shook Cormac's and Luke's hands. He ruffled Julie's hair and said, 'Hi, kiddo.' Lauren stared at us rather rudely and ignored her mother's request to be a good girl and say hello. Julie immediately took advantage and became Miss Perfect, smiling and shaking everyone's hand. Lauren scowled at her.

Linda whispered to me, 'Sorry. She's not usually like this. It's just that she's a bit tired.'

If I had known then how often over the next two weeks I was going to hear that particular phrase, I think I'd have run down the airport hill, tearing at my clothes and howling for my dad to come back and rescue me. Luckily, though, I had no idea, so I just smiled at everyone and rooted in my bag for the tickets and the passports.

Before long, we were climbing the clanky metal stairs onto the plane and smiling politely at the air hostesses. We'd been a little late checking in, so while most of the party could sit together, two had to sit away from the others, right at the front of the plane.

Cormac's eyes lit up when he saw the two front seats. 'Will Max and I sit here, out of the way?'

I was ready to nod my assent when Linda spoke from behind him on the steps. 'No way, sunshine. I bet Jill packed and cleaned for weeks to get here. I know I did. And those seats are our reward.'

Cormac knew he was beaten. It was true that his sole contribution to the holiday preparations had been packing his own clothes, so he set off for the back of the plane with Max and the three children. Linda joined me in front, and we settled in our seats. A few minutes later she turned around to see how the others were getting on. She giggled and took my arm. 'Quick, look back there.'

I looked. Max and Lauren were rowing. It looked as if they both wanted the window seat. Lauren was stamping her foot and scowling.

Cormac was seated right next to the toilet. He didn't look very happy. In the seat beside him was Luke, who, as usual, wore his 'too cool for this world' look. Next to Luke, Julie was struggling with her seat-belt. I went to get up. 'I'd better give Julie a hand.'

Linda put out her hand to stop me. 'Hang on a sec. Who's that responsible-looking adult sitting just near her? Oh, yes. It's her father.'

I nodded. 'Yes, but—'

'Yes, but nothing. They're all fine. Don't be a martyr. Anyway, I need you here. I need your help with this.'

'What?'

She reached into her rucksack and pulled out a bottle of red wine and two glasses. I watched in wonder as she opened the bottle and poured us each a glass. I took mine, and she clinked it with hers. '*Sláinte*. Here's to the best holiday ever. We're going to have a ball. I just know it.'

As she spoke, she smiled her wonderful, enthusiastic, almost innocent smile.

I drank deeply, and for a few moments I felt like a teenager again. As usual, Linda had managed to totally beguile me. I was sure we were going to have a great holiday, just because she had decreed that it would be so. I smiled at her, and, for the first time in ages, I remembered why I'd always liked her so much.

Chapter Thirteen

By the time we landed in Toulouse, I was feeling particularly good about myself, and about the world. That might possibly have had something to do with the half-bottle of red wine that I had churning around inside me.

We gathered our bags and went through the double doors into the arrivals hall. I quickly spotted a jolly-looking man holding a placard with our names on it. He quickly spotted us, and became considerably less jolly-looking.

He lowered the sign and eyed us with barely concealed disdain. First he looked at my new glittery sandals; then his eyes drifted towards Linda's high-heeled, pointy shoes. Next he looked at Lauren's tight cycling shorts and shiny belly-top. Luke, still in his long leather coat, caught his eye next. The poor man's face fell, and he rubbed his head in a frustrated-looking way.

I was beginning to feel that I should apologise for our very existence when Linda nudged me. 'Look at the state of Sourpuss. Who was he expecting? The Swiss Family Robinson?'

I had to laugh as she tossed her head and click-clacked her way over to the poor gentleman. She held out her hand, showing her nails, which were varnished in perfect, narrow, red and white stripes. 'Hi, I'm Linda. This is Jill, Cormac, Max, Lauren, Julie and Luke.'

The man took her beautifully manicured hand in his callused and wrinkled one. He spoke in a perfect English accent. 'Very pleased to meet you. I'm Peter. I'll be your guide for the duration of your holiday.'

Cormac couldn't hide his disappointment. 'Guide? I didn't know we needed a guide. The river only goes one way, doesn't it? How could we possibly get lost?'

Peter shook his head. 'Well, we'll see about that. Anyway. I'm only here for emergencies. I'm always only a mobile-phone call away. I just take you to your hotel and get you settled. In the morning, I fix you up with your canoes and give you your itinerary. Every morning, after you leave, I transport your luggage to the next stop. Actually, if all goes well, you will barely see me at all.' He gave a rather nervous smile and repeated, 'If all goes well, that is.'

His expression indicated that he didn't hold out much hope of all going well. I had a funny feeling that he'd already decided we were the canoeists from hell.

Peter led the way out of the airport and into the car park. It was wonderfully, beautifully warm. The air seemed to caress my skin. The tarmac glistened and shimmered. It was ever so slightly tacky under my feet. The weather at home had been dull and cool for weeks. I thought perhaps I'd be happy to let the others continue without me. I could lie in a deckchair in the airport car park until it was time to go home.

Peter led us to a minibus. It was painted in browny-green camouflage colours. A small sign declared quietly, 'Dordogne Tours.

114

Est. 1978.' This was a serious minibus, for serious canoeing types with khaki shorts and huge netted rucksacks. I had a horrible feeling we had no place there, with our city clothes and wheeled suitcases. Still, there wasn't a whole lot any of us could do about it at this stage. I smiled brightly at Peter, and hoped my fears didn't show on my face.

We all piled into the minibus for the journey to our first hotel. Max and Cormac sat in front with Peter and talked soccer. At one stage Cormac gave a huge laugh, and for one brief moment I caught a glimpse of the light-hearted man I had married.

Lauren had relaxed a bit and was showing Julie her colouring book and her giant pack of a hundred gel pens. If seven is enough colours for the rainbow, I'm not quite sure why anyone would need pens in a hundred different shades. Unfortunately, Julie didn't share my views – her face was a picture of complete envy. She wisely didn't offer to show Lauren her meagre set of markers – Lauren didn't look like the type of child who would feign enthusiasm for politeness's sake.

Luke sat in the last row of the minibus, with the luggage, and gazed out at the landscape with a bored expression. Still, maybe bored was OK. At least he and Cormac hadn't started arguing yet.

I rested my head against the window. I was tired after the journey and the wine. As usual, Linda was on sparkling form, so I shut my eyes and let her chat wash over me. She didn't seem to mind that I wasn't listening.

I awoke to hear Max reading aloud from a guidebook. 'Hey, get this, guys. The name "Dordogne" comes from the Celtic word "Du-anna". And guess what that means.'

He waited, but no one bothered to reply. 'OK, be like that. It means "fast-flowing water".'

I opened my eyes and sat up. 'Hey. Say that again.'

Max turned around in his seat and smirked at me. 'Well, it's nice to know someone's listening. I said "Dordogne" means "fast-flowing water".'

I sat up even straighter. 'I thought that was what you said. But my so-called friend Linda said we'd be canoeing in calm, gentle waters. There was no mention of white-water stuff. I don't do extreme.'

Linda leaned over and patted my arm. 'Come on, Jill, don't panic. Those Celts were mad. They were all on drugs or something. They hadn't a clue. Maybe some parts of the river are a bit rough, but we'll only be in quiet parts. I promise.'

She smiled at me reassuringly. I had too much experience of Linda to be at all reassured. Memories flashed into my mind. Her 'I've invited a few friends over for a quiet drink' turned out to be about eighty loud people carrying enough alcohol to keep a small city singing for a week. Her 'Let's go for a walk with some guys I met' turned out to be a mountain expedition involving hiking boots and ropes and ultimately, twelve cold and wet hours later, the Kerry mountain rescue team.

Still, short of throttling the driver and making him drive us back to the airport, there wasn't a whole lot I could do, so – as usual when Linda was around – I tried to put my worries to the back of my mind and think of something else.

Before too long we arrived at the aptly named town of Beaulieu sur Dordogne. When we got to the hotel, Peter wasn't hanging around. He unloaded us and our luggage in about thirteen seconds flat. We must have looked a rather forlorn group as we stood in the driveway, surrounded by our many bags. Peter didn't seem to care. He jumped back into the van with what appeared to me to be undue haste. 'Just go inside and check in. They're expecting you. I'll meet you right here at ten tomorrow. Have a nice evening.' The wheels of the minibus skidded, sending a small spray of gravel over our feet, as he drove away at speed.

We gathered our bits and went inside. We were greeted by a charming Frenchwoman, who had us settled in no time. While Luke and Julie were watching TV in the room off ours, Cormac and I threw ourselves onto the bed.

'Well?' I asked.

'Well what?'

'What do you think so far?'

He shrugged. 'It's a bit early to say. We have just got here. Max is OK. I always liked him. He's got an incredible knowledge of soccer.'

I made a face. 'Oh, well, he must be a nice guy, then, mustn't he? Maybe he'll have an interest in office machinery, and then you two can be soulmates.'

Cormac ignored my sarcastic tones. 'Linda seems to have calmed down a bit, hasn't she?'

'Mm. I suppose she has.' I wasn't at all sure about that. She was always kind of quiet at first in new places, like she was trying to suss things out. Still, I didn't want to spoil Cormac's positive mood by pointing this out.

He continued, 'And, let's give the girl credit, she's looking great.'

Maybe it was an innocuous comment, but I couldn't let it pass. I'd spent too much of my life watching men drool over Linda, and I certainly didn't want my husband to start.

I couldn't keep the sharp tone from my voice. 'What do you mean?'

He shrugged. 'Hey, take it easy. I just said she's looking great. Don't get your knickers in a twist.'

117

'So you're saying I don't look great?' That was a really stupid comment, but I couldn't stop myself. Just being around Linda brought back all my old feelings of inadequacy.

Cormac sighed. 'You look great too. I told you that this morning before we left home.'

He hadn't, actually, but I was too tired to take that point and run with it.

Cormac sat up and stroked my arm. 'You look lovely, Jill, really.'

I smiled and turned away. Surely a compliment didn't count as such when it had to be dragged out? What had I been thinking of, coming on holidays with my husband and the most beautiful woman I had ever known?

We ate at the hotel that night. Everyone was tired, and I suspect that most of us were a little apprehensive about the next day. I couldn't help thinking that I'd like to spend a few days relaxing by a pool with a good book. The thought of canoeing for ten kilometres sounded like very hard, unnecessary work. Still, that thought was about two months late in arriving, so there was no point indulging it now.

Apart from a minor row, when Julie wanted a second fizzy drink because Lauren had one, it was a quiet evening. Even Linda was unusually subdued. I wondered if there was something going on. I didn't ask her, though – I was too busy watching Cormac to make sure that he wasn't watching her.

We went to bed early. Cormac was asleep in minutes, and began to snore loudly. I smiled at the sound. After sixteen years, I was so used to his snoring that it didn't bother me any more.

I rested my head on one arm and looked at him in the shaft of light coming through the window. His face was comfortable, familiar. Whatever happened between us, he was a part of my life, the man I'd married, the father of my children.

But still, my thoughts strayed once again to Dudley. I remembered his deep sighs when we embraced. His muscly chest. His strong hands gripping my shoulders. His groans of pleasure. The way he held me tight, as if he could never bear to let me go.

Cormac stirred and flung himself over in the bed. His arm landed on my chest and rested easily there. I took his hand and held it to my cheek, like I used to when we were first married.

And all night long I tossed and turned and wondered why on earth I'd agreed to come on this holiday at all.

Chapter Fourteen

Next morning we had a wonderful breakfast. (Which was, of course, all the more wonderful because I didn't have to shop for the food, I didn't have to cook it and I didn't have to clean up afterwards.) Then we legged it back to our rooms, to pack our bags ready for Peter to carry on to our next stop.

Julie was suspicious. 'I don't like that man at all. He has an ugly face and his shoes are horrible. And he has a funny posh voice. And he's a stranger. You told me never to trust strangers. What if he runs away with all our stuff? What if he steals Pink Teddy?'

Luke interrupted. 'That filthy old thing? Peter would deserve a reward if he took that. He should do us all a favour by putting Pink Teddy out of its misery.' As he spoke, he picked up Julie's teddy and pretended to choke it.

'Muuuum!' Julie looked suitably stricken, which was a bit rich, considering poor old Pink Teddy often spent weeks under her bed, unloved and forgotten.

Luke put the teddy down and smiled a beatific smile. It was time to stop picking on Julie, and to start on his mother.

'Look at it this way, Jules. Mum and Dad are sensible people. You can be certain they're well insured. And you know the beauty of insurance?'

Julie shook her head. 'How would I know that? I'm only eight.'

He grinned at her. 'It's very simple. If Pompous Peter nicks our stuff, the insurance company will cough up, and we can buy better stuff.'

Julie's face lit up. She pointed at her much-hated runners. 'So if, maybe, these runners…em…fell into the river or something and got lost, then the insurance company would buy me nice new ones?'

Luke nodded at her and grinned. 'That's it, Sis. You've got the idea. Think expensive. Think very expensive. Think designer runners with lights on and fancy laces.'

I gave Luke a dirty look and eyeballed Julie. 'Don't even think of it. If anything happens those runners, there will be a major inquiry. And then I will make sure they are replaced by something really, really hideous. I promise you I won't rest until I find you the ugliest runners in France.'

Julie knew when I was serious. She put her head down and finished packing her teddy into the suitcase. For the millionth time, I wondered how such a sweet-looking girl, who still loved her teddy when it suited her, could also be so scarily devious.

A few minutes later we were ready. We went downstairs and stepped out into the sunshine. While I was blinking in the bright light and rummaging for my sunglasses, Cormac grabbed my arm. 'What's all this about?' he hissed. 'It's bad enough being saddled with Linda and her family, but who on earth are this shower of misfits?'

121

I put on my sunglasses and surveyed the scene. It was indeed a motley crew that was gathered outside the hotel. Linda, Max and Lauren were there, of course. Next to them were two forty-something men. They were dressed in seriously tight shorts and T-shirts. Both were deeply tanned and fit-looking. At first I thought they must be gym instructors, but then I changed my mind and decided they were stressed-out executives on holiday trying to look like gym instructors. They were hopping about with impatience and speaking in loud Dublin accents.

'Come on. Let's get this show on the road. It's already five past ten. What's this delay about?'

His buddy turned to me. 'We were hoping to be in Tauriac by lunchtime.'

'Really?' I wasn't particularly interested, and besides, I'd be happy to see Tauriac any time before sundown.

'Yeah. We were hoping to get a cycle in this afternoon.'

'Good for you.' I was fairly sure he didn't mean a meander down to the nearest pub. They probably planned to cycle to Paris and jog up to the top of the Eiffel Tower before dinner. I looked at Linda, who wasn't even pretending not to look at the contents of his tight shorts. She caught my eye and raised her eyebrows. I had to laugh.

Besides the Lycra Laddies, there was a young English couple – well, they were young compared to me. I figured they were perhaps in their early thirties. The woman was a thin, pale, worried-looking thing, and the man was a big, red-faced bully.

He was almost shouting at her. 'It will be easy. I promise. Even for you. It's all in the arm action.'

He glanced around and saw a long stick lying on the grass. He picked it up and made a big show of gripping it carefully, with one hand at each end. Then he began to turn it in the air, almost taking out the eye of one of the Lycra Laddies as he did so. The bully was so intent on his arm action that he failed to notice this. 'Look, see how easy it is? Over and around. Over and around. Any fool could do it. Even you could do it.'

His poor wife looked as if she was going to cry. 'I'm not sure about this at all. You know this isn't really my kind of thing. I wish we'd decided on a painting holiday instead. Maybe I should go in the minibus, and meet you at the hotel later.'

Her loving husband addressed the crowd. 'Hear that? Bloody typical.' He glared at his wife and spat his words at her. 'I should have bloody well left you at home doing your knitting. You're always the bloody same. I should have known after the mess you made of the hill-trekking last year.'

His wife put her head down and didn't reply. I was so sorry for the woman that I felt tears come to my eyes. Linda didn't bother with tears, though. She leapt into action.

She sidled across the gravel towards the bully. I knew by the swing of her hips that she meant business. I knew her tactics from long ago. She smiled her best smile. The smile was to give him a false sense of security. She looked him up and down, an admiring expression on her perfectly made-up face. She was like a cat stalking a poor stupid little mouse. I could hardly bear to watch, but still I leaned forward to get a better view of proceedings.

'So,' she said in her sweetest voice. 'You look quite the expert. Have you done a lot of canoeing yourself?'

He smiled back at her uncertainly. He looked at his wife, who seemed to be enjoying what was happening. 'Well, I've done a bit. I've... Well, actually, I've done a lot of research on the internet. I've visited every canoeing site there is. And I've been subscribing to *Canoe Monthly* since Christmas.'

Linda smiled. 'Well, aren't you the clever boy?'

Max gave a huge, loud burst of forced laughter. He had such an infectious laugh that no one could resist joining in with a giggle or two. Well, no one, that is, except for the bully, who suddenly seemed to need to check the straps of his suitcase. Linda winked at the bullied wife, who smiled back gratefully. Linda looked rather disappointed, though. I knew why. It had been too easy. It was almost as if the cat had leapt on the mouse, and the mouse hadn't even tried to get away.

Next Linda proceeded to introduce herself and everybody else. I was sincerely hoping that this would prove to be a total waste of time. I didn't want to spend enough time in the company of these freaks that I'd need to know their names. Still, Linda didn't have it in her to be unfriendly. If she spent ten minutes in a bus queue, she'd end up intimately acquainted with everyone there. We learned that the boys in Lycra were Dominic and Trevor. The bully was called Barry, and his wife was called Laetitia – poor woman, as if being married to Barry weren't misfortune enough.

Just then the crunch of gravel announced Peter's arrival. He pulled up beside us and jumped out of the minibus. 'Everyone ready?'

We all nodded with varying degrees of enthusiasm. 'Well, we'll have to make two trips. Who...'

Before he'd finished speaking, the Lycra Laddies had leapt into the bus and strapped themselves into their seats. Barry dropped the stick he was still holding, grabbed his wife rather roughly by the arm and dragged her onto the bus. I began to feel indignant and wondered if I should protest. Why should they go first? After all, we were the ones with young children. Max just laughed. 'Great, now I get to have another cup of coffee. I'll bring some out for everyone. The river will wait.'

So Cormac, Linda, the kiddies and I sat on the terrace, in the pleasant sunshine, and watched as the other four set off with Peter. Max was soon back with coffee for everyone and yet another plate of croissants. While we waited, Lauren and Julie began a game with stones from the drive. Luke lay back in the sunshine and didn't look particularly unhappy. Max mocked the boys in Lycra, and Linda did a perfect imitation of the bully showing everyone how to paddle a canoe on dry land. They were a good double act.

As I wiped the tears from my eyes, I turned to look at Cormac. He too was laughing long and loud at Max and Linda's antics. Now that he was out of his suit, and away from his office, he seemed younger and happier and slightly more like the man I had married.

For the first time, I really began to look forward to my holidays.

Chapter Fifteen

When we climbed out of Peter's minibus at the riverbank, forty-five minutes later, there was no sign of the boys in Lycra. Linda laughed. 'They're probably in the next hotel already, doing push-ups or something.'

We couldn't see Barry and Laetitia either. Then, just as I wondered if perhaps she'd got sense and left him, or drowned him or something, I heard his strident tones drifting around the first bend in the river. 'No, not like that, stupid. God, how many times do I have to tell you? Don't you *ever* listen?'

If she replied, I didn't hear it. Anyway, I had to put them out of my mind, as Peter was explaining the drill to us.

We were all fitted out with lifejackets, and then we were brought to the boats. Linda, Max and Lauren were to travel together in one canoe. Our family had booked two.

Julie wanted to travel with me. 'Please, Mum. Don't make me go with Dad,' she said. 'He'll go too fast, just to scare me.'

She was probably right, but there was no way I could let

Cormac and Luke travel together. The way they were getting on, it was likely a canoe trip together would end in bloodshed.

I smiled at Julie. 'Sorry, love, you're with Daddy. Luke gets to go with me this time.'

Luke didn't care. He slouched along the riverbank, looking as if being with either parent was a fate worse than death.

We were given watertight containers to hold our valuables, and that was pretty much that. Cormac was raring to go, and he looked as if he wanted to catch up with the boys in Lycra. I was slightly worried, though. 'Er, there's just one thing,' I said, as Peter prepared to leave us to our fate.

'What's that?'

'We haven't a whole lot of canoeing experience.'

Actually, we had precisely no canoeing experience at all, but I thought I'd better not share that knowledge with Peter, since he was allowing us to head off into the sunset in his precious canoes.

That got his attention. 'How much experience have you, since you mention it?'

'I saw a canoeing race on *Jackass* once,' offered Luke helpfully. 'It was class. They did all this cool white-water stuff. In the end they went over this huge gorge and smashed five canoes.'

Now Peter started to look seriously worried. I hadn't planned that. I didn't want him deciding we weren't fit to be left in charge of his huge lumps of yellow plastic. I spoke as confidently as I could. 'Oh, don't worry. Cormac has plenty of experience of boats – from his last holidays. It's just me. I'm a small bit rusty. Maybe you could remind me – how exactly do you manoeuvre these things?'

Peter gave a laugh that someone slightly more paranoid than me would have perceived as evil. 'Oh, don't worry. You'll figure it out. After all, you've got two weeks.'

He gave each of the three canoes a push, waved goodbye and jumped into his minibus. As we wobbled away from the riverbank, I wondered if it was too soon to admit defeat and call him back. I dithered for a moment too long, and by the time I'd made up my mind to call him over, he was gone.

The first half-hour was rather difficult, to say the least, and in the end I was glad Peter wasn't around to watch our pathetic attempts to propel our trusty yellow vessels. Luke was handy enough, and managed to get a rhythm going, but his steering wasn't so hot, and we seemed to spend a lot of time floating along the riverbank, ducking low to avoid having our eyes taken out by overhanging trees. Lauren had a ball, seated comfortably between her parents. Max and Linda were paddling furiously, but they seemed to be making hardly any progress for all their effort. Cormac and Julie went for the slow and steady option, with Julie offering plenty of advice but doing very little actual work.

Max was the first to crack. 'OK. It's official. This is very hard work. Next place we see, we're stopping for coffee. Or maybe even something stronger. Agreed?'

Cormac wasn't so sure. 'I don't know, Max. Do you think we've gone far enough? We have to do ten kilometres today, you know.'

Linda was tired too. 'Who cares? I'm for stopping. We must have gone miles already. We're probably nearly there by now. And if we go too far this morning, what will we do after lunch?'

Luke and I were in the lead at this stage. We stopped paddling and turned back to look at the others straggling behind us. 'What do you think, Lu?' I asked him. 'Do you think we've gone far enough?'

He shrugged. 'How'm I meant to know?' This was his standard answer to pretty much any question I'd asked him in the last two years, and, as usual, it drove me crazy. I felt like hitting him on the head with my paddle. I resisted the urge, partly because, if Luke went on strike, I'd have to paddle on my own.

Just then I spotted a small wooden sign on the riverbank, pointing back the way we had come. I squinted my eyes to see it in the dappled shade. It read, 'Beaulieu 3/4 km'.

I laughed. 'Should we tell them, do you think?'

Luke considered for a moment. 'Nah, better not. There could be a mutiny.'

He steered us towards the sign and grabbed an overhanging branch, which he pulled down to obscure the writing. Then we waited for the others to catch up. As soon as they passed us, he let go of the branch, and we scooted to the front of the pack once more.

The day passed pleasantly, with plenty of stops for drinks and food. We didn't catch up with our fellow travellers, which suited me just fine.

After what seemed like a very long time on the river, we finally pulled into Tauriac. We had travelled the huge distance of ten kilometres. It felt like about ten thousand. I had a funny feeling that swimming it would have been less arduous. My back ached, my behind was sore from the hard seat and my hands were blistered from the paddles.

Luke and I were in the lead, as usual, so we were the first to see the wonderful sight of our beloved leader, Peter. He was reclining in a deckchair on the bank of the river, looking very pleased with himself.

'Hey, Peter, grab the rope,' I called as we drew level.

Peter slowly put down his book, removed his sunglasses and looked at us calmly. 'What was that? I couldn't quite hear what you said.'

'Quick, grab our rope.' There was, of course, no need for panic. It wasn't as if Niagara Falls were around the next bend (or so I hoped), but I felt my voice rising anyway. 'Please, Peter, grab our rope.'

The river was determined to drag us further, perhaps on to the next village, but I was having none of it. I'd had quite enough canoeing for one day. I took a moment to wonder why the canoeing was so hard, since the river was determined to drag us along anyway. Then I figured it out – all the effort was just to keep ourselves in a straight line, clear of the riverbank.

We struggled against the current and somehow managed to remain pretty much in the right position as Peter ever so slowly sauntered across the grass to us. I could see he was enjoying himself, grinning slightly to himself at our desperation. He seemed to enjoy causing pain. I wondered what he used to do before becoming a canoeing guide – perhaps he had been a dentist. I tried to smile as I held the rope with one hand and helped to paddle backwards with the other. Eventually, Peter took the rope and tied us to dry land. He looked at his watch. 'Hmm. Four hours. Not quite the slowest ever, but you're close.'

'We had a three-hour lunch,' I muttered through gritted teeth, as I climbed ashore.

Luke followed me, and we sat on the grass, trying to look as if we'd been there for hours, as the other two canoes appeared around the last bend.

Linda looked more tired than I'd ever seen her before, but she managed a smile nevertheless. She never liked to admit to any weakness. I went to grab her boat, but Peter edged me aside.

'Please, allow me.' I was too tired to argue. Once more he did his leisurely stroll to the water, as Max and Linda struggled against the gentle current. Linda threw him the rope. It was a good throw, but somehow he managed to miss it, so she had to reel it in and try again. What was it with this guy?

Linda threw him the rope once more, and this time he caught it. She smiled at him. 'Have you got it this time?'

He smiled back. Even he couldn't resist Linda's charm.

'Yes, I've got it.'

'You're sure?'

'Yes, I'm quite—'

Peter was so busy looking down the front of Linda's T-shirt that he never saw what was coming next. Before he could finish speaking, Linda gave the rope a sharp tug. He completely lost his balance, and after a few hopeless revolutions of his arms, he toppled slowly into the river. He was a big man, and the splash he made soaked us all, but it was worth it.

He surfaced a second later and swam the few strokes to the shore. Linda, who was there before him, offered him her hand. 'Oh, Peter. I don't know how that happened. Silly me. I mustn't know my own strength.' She smiled again, but this time he was taking no chances. He resisted the smile, and her offered hand, and scrambled ashore on his own.

He glared at Linda. 'That was very childish. Imagine if I couldn't swim. I could have drowned.'

Linda smiled one more time. 'Oh, don't worry, Peter, I'd have saved you. I can even do mouth-to-mouth resuscitation.'

Most red-blooded men would have jumped into the river unaided if promised resuscitation by Linda, but by now poor Peter was so spooked, he didn't seem to think of this. While he was distracted, I caught Cormac and Julie's rope, and they climbed ashore. Peter tied all three boats together and muttered under his breath. I wondered if it was possible to be expelled from a canoeing trip.

Peter flattened his hair, removed a piece of green slime from his cheek and spoke haughtily. 'Your hotel is just over there, behind those trees. Your bags are in your rooms. I'll see you in Carennac the day after tomorrow.'

He spoke as if he sincerely wished we would never make it to Carennac. We laughed, and, having removed our belongings from the watertight containers, we set off on the short walk to the hotel.

We dined early. Luckily there was no sign of Dominic and Trevor – even talking to those two made me feel tired. They were probably drinking wheatgrass cocktails in some macrobiotic vegetarian restaurant at the other side of town. Or maybe they'd decided to do the two-week trip in one afternoon, and were already at home planning next year's holidays.

Linda was worried about Laetitia. 'I hope Barry didn't finish her off with his paddle. That man seemed to have a lot of excess anger. And it was all directed at her.'

I made a face. 'Yeah. Poor Laetitia. Still, maybe she flipped and finished him off instead. I hope she pushed him overboard and is headed for the Atlantic as we speak.'

Linda laughed.

The meal was pleasant. We all had healthy appetites after our exertions – all except for Lauren, who hadn't exerted herself at all. Even though Julie hadn't done a whole lot of paddling, she had made the odd effort. The only time Lauren had been seen with a paddle in her hand was when she was using it to hit Julie because she wouldn't let her have half her ice-cream at lunchtime.

132

After dinner, Julie scraped her dessert plate and looked at me carefully. 'Can I have another dessert, please?'

I shook my head. 'Of course not. One dessert is enough for anyone.'

'Lauren had two.' That was true, but I'd been nurturing the feeble hope that this had escaped Julie's attention.

Linda patted Julie on the arm. 'Yes, love. You're right. She did have two desserts, but that's only because she's hungry. She didn't like her dinner.'

Julie gazed steadily at me. 'Mum, if I leave my dinner tomorrow, can I have two desserts?' She knew there was no hope of this happening. She was just stirring trouble.

I smiled at her. 'No, my darling. If you leave your dinner tomorrow, you'll go to bed with no dessert at all. How about that?'

She knew when she was beaten. I wondered if she'd appreciate my tough love when she got older. Probably not. I'd always be remembered as the evil mother who was too quick to dish out punishments and too slow to dish out desserts.

When we'd finished eating, we retired to a small lounge in the hotel. Cormac and Max were getting restless.

'I wonder what the rest of the town's like?' asked Max.

'Bet there's some great pubs.'

'Wouldn't it be a shame altogether if we didn't check them out? Especially when we're leaving the day after tomorrow.'

They were like a pathetic double act. I wondered if they had practised their routine earlier.

Then Luke interrupted. 'I'll watch the girls if you all want to check out the town.'

Linda's eyes lit up. She got bored easily, and I could see she'd already had enough of our picturesque, but very quiet hotel.

'That's really sweet of you. Thanks, Luke. How about it, guys?'
Without waiting for an answer, she stood up. 'I'll just get my—'

She was interrupted by a huge wail from Lauren. 'Nooo!'

Max ran to her. 'What is it, pumpkin? Did you hurt yourself?'

Lauren wailed even louder. 'Noooo! I'm not staying with him.'
She pointed at Luke.

Linda took Lauren on her knee. 'But, darling—'

She didn't get to finish. 'I'm not staying with him. I hate him,
and his hair is disgusting.'

I couldn't argue with her on the last point. Luke's hair was
indeed disgusting, with its asymmetrical fringe hanging lankly
over his left eye. Still, I didn't feel it was fair to agree with her.

Linda hugged Lauren and kissed her hair. 'That's not very
nice, darling. Don't say that.'

Lauren made a hideous face. 'I will say it. I hate him. I hate
him. And his hair is very, very disgusting.'

Linda stroked her daughter's hair and smiled at Luke. 'I'm
sorry, Luke. She doesn't mean that. She's just tired, that's all.'

So put her to bed, and then we can go out in peace. I didn't
say that, of course.

Luke shrugged and pretended he didn't care. I knew, though,
by the way he tossed his gammy fringe, that he was rather upset.
In a strange way I was pleased. Sometimes I wondered if there
still was a human being inside his cool exterior.

In the end, Max bought more beer, and we drank it in the
hotel. I put Julie to bed around nine. Lauren fell asleep in Linda's
arms and remained there for the evening. Every now and then,
Linda stroked her head and cooed softly to her.

I couldn't help shaking my head in wonder. Linda had always
dominated our class at school – even the teachers had bowed to
her will. At college, she had been like the centre of the universe.

At discos she had practically had men falling at her feet, ready to do her will. And now, here she was, cowed by the force of the will of a three-foot-nothing, precocious little madam. She really wasn't a very competent mother.

For a while, I felt sorry for Linda. Then I wasn't so sure. For the first time ever, it looked as if there was something I could do better than Linda. And, mean though it was, that made me feel really, really good.

Chapter Sixteen

In the morning, Lauren was all sweetness and light again. She even smiled at Luke over her cornflakes and offered him one of her ever-present sweets. Luke could be unpredictable. In this case, I didn't know if he was going to be charming or obnoxious. I held my breath. I needn't have worried, though. This time he was a good boy. He smiled back at Lauren, even though he must surely have felt like grabbing the sweets and ramming them in her bold little face.

I gave him a grateful smile. Maybe there was hope for him, after all. Maybe today was going to be a good day for all of us, especially since it was a rest day, which meant that I didn't have to paddle a single stroke.

Once again, there was no sign of Dominic and Trevor. No doubt they'd left to run a marathon at dawn, while I was turning over and settling in for another few hours' sleep. Laetitia and Barry arrived for breakfast just as we were leaving. Barry kept his head down, but we still noticed that he had a huge black-and-purple eye. Laetitia was holding on to his arm and simpering at him. I resisted the temptation to ask what had happened, but Linda failed – she never had great self-control. 'Ouch, Barry. That looks sore. Did you walk into a door?'

He shook his head and made as if to walk past us. Laetitia spoke, though. Her voice was thin and kind of whiny. She hadn't noticed that Linda was being smart. 'Oh, no. It wasn't a door. He rowed into the bank and hit a tree-trunk.'

I stifled a giggle. Then Laetitia continued, 'Luckily I wasn't even in the boat, so he couldn't blame me.' She began a high, fluttery little laugh, but cut it short as Barry pulled at her arm.

'You were supposed to be holding the boat steady while I got out, remember? And it wouldn't have happened anyway if you hadn't had to stop to go to the toilet. Again.'

Laetitia gave us a nervous little smile and allowed herself to be pulled into the dining room.

Cormac and I had a lovely lazy day by the pool. Poor Linda and Max were tormented by Lauren, who'd found a sheaf of glossy brochures on the hotel reception desk. She waved them repeatedly in her parents' faces, whining constantly. 'But, Muuuummy, I want to go to this place. It's got a cool playground.'

I edged my sun-lounger ever so slightly away, and tried to ignore the constant scenes.

After dinner that evening, Max and Cormac parked themselves in front of a small television, watching an obscure soccer match. I was happy to sit in the lounge and sip the last of my wine, but Linda was having none of it.

'Come on, Jill, it's girls' night out.' I had to laugh. If it were up to Linda, every night would be girls' night out.

I didn't bother to protest as she instructed the men to put their daughters to bed sometime before midnight. Then she led the way into the village, and into the first pub we came to.

My first big mistake was letting Linda go to the bar counter. My second big mistake was drinking the huge glass of tequila she placed before me. After that, I didn't care about mistakes any more.

Linda was in great form. She told me a hilarious story about how she had bluffed her way into a new office job by composing a rather creative CV.

I laughed. 'But surely they realised you were lying when you started the job?'

She shrugged. 'Nah. The job is so simple a monkey could do it.'

That sounded a bit boring to me, but then, who was I to talk? I hadn't done a day's paid work in years.

'Did you ever think about going back to teaching?' I asked her.

She gave a theatrical shudder. 'No way. I don't know how I lasted as long as I did.'

I had to laugh. As far as I could remember, Linda's teaching career had lasted for about four months, and had ended in ignominy when she escorted a group of girls to Tramore for the day and managed to lose seven of them. The girls showed up safe and well the next day, but by then Linda's employers had decided that perhaps teaching wasn't the best career choice for her.

She continued, 'Becoming a teacher was a huge mistake. I don't know what I could have been thinking. I'm not sensible enough to be a teacher.'

I couldn't argue with that.

She went on, 'You, now. You'd have made a great teacher. You have so much patience. You must regret leaving college without finishing.'

I sighed. 'Regret' wasn't a big enough word for what I felt about abandoning college with an arts degree and nothing else. I had ended up in a succession of nice but undemanding office jobs, and when Luke was born, I had been more than happy to retire from my so-called career.

'Anyway,' Linda said, 'do you ever think about going back to work, now that the kiddies are getting bigger?'

I shook my head. 'No, not seriously. I like being at home.'

She gave a bright laugh. 'Ha! Good old Jill. You never changed, did you? Stay at home, where it's nice and safe.'

I knew it was partly the drink talking, but nevertheless, her words stung. I felt that she was being totally dismissive of me, and as I too had a skinful of drink inside me by then, I couldn't let it go.

I spoke more sharply than I had intended. 'Hey. Leave it out. That's not fair.'

She put her hands up in mock surrender. 'Relax. I didn't mean to offend you. I just said you liked to be nice and safe. It's true, isn't it? It's just the way you are. And that's one of the things I like about you. You never take chances, do you?'

Now that really hurt, and the fact that she was telling the truth didn't help at all. All my old jealous feelings began to resurface. I knew she was more daring, more exciting than me. Why did she have to rub it in?

I was filled with a sudden urge to impress her, to shock her, to show her that she wasn't the only one with a bit of spark and excitement in her life. And I could think of only one way to do this. My voice rose. 'Well, actually, for your information, only a few weeks ago I met a man in a bar, and I went back to his hotel room and we had mad, passionate sex.'

I became aware of a sudden silence behind me. I turned around to see two elderly Englishmen grinning broadly at me,

139

while their women companions adjusted their handbags, pursed their lips and tutted out loud.

Linda laughed. 'Hey. Good one. You really got my attention there.'

I didn't laugh with her. But then, why would I?

She leaned towards me and looked at me closely. 'You *are* joking. Aren't you?'

I shook my head. The damage was done. It was hard to impress Linda, so I might as well exploit it now that it had happened. 'I just felt like a bit of a fling. You know how it is.'

I was delighted with Linda's reaction. She was actually open-mouthed. 'You mean you picked up a stranger and went to bed with him?'

That, of course, wasn't strictly true. It had been a very, very long time since Dudley had been a stranger to me. But there was no way I was telling Linda the full truth. Luckily some shreds of sense remained in the drink-addled depths of my brain.

I nodded, like it was no big deal.

Linda's eyes were still wide with wonder. 'And are you going to see him again?'

Now there was the million-dollar question. I sincerely hoped I would see him again. But what were the chances of that?

I sighed. 'I don't know, actually.'

'Do you want to see him again?' Linda seemed to have forgotten that I was a supposedly happily married woman.

'I suppose.'

'Have you got his number?'

Of course I had. It was on a scrap of paper at the bottom of my handbag, right next to the travel-sickness tablets. I nodded.

'So ring him.'

She made it sound very simple. And, since I'd just had six large

140

tequilas, I thought it was very simple too.

I rooted in my handbag and pulled out the number and my mobile phone. I dialled and listened. He had his voice-mail on. My insides gave a funny little jolt when I heard his voice.

'Dudley here. Leave a message.'

I mouthed at Linda. *It's voice-mail.*

'So leave a message.' This was in a huge stage whisper.

I hesitated. Then I poured forth a stream of alcohol-induced babble. 'Hi. It's Jill. From Cork. Remember me? Just phoning you, you know. Not sure why. Just wanted to say hello. So, hello. I'm in France. On the Dordogne. That's a river, you know. I'm in a place called Tauriac, but we're going to Carennac tomorrow. We're going to canoe all the way there. Why don't you...?'

I was going to ask Dudley to ring me back. I never finished the sentence, though, as the phone began to beep loudly and then went dead.

My battery had let me down. Or had it saved me?

Linda took a big drink of her tequila. She looked at me closely. 'Well, you're a dark horse if ever I saw one.'

I smiled at her. I liked her admiring tone. I liked the way I had impressed her. But, deep down, I was sure I had made a terrible, terrible mistake.

Chapter Seventeen

Next morning, I had a hard, sharp headache, and I felt slightly queasy. And very guilty. What on earth had I been thinking of, phoning Dudley? What would he make of my drunken ramblings? What if he phoned me back? What if Cormac or one of the children answered?

I was too unwell to ponder this prospect for long, so I put it to the back of my mind, where there was still a nice, warm, fuzzy, tequila-soaked corner of near-oblivion.

After picking at my breakfast, and knocking back a few painkillers when no one was looking, I helped to pack up the bags and left them in the lobby, ready for Peter to pick up. We walked the few hundred metres to the riverbank, packed ourselves into our boats and set off.

I travelled with Luke again. The painkillers had done their work, and I was looking forward to a nice chat. For a while, we chatted about Lauren's bad behaviour. It was nice that my son and I had something in common – a rapidly growing dislike of

Lauren. Then I asked him about his thoughts on his Junior Cert, which was eleven months away. He answered politely, and then said, 'Er, Mum, would you mind if I listened to my music for a while? I've got this great new album, and I've only heard it once.'

Of course I minded. This was meant to be quality time with my son. I had been enjoying our chat. I thought of all the times when he was small, when he had told me endless, not-very-interesting tales of his day at school. I thought with regret of all the times I'd hurried him on or nodded absently, only half-listening. Would he understand if I shared those thoughts with him now? Probably not. So I had to pretend to be Cool Mum, who didn't mind about much at all.

I put on a fake cheery voice. 'You just go ahead and listen to your music. Don't mind me.'

He turned back to grin at me. 'Gee, thanks, Mum. You're all heart. Tell you what: when the time comes, I promise to pick you a really nice nursing home, OK?'

I dipped my paddle into the water and sent a sparkling spray over his cheeky face. He laughed as he released his old Walkman from its watertight container and plugged himself in.

It was relaxing, in a way, not having to talk. And, when I managed to forget about the previous night's phone call, it was almost pleasant. We paddled slowly and easily, like old pros. I sat back and didn't kill myself with exertion. I watched Luke's shoulders. I hadn't noticed them getting so broad. And his neck had filled out – almost like a man's. How had that happened? Part of me still saw him as a little boy.

We slid along smoothly, with only the occasional missed stroke causing a splash. I could hear the faint tones of Luke's music and occasional bursts of laughter from the other boats, which were never too far behind.

We stopped for coffee, then ice-cream, then more coffee, and then lunch. Lunch was a slow, lazy affair, with lots of wine and olives and fresh, warm bread. Despite earlier promises to myself, I drank a few glasses of wine. Afterwards we lay on the grass. The adults snoozed intermittently, while Lauren and Julie fed the ducks. Luke amazed us all by practising his French on two young girls sitting nearby. They giggled and corrected his mistakes gently. He lay on the grass beside them and looked as cool as he possibly could.

Much later, Cormac sat up. 'Look at the time. It's almost three. We'd better get going.'

Max was lazy. 'Ah, wait. What's your hurry? If we wait long enough, maybe Peter will come and pick us up in the bus.'

I wasn't having that. 'Come on, Max. I'm not letting Peter think we're not up to this. Think how he'd gloat. Let's go.'

Max opened his eyes. He grinned at me and held out his hand. I hesitated; then I took it and pulled him to his feet. He held my hand for a few seconds longer than was necessary, and for the briefest of moments, he stroked the back of my hand with his thumb. Then he gave me a strange look, before letting go and heading down towards his boat.

I was disconcerted. What had that been about? Or had I just imagined it? How could anyone who was married to someone as beautiful as Linda possibly be interested in me? Or was it just that men had a feel for these things? Could Max somehow tell that I'd recently had that fling with Dudley? Did I have 'EASY' tattooed on my forehead? Or had Linda told him? Surely she wouldn't betray me like that? Wasn't there some kind of code of honour between women about this kind of thing?

I brushed those foolish thoughts aside and decided that it was only guilty conscience that was leading me astray.

Just then Julie called out, 'Come on, race to the boats,' and there was a mad scramble as we legged it down the riverbank. As I went to put my purse into the watertight container, I turned to see Max and Linda engaged in a long, passionate kiss. They disengaged slowly, and he stroked her cheek. He looked over her shoulder and smiled at me. I turned away. I felt stupid for reading something into the way he had held my hand. Life had been easier before I became an adulteress.

Linda snuggled against Max's chest. 'How about if I travel with Jill this time?'

I shrugged. I didn't mind. It would be nice to chat to her on her own for a while – especially now that we were relatively sober.

In the end, it was decided that Cormac, Max and Lauren would travel together, with Luke and Julie in another boat. Cormac came over and whispered in my ear, 'I'll take the back seat. Maybe my paddle will slip occasionally, and poor Lauren will get the odd dig.'

Luke had overheard. 'Go, Dad,' he laughed. 'Be sure to get one in for me.'

Julie had also overheard. 'Daddy, that's very bold. I'm going to tell Lauren.'

I knew she wouldn't. I smiled at my not-so-dysfunctional family. 'You all go on ahead. Linda and I will catch up.'

Just then Linda came over. 'No, we won't. You all just keep on going. Don't bother to wait for us. We'll meet you at the hotel in Carennac this evening.'

We waved the others off. 'Bye, my darlings,' called Linda after them. 'Miss you already.' She saved the last word until they were out of earshot. 'Not.'

Then she turned to me. 'God. My head is done in between the two of them. Lauren is forever moaning about something, and Max isn't a whole lot better. What is it about children and men?'

I laughed. 'They have a lot in common, that's for sure.'

Linda grinned. 'Anyway, forget about them. We have the whole afternoon to ourselves. Let's start with coffee. Mine's a latte, if you're buying. After last night, I need regular fixes of caffeine.'

We had a seriously lazy afternoon. For every ten minutes of paddling, we got twenty minutes' rest. Mostly we just drifted along with the gentle current, trailing our fingers in the black-green water and watching the trees slip by. We talked about everything – except last night's confession and the stupid phone call.

In the end, though, I had to bring it up. It was hanging too heavily between us.

'Er, Linda. About what I told you last night. I...'

She turned around and raised one eyebrow. 'You what? You made it all up?'

It was tempting to agree, but I knew she wouldn't believe me. 'No, unfortunately, I didn't make it up. It happened, all right. But it's not like – you know…it's not like we're having an affair or anything. It was just one stupid fling. It means nothing.'

'And Cormac? Where does he stand in all this? Does he know?' This time she didn't turn around.

'No. Of course he doesn't know. What kind of an eejit do you take me for?'

She kept her eyes firmly fixed on the river in front of us. 'So why did you do it?'

I sighed. 'Well, you know what Cormac is like. He's all wrapped up in his work. Nothing excites him like his customers, and his fancy new premises, and the latest line in office furniture. I love him, but I suppose I just got bored.'

Still Linda didn't turn around. 'He's a good guy, Jill. Look after him. You don't know how lucky you are.'

I wasn't quite sure what she meant by that. I decided it was time to close the conversation. 'Anyway. It was just a fling. It won't happen again.'

I wondered if I wanted that to be the truth.

We paddled for another while. Frequent easy silences were interspersed with non-controversial chat. At one stage, the conversation drifted to cosmetic surgery. I was laughing at some celebrity who'd had a series of painful operations in a feeble attempt to roll back the years. Linda didn't think it was all that funny. 'Hey, don't mock. That's what's in store for all of us.'

I was horrified. 'You wouldn't consider plastic surgery, would you?'

She shrugged. 'Why not?'

'Because it's pathetic. I don't fancy getting a face full of wrinkles, but when the time comes, I figure I'll cope somehow.'

Linda spoke sharply. 'Well, not me.' She rested her paddle on one knee and used her fingers to feel the skin around her eyes. 'If my skin sags any more, I'm getting the best face money can buy.'

'But you've always had such beautiful skin.'

'Exactly.' She spoke forcefully. 'And I plan to keep it that way.'

Suddenly, I realised what was happening. Growing older and losing the dewy flush of youth was no fun for anyone, but for the truly beautiful, like Linda, it was a devastating blow.

She continued, 'I have to keep my looks. Otherwise...'

She stopped. 'Otherwise what?' I asked.

She gave a long sigh. 'Otherwise I lose Max. It's a package – keep my looks, keep Max.'

I was horrified. 'But he can't—'

147

Linda gave a sharp little laugh. 'Oh, he hasn't actually said as much. But he doesn't need to. He has an eye for a pretty face. In fact, he can't resist one. Didn't you notice him with the waitress, the first night? He was all over her.'

Actually, I hadn't noticed. But I did remember that Linda had been unusually quiet that night. And I remembered the way Max had held my hand that very afternoon. And I'm not even pretty. And now that Linda knew I was an adulteress, what would she think if she knew about that? Would she see me as a threat to her marriage?

I spoke tentatively. 'Does he just flirt? Or is there more to it?'

Her reply was cold and bitter. 'You mean does he do more than a sly grope when he thinks I'm not looking? You mean does he drag his willing victims into his bed and have his wicked way with them?'

That, I supposed, was exactly what I meant. 'Er, I wouldn't have put it that way, but yes.'

She gave another cold little laugh. 'Ha. How would I know? I'm only the stupid little wife.'

'But, Linda…'

She turned to face me and spoke more softly. 'Hey, don't worry about it. You worry too much. You always did. It's fine. Max is just all talk. We both know that.'

Did she believe that? Did she expect me to believe that? I wasn't sure. I began to wonder just how well I actually knew Linda. Or Max. How could he treat her like that? How could she let him?

But who was I to be taking the moral high ground? If there were stones to be cast, I'd better make my way to the back of the queue.

I put my head down and paddled. All this serious talk was exhausting.

Linda turned around and smiled again. 'Anyway, Jill, when I have my Botox party, you'll be the first to be invited.'

For the rest of the journey, Linda was determinedly bright and positive, laughing and joking with her old sparkly wit. It was almost as if she regretted letting me see the small chink in her armour of happiness.

Much later, I was reclining in the back of the boat with my eyes half-closed, and Linda was steering with the odd jab of her paddle, when I heard a call. 'Mum, you're here.'

I opened my eyes to see Julie and Lauren on the riverbank. Lauren immediately began to cry. 'Muuuummy, come back. Please come back.'

Linda jolted into action. 'Shit. I wasn't paying attention. I thought we had miles to go yet. Quick, paddle harder.'

We paddled furiously for a few minutes and arrived safely on shore. Peter was reclining under a tree, with a half-smile on his face. He'd probably hoped we'd paddle on out of his life forever.

Linda tied the boat, and I hugged Julie. 'Clever girl. You saved us.'

She smiled. 'At first I wasn't going to call you. I thought if you went too far, I could get two desserts tonight. Or maybe even three.'

I gently tapped her bottom. 'You cheeky little thing. So why did you call out? Why didn't you let us go on forever, and then you could have two desserts every night for the rest of your life?'

''Cause I'd miss my good-night kisses.'

I laughed and hugged her again. 'Come on, will you show me the way to the hotel?'

'OK, it's just down here. The bathroom's so cool. There's a funny thing there. I thought it was a kiddies' toilet but Daddy says it's for washing your bottom. Isn't that gross? Imagine if a big dirty man had his bottom in there last night. I'm not using it, anyway. And in the garden there's a pony. He's sweet. I don't know his name, but I've decided to call him Lucky. And on the stairs...'

Behind us, I could hear the now-familiar sound of Lauren's wail. 'But I want a Coke. I was good, and I want Coke. You said.'

Julie pulled me by the arm until her mouth was nearly level with my ear. She gently moved my hair out of the way and then whispered, 'Lauren's never good, is she?'

I thought she was probably right, but I didn't feel I should agree out loud.

Julie persisted. 'I'm a good girl, aren't I? And Lauren isn't.'

My little girl was no angel, but next to Lauren, she was a shining star of childlike virtue.

I smiled at her. 'Well, I'm sure she's good sometimes. Just not as good as you.'

Chapter Eighteen

I had a lovely long shower that evening. When I was sure I'd
used about a hundred gallons of hot water, and half a bottle of
shampoo, I stepped out and wrapped myself in a huge fluffy
towel. I was racked by guilt and the remains of a hangover, and
I needed comfort.

Just as I was reaching for another towel to wrap around my
hair, I was interrupted by an unfamiliar sound.

It was my mobile phone ringing. It seemed strange and
intrusive in this peaceful place. Its polyphonic *Swan Lake* ring-
tone, which I'd spent ages selecting from a list of about a
thousand, suddenly sounded cheap and nasty. I felt a sudden dart
of fear. It had to be Dudley replying to my call. Who else would
be ringing me on holidays? Or could it be his wife? Maybe she
had listened to the message I'd left for him, and was phoning to
threaten me with death and destruction and horrible plague-like
diseases.

What kind of eejit was I to have phoned him in the first place?

At my age, I should know better. How had I let Linda bully me into that one?

But that wasn't really fair. This time I couldn't blame Linda. I hadn't needed a whole lot of persuasion. In fact, I had positively jumped at the idea.

I scrambled for the phone, and reached it just as the last swan was about to expire.

'Hello?' My voice was tentative, afraid.

A rush of relief washed over me when I heard Rita's voice. 'Hi, Jill, how's it going?'

If she had been in the room with me, I think I would have kissed her.

'Great, thanks. Why are you ringing?'

She gave a big laugh. 'That's a nice reception, I'm sure.'

'Sorry. I just got a bit of a fright, that's all. I wasn't expecting you to ring.' *I thought it was the first love of my life, replying to the stupid drunken message I left for him last night.* I couldn't say that, of course. As far as Rita was concerned, Dudley was an old flame whom I'd met briefly in the lobby of the South Court a few weeks earlier. She knew nothing of how our relationship had progressed since then.

She was instantly concerned. 'Oh, Jill, I'm sorry. I didn't mean to alarm you. Everything here is fine. I just thought I'd ring to see how you're getting on. That's all.'

All of a sudden I could picture her, sitting with her feet up on a comfy chair, in her favourite telephoning position, with a huge cup of strong black coffee on the table next to her. I thought how nice and uncomplicated it would be to be sitting there with her, with nothing more on my mind than what to have for dinner.

'Everything's fine. We're having a lovely time.'

'And the lovely Linda?'

The lovely Linda was downstairs in the bar, waiting for me to join her in a huge feed of drink, and I felt rather disloyal to be discussing her. Still, though, I knew Rita was genuinely concerned. She wasn't just phoning in hopes of picking up some juicy gossip.

'Well, Linda's fine. We're getting on well.'

'So all that fuss was for nothing? Time must have mellowed her. Is she completely different?'

I had to think for a moment. Then I realised what had happened. 'Actually, she hasn't changed a bit. She's just like before. Crazy and funny as ever. She hasn't even aged that much.'

'God, I really hate her, and I haven't even met her. Bet her pelvic floor's still intact.'

I laughed. 'Well, we haven't discussed that, but you're probably right. But I don't care about that. You see, I've changed, so it doesn't matter that she hasn't. I don't mind that she's the life and soul of everywhere she goes.' This was, in fact, true. Most of the time.

Rita sounded genuinely pleased. 'That's fantastic. Well done, Jill.'

'Thanks. But don't worry, it's not quite perfect. Every time she walks into a room, all the men turn and stare. Their tongues practically hang out. In her presence, men turn from rational human beings into a big shower of stupid, slobbery puppy-dogs. I canoed with her today, and a group of young fellas nearly toppled their canoe, they were so busy ogling her. But I don't mind as much as I used to.'

Rita's voice was warm. 'I'm really glad to hear it. And how about everyone else? Any huge rows, or are you all getting on famously?'

'Yeah. I suppose we are, kind of. Luke's not complaining, so that means he's OK. And he's not irritating Cormac as much as he does at home. Cormac and Max have soccer in common, and now they're bosom buddies. They can turn a proposed transfer deal into a three-hour conversation, complete with complicated diagrams on beer-mats. Linda's daughter is a brazen little pup, though.'

'And how does Julie cope with that?'

'She's just loving it. She's decided Lauren is the "bold girl" and she's going to be the "good girl". She's being so angelic that sometimes she makes me want to throw up.'

Rita laughed. 'I can just picture her. Hey, guess what? Your friend was in last night's *Leader*.'

'Which friend?' I had a funny feeling that I knew exactly who she was talking about.

'The handsome Dudley, of course. He was at some do in town with his wife. There was a big society piece about them – the new big-shots in town.'

I had to ask. 'What's she like?'

'Well, you know the type. Looks about fifteen years old, absolutely stunning, hair like spun silk, figure to die for, slinky red dress that left very little to the imagination.'

'Mmm. Sounds interesting.'

I tried not to sound interested. I couldn't help wondering why Dudley had bothered with me if he had this wonderful creature tucked away somewhere. Maybe it hadn't been a bored aberration. Maybe it hadn't been just about sex. Could he possibly still feel something for me, after all these years? Had he come to think that ditching me twenty years earlier was a big mistake?

Rita continued, 'She had a rock on her wedding finger that would take your eye out if you weren't careful. And a necklace you wouldn't expect to see outside the Oscar ceremonies – all gold and monstrous diamonds. And she's called...wait for it...'

I could hear the rattling of a newspaper and a long bout of giggling, and then she continued, 'Miranda Whittingstall-Smythe.'

I gave a huge snort of laughter. 'That's not a name. That's a declaration.'

Rita laughed with me. 'And that's not all. They've bought a huge new house out in Ballyclough. Apparently it's a palace – all marble hallways and electric gates and bathrooms with jacuzzis. The garden is modelled on the one from some stately home belonging to Miranda's uncle. It even has a river running through it.'

I stopped her. 'Hey. How do you know all this? Surely the paper didn't give this much detail?'

Rita laughed. 'No, of course that wasn't all in the paper. I have my own private sources. Our painter was doing some work out there last week. Luckily he's the biggest gossip in the history of the world. He says Miranda's a total bitch. And it seems the bold Dudley's been married twice before. You'd think he'd know better. You'd think, with all that practice, he'd be good at picking wives by now.'

'Yeah.' I didn't like the sound of that. Was he just an incorrigible womaniser? Would Miranda somehow hear about me? Would it be my fault if she left the palace in Ballyclough and became ex-wife number three? And if she was a total bitch, why should I care anyway?

I had to change the subject. 'So tell me, Rita. Are you in Kilkee yet?'

'Yeah. We came down last week.'

'And how is it?'

'You know, the usual. Still, Jim's happy. And the girls love it. They have lots of friends here, and it's safer than home, so they get more freedom. Fiona's almost nice. She's nothing like the evil person she is at home.'

'Come on. She's not evil. She's just a normal teenager.'

'She's only twelve – not even a teenager yet. Imagine if she gets worse. I think I'll leave home on her thirteenth birthday, just in case.' We both laughed.

We chatted for a while. I told her about Linda 'accidentally' pulling Peter into the water, and about Barry and Laetitia. She told me about the competitive ladies who bragged about doing the cliff-walk twice before breakfast.

Eventually we said our goodbyes. It had been nice talking to Rita. She always made things seem less complicated. The warm feeling lingered as I sat on the bed and dried my hair. I put on one of my new dresses, and used my new make-up. I checked in the mirror and was impressed.

Then I went downstairs, all ready for a nice, uncomplicated evening.

Ha. Fat chance.

Chapter Nineteen

When I got down to the lobby, I stood for a second wondering where to go, before the sound of Linda's tinkly laughter indicated where the others were. I was heading for the room just off the reception area when I was interrupted by a tap on the shoulder. It was the little old woman who ran the hotel. She was probably worth a fortune, but she was wearing a faded overall and shoes that must have been about a hundred years old. She held a small, folded piece of paper towards me and smiled a broken-toothed smile. 'Madame. For you.'

I smiled back and took the piece of paper from her gnarled old hand. I couldn't pretend any great interest. It was probably just a bar tab, or something equally boring.

The old woman watched as I unfolded the paper. It was just a few words, carefully printed as if to disguise the identity of the writer.

Decided to surprise you. I'm in room 15. Come on up. D.

I gave a small gasp of surprise. I felt suddenly weak and reached out to hold on to the reception desk for support. The little old lady patted my arm and smiled again. I wished she'd stop smiling – her teeth were truly revolting.

She gave a cackle that, in my sensitive state, sounded distinctly evil. She pointed (as far as anyone with curled-up fingers can point) upstairs. 'Up. Upstairs. *A gauche.*'

Gauche was right. That was exactly how I felt. I smiled weakly back at the old woman, and she vanished behind the old reception desk, flashing me one last dentist's-nightmare smile as she went.

How could this be? How could he have found me? I had mentioned I was going to be in Carennac, but was that enough? Still, it was a small town, and there couldn't be that many hotels. A clever man like Dudley would have no problem finding me if he wanted to.

But why would he want to find me now? Why would he risk coming while Cormac was here? Did he want to declare his undying love for me? Was he going to leave Miranda with the double-barrelled name and the big rock on her finger? Did he want a big showdown on the banks of the Dordogne? Was he going to be like Richard Gere in the stupidly, wonderfully romantic closing scene of *An Officer and a Gentleman*? Was he going to pick me up in his strong brown arms, fling me into a canoe and paddle off into the sunset with me?

And, more importantly, did I want him to?

I read the note again and slipped it into my pocket. I peeped through the half-glass door of the bar and saw Cormac, Linda and Max deep in noisy conversation. Linda was waving her arms in the air and laughing. Luke and the girls were parked in front of a television showing a music video that looked rather too raunchy for their tender eyes. No one saw me.

I turned around and went slowly upstairs. My feet made no sound on the heavy carpet. The noise from the bar faded. It was as if nothing in the world existed except for me, the stairs and my surprise visitor. I felt almost sick from fear and excitement. When I got to the top of the stairs, I was breathless. I followed a small hand-painted arrow and found myself standing outside room 15. I stood for a while, looking at the heavy, dark mahogany door. There was music playing inside. Something slow and classical. Perfect for a seduction?

I shook my head angrily. This was crazy. Why was I letting myself get carried away like this? It was probably just a foolish mistake. Why on earth would a man like Dudley leave his wife and his family and his fancy new home, and fly to France to seduce someone he had dropped so carelessly so many years earlier? Surely the old woman had got it wrong. Surely the note was meant for someone else. I had blundered into the middle of someone else's romantic intrigue. This could be terribly embarrassing. Some poor man was probably waiting inside for a stunning young maiden to knock on his door. He was in for a right shock, that was for sure, when he saw a nervous nearly-forty-year-old, panting with years of unquenched passion, waiting on the threshold of his boudoir. I looked around. I half-expected to see a vision of youthful beauty floating along the corridor towards me. But there was no one there.

I took a deep breath. Best to get this over with quickly, clear up the misunderstanding and go back downstairs to my friends and family.

And yet, part of me fervently hoped that there was no mistake, and that Dudley was in the room, separated from me by only two inches of dark-brown wood and some warm evening air. Part of me wanted to rush into his arms and surrender to wild, foolish passion, and worry about the consequences later.

I tapped lightly on the door. Too lightly, it seemed. Nothing happened. I tapped again. Still nothing. Was this a stupid prank of Linda's? She was capable of such things – and worse. But no. I was certain I hadn't mentioned Dudley's name to her, so she wouldn't have known to put a 'D' on the note.

I took another deep breath and tapped one more time. This time I was rewarded with the slap-slap sound of bare feet on wood. Oh, no. A naked man was about to open the door to me. Could it possibly be Dudley? I held my breath and closed my eyes. The door was flung open. I couldn't bear to look.

I was enfolded in a huge hug, and almost dragged into room 15. A familiar voice spoke in my ear. 'At last! Where were you? I had nearly given up hope. I've been waiting here for hours.'

That wasn't Dudley's voice – or, indeed, the voice of any man. I freed myself from the hug and took a small step backwards. I opened my eyes to see my sister Deirdre standing before me, clad in a fluffy hotel bathrobe and grinning broadly.

I smiled weakly. 'Deirdre. It's you. What on earth are you doing here?'

She smiled happily back at me. 'Well, that's a fine welcome, I'm sure.'

'Sorry. It's great to see you. Really. I'm just surprised, that's all.'

She gave me a funny look. 'Who did you think was here?'

I certainly wasn't going there. My notions of a romantic idyll with my handsome lover now seemed vaguely ridiculous.

I shrugged. 'No one, really. I thought the note was meant for someone else.'

She seemed happy with that explanation. She sat on the bed and began to paint her toenails a deep shade of scarlet. That was almost as big a surprise as her being there at all. Usually, Deirdre's only nod at caring for her appearance was keeping herself clean. In all the thirty-eight years of our acquaintance, I'd never seen her anywhere near a bottle of nail varnish.

I sat on a chair by the window and looked at her again. I hadn't seen her since Julie's Communion party, even though I'd guiltily phoned her on a number of occasions. Each time, she'd politely but firmly deflected my concern for her. Since then she'd allowed her always close-cropped hair to grow into a nice wispy style. I got up again to view it from a better angle. Could it be true? I had to ask. 'Is it the light, or are they highlights in your hair?'

She laughed. 'They're highlights, all right. Light golden blonde. Eighty euros' worth, actually. I nearly had to be resuscitated when the hairdresser told me. Is that what people always pay?'

I laughed too. 'Yes, Deirdre. That and more.'

Deirdre is the smartest person I know, and yet her innocence was delightful. I leaned towards her. 'And is that mascara?'

She grinned. 'Blue-black. Nice, isn't it?'

I sat on the bed beside her. This was a new Deirdre – a far cry from the sad, almost depressed girl I'd last seen in May.

'OK. Spit it out. What's going on? Who are you, and what happened the sister I know and love?'

I hoped she was going to say she had a boyfriend. As far as I knew, that too would have been a first.

She smiled. 'Well, I'll tell you about the makeover later. It's a bit complicated – to say the least. But now I'll tell you why I'm here. How's that?'

I shrugged. I knew it was the best I was going to get. 'Fine, I suppose.'

She replaced the cap on the nail-varnish bottle and stretched out on the bed, with her toes carefully extended. 'Actually, it's not much of a story. I haven't got going on my studies yet, so I've been at a bit of a loose end. My apartment won't be ready for another month, so I've just been hanging around at home. I think I've been driving poor Mum and Dad crazy.'

I smiled. I could picture Mum and Dad sighing in frustration over their beloved but far too particular and exacting daughter.

'So I decided to join you. And here I am.' She smiled again – an innocent, guileless smile.

I shook my head in wonder. Clearly it had never even occurred to her that I might not welcome her tagging along on the trip. Luckily, that wasn't the case. I was delighted to see her.

We'd always been close, in our own funny kind of way, but due to our different lifestyles we hardly ever spent any time together. And I've often regretted the fact that I spent far too much of my youth tearing around Cork after Linda, too busy to have much time for my serious, studious younger sister.

I looked at my watch. 'Are you nearly ready? Dinner's at eight.'

She jumped up. 'Yep. Just give me one minute.' She pulled a dress from the wardrobe and slipped it on, all casual-like, even though I hadn't seen her in a dress since my wedding day sixteen years earlier. Then she put on a pair of navy-blue strappy sandals – with real high heels and pointy toes. She ran a hand through her already perfect hair. 'How do I look?'

I stepped back for a better view. 'You, Deirdre, look amazing.'

It was true. Her fantastic slim figure, which was normally hidden by jeans and baggy shirts, was perfectly shown off by the slinky, midnight-blue dress. I had no idea what could have brought about this change in my sister, but at that moment, I didn't care.

'Come on,' I said. 'Let's go to dinner.'

As we went downstairs, I suddenly thought again of Dudley. How stupid could a girl be? How could it possibly have been him lying in wait for me in room 15? What on earth had I been thinking? What kind of a vain, misguided idiot was I? I shook my head to clear it of foolish thoughts, and followed my beautiful sister into the bar.

Everyone was delighted to see her, and ten minutes passed as they queued up to tell her how marvellous she looked. Julie sat beside her, stroking her hair and the soft fabric of her dress in silent wonder. Lauren told her she looked just like her Dream-Date Barbie. Apparently this was meant as a compliment. Linda, who was used to being the centre of such admiring attention, didn't seem to mind being relegated to a supporting role. She was loud and generous in her praise of Deirdre's new look. I sat between them, pleased that things were turning out so well, and tried not to think too much about the way Max was looking at my younger sister. His face showed something much deeper than the simple admiration everyone else was expressing. Would I have to be a reverse fairy godmother? Would I have to turn Deirdre back into a slob to protect her from Max's lecherous ways?

Soon we were called into the dining room, where we had an unremarkable, but most entertaining meal. Afterwards the children retired to their bedrooms and the adults retired to the bar for a change. After a while, I could see that Deirdre was exhausted. I leaned over to her and said, 'Why don't you go on up to bed?'

She yawned. 'I'd love to. But I wanted to talk to you on your own. Do these people ever get tired?'

I laughed. 'Yes, they do. Unfortunately, not until about five in the morning, though.'

Deirdre shuddered. 'How could they even want to stay up so late?'

I laughed again. 'I'm not sure. Anyway, you and I could never outlast them. I think we'd better just leave them to it.'

She nodded happily, and we made our excuses and went out into the lobby.

'What's it to be?' I asked. 'Your room, or a walk?'

'Definitely a walk. My room is still a health hazard after those nail-varnish fumes. Mum always said you have to suffer for your beauty, but asphyxiation is a bit extreme, don't you think?'

I laughed. 'Don't worry, Deirdre. If nail-varnish fumes killed, half the female population of the Western world would be dead by now.'

She shrugged. 'Well, whatever, but I'm not going back there for a while.'

So we set off for a stroll along the riverbank.

Deirdre, ever the businesswoman, didn't bother with small talk. 'I'm going to have a baby.'

I stopped walking and looked at her in wonder. 'You're pregnant? Wow, Deirdre, that's fantastic!'

Then I wondered at the wisdom of that statement. 'Or is it?'

I knew Deirdre would make a good, if rather scatty mother, but since there was no evidence of a father around, maybe pregnancy wasn't such good news after all.

She laughed. 'Hey, don't get too excited. I'm not pregnant yet. I've just decided I'm going to have a baby, that's all.'

'And is this baby going to have a father?'

She spoke disdainfully. 'Did you not do biology at school? Of course it's going to have a father.'

'And who is it going to be? Do I know him?' I sounded like a cranky, judgmental old granny, but I had to know.

'Well, actually, I'm not quite sure yet who the lucky man is going to be.'

'Why this, all of a sudden?' I asked.

'It's not so sudden, actually,' she said. 'I've been thinking of it for a few years, and now that I'm out of the workplace for a while, it seems like the perfect time. I could get pregnant, have the baby, and when the baby's a few months old, it'll be time to go back to work again.'

I didn't know whether to laugh or cry. In Deirdre's world of work, there was a solution for every problem. She had never seemed to grasp the notion that real life wasn't usually quite so simple.

I spoke as gently as I could. 'You know, Dee, despite what you see on the television, getting pregnant isn't always that easy. It might not work out for you.'

'I know, but I've been checked out. The doctors say there's no indication of any problems.'

I got back to the real problem again. 'And the lucky father?'

'Well, at first I was going to use a sperm donor. That seemed like the logical way.'

I had to laugh. With Deirdre, everything had to be logical. She didn't yet know that logic and babies had very little in common. 'And?'

'I went to a clinic in London a few months ago, but it was kind of scary. I got handed all these files describing the donors. I took them home and read them, but it was just like reading a bunch of CVs. It was so impersonal. I couldn't even begin to decide. Did I want a guy whose only health problem was a tendency towards haemorrhoids? Was prematurely grey hair too high a price to pay for an IQ of one hundred and forty? Could a guy whose hobbies were plane-spotting and assembling model aircraft be a suitable father for any child, even if he did have a clean bill of health and all four of his grandparents had lived to their nineties?'

I had to laugh. 'Plane-spotting is always a bit suspect. I think you'd be wise to steer clear of that guy.'

'Yeah, me too. He sounded far too creepy. In the end, I found one guy I'd love to employ as my personal assistant at work, but none that I wanted to breed with. So then I changed my plan.'

I breathed a sigh of relief. 'I think maybe that's a good idea. Are you going to try to adopt a baby from China?'

She shook her head. 'Actually, that's plan C. But it only comes into force if plan B doesn't work out.'

Poor Deirdre. What a clinical way to approach the issue. Didn't she know that most babies are conceived accidentally, after wild bouts of drink-related passion? That many people put way more thought into changing their hairstyles, or buying new tiles for the bathroom, than they ever did into the prospect of having a baby? That most babies are happy accidents?

I hardly dared to ask the next question, but I forced myself to be brave. 'So what exactly is plan B?'

'I'm going to try and meet someone, and get pregnant.'

I felt like laughing again, but I decided this wasn't really appropriate. After all the clinical discussion, she was going about it in the old-fashioned way after all.

'So that's what this is all about. The new look, the slinky clothes. It's all to trap some poor man into getting you pregnant.'

'Well, you make it sound horrible and calculating, but I suppose that's kind of what I plan.'

A sudden image slipped into my mind, of a tropical bird only preening her plumage when it was time to attract a mate. I decided not to share this vision with Deirdre.

'And tell me, are you going to share your plan with this man, or are you just going ahead on your own once he's provided the vital ingredient? Is it going to be a case of "Thanks for the sperm, now get out of my life"?'

'Don't say that, Jill. It's not fair. You make it sound sordid and dirty.'

I realised with a shock that she was close to tears. 'I'm sorry, Deirdre. I didn't mean to be so harsh. It's just that I'm not sure this plan is going to work, that's all. I'm only thinking of you.'

'It's OK. I have to be honest and say I haven't fully worked out the details. At first I thought I'd just trick some guy into having sex, and then vanish from his life, without him ever knowing about the baby.'

I spoke quietly, trying to soften my words. 'Is that fair, though?'

'Fair on who?'

'On any of you. You, or him. It certainly doesn't seem fair on the baby.'

She sighed. 'Probably not. Anyway, now I'm thinking that's not the best idea anyway. Now I'm kind of thinking that maybe I should get to know some guy, tell him my plan and persuade him to donate some sperm.'

I giggled. 'You mean donate it into a jar or, em, sort of go straight to the point?'

She laughed too. 'I told you. I haven't dealt with the details yet. I'll let you know when I've decided.'

I grimaced. 'Must you?'

She ignored me. 'Maybe there's a guy out there somewhere who'd like to have a baby, and might even want to be part of its life, without necessarily being a part of mine.'

This all sounded sad and desperate to me, but I was afraid to say so. I could see that she was upset, underneath her jaunty manner. 'Maybe you're right.'

She gave a sudden giggle. 'Mum and Dad aren't very happy with my idea.'

I stopped walking. 'You didn't?'

'Didn't what?'

'You didn't tell Mum and Dad that you're going to deliberately get pregnant by some obliging stranger?'

She shrugged. 'Why not?'

I shook my head in frustration. 'Deirdre. You big eejit. You should have said nothing. And when the time comes, they'll be so happy with the baby, they won't ask too many questions. That's the best way. The only way.'

She seemed mystified. 'But why? Why not tell them the truth? They're my parents.'

Her innocent smile was both endearing and annoying in the extreme. I felt like punching her and hugging her. 'Will you never learn? Don't you know that there are certain things you never, ever tell your parents? They're parents. They're meant to be kept in the dark most of the time. They can't cope with the truth. They're best left with total lies, or, at worst, a carefully air-brushed version of the truth.'

Deirdre gave me a sly smile. 'Is that the way you feel about Luke and Julie?'

A good point. And not one I was prepared to entertain. I loved my mum and dad dearly, but, like most children, I was sure I could be a far better parent than them. 'That's completely different.'

Deirdre smiled and began to walk faster. 'Anyway, back to the topic at hand. I'm hardly likely to find someone suitable around here. Mr Perfect is hardly likely to come paddling down the Dordogne, all ready to jump into my welcoming arms and make babies at the drop of a hat.'

'Or at the drop of his trousers?'

Deirdre laughed at my joke. I couldn't, though. I'd suddenly had the most horrible thought.

Mr Perfect might not show up, but Max was very much present. I'd seen the way he looked at Deirdre, and I strongly suspected that he wasn't the type of guy to let something silly like a few marriage vows come between him and his pleasure. Maybe

Deirdre would fall for his easy charm? Maybe she wouldn't fall for it, but would accept his sperm anyway?

How would it be if my oldest friend's husband were to father my sister's baby? We'd be a big hit on talk shows, of course, but apart from that I had a funny feeling it might not be a good idea to proceed this way.

How could I keep them apart? Would I really have to dress Deirdre in her old baggy clothes, and throw away her make-up bag and her hairdryer, in order to keep her from Max's clutches? Could I kind of casually mention that Max was a carrier of some dreadful, incurable disease? Would a few days in the company of Lauren be enough to warn Deirdre away from Max as a potential father?

This holiday was becoming too complicated by far.

Deirdre didn't seem to notice my distress. She spoke brightly. 'I'm just going to settle into my new look and enjoy myself, and when I get back to Cork, I'll start the search in earnest.'

I wondered if some concerned citizen should warn the men of Cork what she was up to.

'I hope it works out for you, Dee. I really do,' I said. I meant this. It might be a totally crazy, misguided idea, but she was my sister, and I wanted her to be happy.

I put my arm around her. She was shivering. 'Hey, you're frozen.'

She gave a huge laugh. 'Course I am. This dress wasn't designed with warmth in mind. I wonder, do blue, goosepimply shoulders add to its appeal?'

I shook my head. 'I suspect not.'

'Let's go back, then. I think one small fleece might have sneaked into my suitcase when I wasn't looking.'

We walked back to the hotel, arm in arm. I felt closer to her than I ever had before.

Cormac had gone to bed, but Linda and Max were still in the bar. Max jumped up. 'Ah, the wandering girls are back. Let me get you a drink. What are you having?'

Did I imagine that he was looking very closely at Deirdre? Was this the beginning? He'd made a kind of half-move on me already, the day he held my hand, but had he now decided to go for the younger model?

I looked at Linda, but she was fiddling with her room key and didn't meet my eyes. Deirdre was smiling at Max in her bright, open manner.

I had to save her, whether she wanted to be saved or not. 'Sorry, Max. No drinks for us, thanks. We're finished for the night. We need our beauty sleep.'

He shook his head in wry amazement. 'Beauty sleep? But how could you be more beautiful?'

An innocent enough remark, but now I was giving his every word extra meaning. I looked at him coldly. 'Sorry, Max. We're going anyway.' I took Deirdre's arm. 'Come on, little sister, it's past your bedtime.'

She didn't seem to mind. We said our good-nights and went upstairs.

It had been yet another very long day.

Chapter Twenty

Peter kitted Deirdre out with a small single-person kayak. Over the next few days, Cormac and Luke regularly offered to swap with her so she could travel in a larger canoe with Julie or me. Deirdre always refused, though, and I knew exactly why. She was having a ball. Deirdre, who'd always hated sport with a vehement passion, had finally found something she loved to do. She grasped the skill of paddling in about five minutes on the first day, and proceeded to perfect her technique on the ensuing days. Usually we all started together, but she'd be gone ahead out of our sight in seconds. Once or twice she left us so far behind that she ended up paddling with Dominic and Trevor, which was a sight to see as they struggled to keep up with her. Then she'd paddle back to us, against the flow of the current, before heading off downstream again. Cormac said she reminded him of an over-enthusiastic puppy-dog. I'd have been cross with him if the comparison hadn't been so accurate.

Every evening, Deirdre appeared in a new, flattering outfit.

She was becoming gently tanned and fit-looking. She looked more relaxed and happier than I'd ever seen her. Which would have been perfectly fine if Max hadn't responded by becoming ever more attentive to her. He paid her increasingly personal compliments, which she lapped up like the innocent she was. Linda acted as if she didn't notice, but I could see she wasn't happy. I spent every evening trying to manoeuvre the seating arrangements. It was like the old joke about the cannibals and the missionaries in a boat, with all kinds of forbidden permutations. Cormac and Luke had to be kept apart so they wouldn't fight. Max and Deirdre had to be kept apart so he wouldn't seduce her. If Linda and I were together, we always ended up drinking too much, and without a sober me to hold her back, she became loud and boisterously funny. And if Julie got too close to Lauren it always ended in tears, as Lauren bullied and irritated Julie with her spoiled pettishness.

After dinner one evening, Deirdre stood up decisively. 'I'm not hanging around the bar tonight. I'm going for a walk. Anyone want to come?'

Nobody answered for a moment. I was wrecked, and looking forward to one quiet drink before bed. And then Max jumped up. 'I'll go with you. I could do with some air.'

Suddenly I wasn't tired any more. I looked around the table. Linda was watching Max closely, but saying nothing. Deirdre smiled at Max. 'Great. Let's go, so. We'll see all you couch potatoes later.'

I had a sudden horrible fear that this was planned. Were we being treated to a carefully rehearsed scene? Maybe Deirdre wasn't as innocent as I thought. I looked back at Linda. She was examining her fingernails closely. Max was helping Deirdre into her cardigan. Was he going to help her out of it again as soon as they got into the woods? I couldn't stand back and watch Deirdre make what surely would be the biggest mistake of her life.

I jumped up. 'I've been drinking more than is good for me. I'll go for the walk with you.'

Deirdre and Max looked at me. Was that disappointment I saw on their faces? He certainly didn't look very happy, but Deirdre's face was harder to read.

Max sat down suddenly. 'Actually, I won't go after all. I'll let you two off for some sisterly chat.'

Deirdre shrugged. 'Whatever. Come on, Jill, or the night will be over.'

We walked outside and down the narrow, deserted street. I felt like shaking Deirdre. How could she be so dense?

She spoke first. 'What was all that about?'

I decided to act innocent. 'All what?'

'You didn't want to come for this walk, so why did you?'

I was tired of the innocent act. 'Because of Max.'

She laughed. 'You mean you think…? You think Max and me? What are you on?'

'Can't you see, Dee? He's all over you like a rash.'

She laughed again. 'No, he's not. He's just charming, that's all. A bit of harmless flirting never hurt anyone.'

Once again I felt like shaking her. 'And you think he wanted to come out here for a harmless bit of flirting?'

She shrugged. 'He only wanted to go for a walk.'

Now I was really cross. 'Wake up, Deirdre. I'm not totally stupid. You want a baby, and Max has all the right equipment and will happily jump on anything in a skirt. It would be perfect. Everyone would live happily ever after. Oh, except perhaps for Linda.'

Deirdre stopped walking and looked at me. 'Oh, God, Jill. You can't think that. Give me some credit, please. He's married. Believe me, Jill, I wouldn't go near him.'

Deirdre was a famously poor liar, and I knew she was telling the truth. I smiled. 'Sorry, Dee. I suppose I did overreact. But be careful. I'm sure his motives aren't quite as pure as yours.'

She grinned at me and held her hand up in a salute left over from our childhood. 'Scout's honour. I won't let Max lay a finger on me. OK?'

I nodded. We walked on for a while. Then Deirdre spoke again. 'Poor Linda. Imagine having an unfaithful husband.'

I couldn't imagine that. But my husband had an unfaithful wife. Was that the same thing?

She spoke again. 'How come you're on holidays with Linda, anyway? I thought you two weren't friends any more.'

I shrugged. 'We never fell out. We just kind of drifted apart.'

'Just as well, really.'

'What do you mean?'

'Linda was never good for you. She controlled you. You did everything she said. Always. You never had a mind of your own when she was around.'

She was right, of course; but, as usual, I was driven to defend Linda. 'No one ever understands Linda. She's fun, and wild, and exciting.'

'You mean she's mad?'

I had to smile. 'I suppose that is one possible interpretation.'

Deirdre was on a roll now. 'She uses you. She always did. You're the dull backdrop to her sparkly personality. And what did she ever do for you?'

I thought for a moment. 'She gave me the best times of my life. If it weren't for her, I'd never have done anything. I'd have sat at home doing my knitting. Can't you remember her, Dee? She was always so exuberant and creative. She fizzed with energy.'

Deirdre wasn't impressed. 'She fizzed? You picked her for your best friend because she was fizzy?'

'Actually, I never picked her. She picked me, remember?'

'You know what? I do remember that. She picked you as soon as she showed up in town. She charmed you from the very first moment. And she was well rewarded. You trailed around after her for years, like an obedient little mouse.'

Once again, Deirdre was right. Her words stung, but they were true. I had to defend Linda. And myself. 'It wasn't always like that. She could be incredibly generous.'

Deirdre wasn't impressed. 'How? Give me an example.'

I had to think. 'Well, there was this time at school. We were in first year. I was in the science lab with Linda. We were supposed to be tidying it. I started messing with the sweeping-brush, and I knocked down a huge box of new equipment. Everything smashed all over the floor. It must have been hundreds of pounds' worth.'

Deirdre looked at me. 'Mrs Simons must have gone crazy. She used to make a fuss if we even broke one of her precious pencils. Mum and Dad must have been called in. How come I don't remember that?'

'Because Linda took the blame.'

'And you let her?'

I shrugged. 'Like you said, I did everything she asked. She convinced me that, since she was always in trouble anyway, it wouldn't be so bad for her. She got two weeks' detention. I felt really bad, but she just laughed and said she needed to catch up on her schoolwork anyway. And I got off scot-free.'

Now Deirdre was impressed. 'Wow. That was really nice of her.'

I nodded. 'I know. Linda has a generous spirit that often gets overlooked. And she was always doing stuff like that. Like the way she always defends Laetitia here, when no one else bothers. She's got a good heart.'

Deirdre smiled. 'You're right. She has. But she's mad too, OK?'

I laughed. 'OK. I'll give you that one. She's a bit mad too.'

We walked on for another while. Our route, like our conversation, might have been going in circles, but the darkened streets were so pretty, it didn't really matter.

As we passed a small well for the third time, Deirdre spoke again. 'Cormac's chilled out a bit. He's almost human again.' This was a somewhat barbed compliment, but the only one I could remember her ever giving him.

'Mmm. I suppose you're right. He's always like this on holidays. After a few days, he actually forgets about his stupid business and lets his hair down for a while.'

'So you're happy?'

How could I answer that one? I had a husband, two kiddies, a nice home. I had everything most girls dream of. But if I was happy, why did I go to sleep each night with thoughts of Dudley?

I decided to avoid her question. 'Cormac used always be like that, you know. When we first met, he was romantic and charming and fun.'

'How come I don't remember that?'

'You were away in London at the time, doing one of your degrees, and I was in Limerick. Cormac and I were so happy then.'

'So what happened?'

I sighed. 'I don't know, really. Everything was fine when Luke was a baby, and then Cormac set up the business, and it began to consume him. The old thing about his irresponsible father

176

came home to roost. Cormac was going to be the best provider in the world, no matter what it cost him.'

'And you just let that happen?'

'It's not like he changed overnight. It was gradual, so I didn't even notice at first. And then, I don't know, things kind of deteriorated slowly. Cormac was hardly ever at home, and when he was, there were always rows with Luke. Even when Luke was tiny, there was always friction when they were together.'

'He was so busy providing for Luke's future, he forgot to love him in the present?'

I shook my head. 'That sounds very harsh. Cormac does love Luke, he's just good at hiding it.'

'Yeah. Very good indeed.'

I ignored her. 'And then, I suppose, there was no magic left. We became a settled married couple for whom romance was only a distant memory.'

'Give me an example.'

I smiled. Sometimes I felt that Deirdre had been studying for so long that her whole life was seen in the form of exam questions: *Define, and illustrate with examples.*

'Well, in the beginning, he used to buy me great presents.'

'There's more to life than presents.'

'I know. But it wasn't the presents. It was the fact that he spent time choosing them for me. They were often silly little things, but they were precious because they referred to private jokes between us.'

'And now he brings you nothing?'

I gave a snort of laughter. 'Oh, he still brings me stuff. He was in Holland in February, and he brought me back the in-flight magazine and the soap from the hotel.'

Deirdre laughed. 'Oh, I see what you mean.'

I was glad someone did, because I wasn't very sure myself what I meant. I was vaguely discontented, but was that reason enough to complain? Should I just grin and bear my life, and be glad that it wasn't worse? Or should I grasp at life and live it gloriously? Was there a wonderful future for me with Dudley? And was it passing me by as I wallowed in domestic torpor?

Deirdre put an arm around me. 'Maybe you could persuade Cormac to work a bit less. He could get a manager in.'

'He has a manager. Johnny. You met him at the Communion party.'

Deirdre laughed. 'Let me rephrase that. Maybe Cormac should get a *proper* manager in. Poor timid Johnny isn't much good. I bet he doesn't even dare to buy a few postage stamps without getting Cormac's permission first.'

She was right. Cormac would never give Johnny any real responsibility.

Deirdre continued, 'Maybe you could go for family therapy. Or couples therapy. Maybe you and Cormac could get some of the old magic back.'

I smiled. For Deirdre, there was always an answer, even for completely impossible problems like mine. Part of the problem was that I was no longer sure I wanted to get the magic between Cormac and me back again. Maybe it could never be got back, anyway. Was it time to try for some all-new magic between Dudley and me?

'Cormac's not a bad guy,' Deirdre went on. 'He's just a bit disconnected, that's all. And, hey, look on the bright side. At least you didn't marry that other eejit.'

'Who do you mean?' I knew exactly who she meant.

'That smooth American guy with the funny name.'

'Dudley?'

She grinned. 'That's the one. Whatever did you see in him?'

Should I point out that whatever it was I had seen in him, twenty years ago, was still clearly visible to me?

'He was good-looking.'

'Yeah, but besides that?'

'Funny.'

'Anything else?'

'Clever.'

'Keep going.'

Did I have to? *Exciting, sexy, gentle, incredibly sexy, rich, cultured, did I mention sexy?*

Deirdre interrupted my mental list. 'Maybe he was all those things, but...'

'But what?'

'I don't know. There was always something about him. He never struck me as being quite honest. Whatever happened between you two, anyway? One minute you were madly in love, and next minute it was all over, and you'd vanished off to Limerick, and we hardly saw you for years. Where did it all go wrong?'

Where, indeed? I really didn't want to go there. I smiled and tried to sound old and wise. 'Oh, you know. It was just one of those things.'

Chapter Twenty-One

Time passed. The days, like the blisters on my fingers, began to blend into one another. Sometimes the river took us between steep cliffs. Other days we drifted gently on languid waters between rows of lush green trees. Occasionally we found small, shingly beaches, where the children swam and splashed in the warm sunshine, and acted like children in feel-good movies.

Soon we were on our last rest day. We'd arrived in a village near Souillac rather late the evening before, due to a particularly long and liquid lunch, and as a result I was tired. I was quite looking forward to a day of doing nothing much. There was a sun-lounger next to the hotel swimming pool that had my name on it. Deirdre, the born-again kayak convert, got up early and decided to take her boat out for a while, since otherwise she'd only have one day's paddling left.

After a leisurely breakfast, Linda and I found ourselves adjoining places and settled down for a morning of reading and idle chat. Just as I was on the third page of my novel, Lauren appeared. (She'd refused to go to bed the night before, and as a result she'd slept late.) She pushed her mother aside and lay on most of the lounger. She was quiet for about ten seconds. Probably a record for her.

'Muuuummy.' Even the way she said that word, elongating the vowel as far as she could, drove me crazy.

Linda ignored her.

'Muuuummy.'

Linda turned the page of her book. I suppose she'd had years of practice at tuning out her daughter's wails.

'Muuuuuummy.'

Answer the bloody child or I'll push her into the pool to quieten her.

I didn't say this, but maybe my vibes of hatred were strong enough to get through to Linda.

'What is it, love?'

'What time are we going out in the boats?'

'We're not. Remember? I told you yesterday. Today we have a day off. You can play in the pool with Julie.'

Of course, as soon as Lauren heard that there was to be no canoeing, the contrary child decided that was the only thing in the world that she wanted to do. (The day before, there had been a tantrum because we *were* going canoeing.) She threw a total wobbly. It was like a tantrum in a cartoon – all red face and clenched fists and stamping feet. Just about tolerable in a two-year-old, but totally out of order in a child of seven.

Then the wail started. 'But I want to go in the boat, Mummy. I want to go in the boat. I want to go in the boat.'

Linda turned to me and whispered, 'She's tired, the poor little pet.'

I bit my tongue and didn't reply. No point falling out at this late stage of the holiday.

181

Julie came out of the pool and sat on a corner of my lounger. Drops of water dripped from her hair onto my legs, cooling them nicely.

She watched the scene for a while. Then she leaned over and whispered in my ear, 'I think Lauren should take a chill-pill, Mum. Don't you?'

I frowned at her to quieten her, but also patted her gently on the arm to show that I wasn't really cross.

The wailing continued, varying occasionally in pitch as Lauren stopped to draw breath and then began again with renewed vigour. I was sure that Linda would give in to her. In fact, I sincerely hoped that she would. My ears were beginning to suffer from the onslaught. To my surprise, though, Linda didn't give in.

She leaned over and told me why. 'This is one battle Lauren can't win. She can't possibly go in the boat on her own, Max refuses to take her, and my behind is red raw from sitting on that hard plastic seat.'

I laughed. 'That's what you get for being so skinny. My behind is fine – I've got more padding.'

Linda continued, 'It's a pity Deirdre left so early. She could have taken Lauren with her in our boat. She probably would have been glad of the company.'

'Yeah. It is a pity, isn't it?' I tried not to smile. The blindness of some parents was hard to believe. Could Linda not see that Deirdre was totally allergic to Lauren? Surely an hour in her company in the confined space of a canoe would put Deirdre off the idea of ever having children of her own.

By now, Lauren had stamped and howled her way to the other side of the pool. There she sat on the grass verge and kept up a constant low-key kind of wailing.

After a few minutes, Linda got up. 'God, Jill, I'm sorry about this. I'll sort her out.'

She went over to her wailing daughter, sat beside her and cuddled her.

Just then, Cormac and Luke appeared. Cormac looked across at Lauren. 'God, what's that racket? It's doing my head in. I've heard angle-grinders that made less noise. That child had better be really hurt.'

I gave him a wry smile. 'Not exactly.'

'What's Linda doing about it?' He blamed Linda for Lauren's bad behaviour, and, though I had often argued the point with him, I knew he was right.

I laughed. 'She's probably promising her the sun, moon and stars if only she'll be quiet.'

The wailing continued. 'Huh. Sun, moon and stars mustn't be enough. Looks like she's holding out for a bottle of Coke and a bag of crisps too.'

Luke sat on the terrace beside me. 'What's wrong with her, anyway?'

'She wants to go on the river.'

He laughed. 'How about *in* the river? You take an arm, Dad, and I'll take a leg. That would sort her.' He went to get up, but I restrained him. It was a pity that the only thing my husband and son wanted to do together was illegal.

'Forget it, Luke. Much as I'd like to see that, I think you'd better not.'

He shrugged. 'OK. Whatever. Just let me know if you change your mind.'

I smiled at him. 'OK. But don't hold your breath.'

By now, Lauren was only giving the odd exaggerated sob, and soon she'd stopped crying altogether. I didn't dare to think what

Linda had paid for the silence.

When Max appeared, the whining began again. He ignored it for a while as he read his guidebook, but eventually he looked at his wailing daughter. 'OK, Laurie, if you're a good girl, we'll get a taxi to Souillac. You'll like it there. I'll bring you and Julie on the tourist train around the town, how about that?'

Julie's face lit up at the prospect – she was apparently not worried by the fact that Lauren was never a good girl. Nevertheless, the three of them set off shortly afterwards, and Linda and I had a pleasant hour or two of peace.

I was half asleep when they returned. Julie was all excited. 'It was so cool, Mum. You should have come.'

Lauren was equally enthusiastic. 'It's the very best thing.'

The girls went for a quick dip, and Max appeared to tell us what had really happened. It turned out that they had been on the small tourist train with a party of very serious and staid German pensioners. Everyone got a set of headphones to plug into a console in the roof, so they could hear the commentary in their own language, and the train set off to tour the historic sights of Souillac. Unfortunately, the trip was rather spoiled by the fact that Lauren and Julie spent the entire time fiddling with each other's headphones and laughing uproariously as the commentary changed from Japanese to French to Italian. It seemed the German pensioners had been rather less than impressed, and when the trip was over it looked as if a deputation had approached the driver looking for their money back. Max had grabbed the girls and left them to it.

Shortly afterwards, we retired to the terrace for lunch. It was a wonderful place. The terrace was shaded by a small wooden pergola, twisted with vines. I sat with my back to a cool stone wall and looked out at the wonderful view. There was rich green woodland, and rolling hills, and of course the river, which seemed to be following us. Just at the horizon, a huge field of sunflowers was in glorious, golden bloom. I sipped my ice-cold white wine and managed to forget, for a while, the ever-present tensions in our motley crew of travellers.

After the meal, I was ready for my lounger again. Four more hours lying in the sun reading sounded just about right to me, but Linda was having none of it. She always needed excitement, and after a whole morning sitting by the pool, she was jittery and agitated. I had the sudden thought that, if Linda were a school-girl now, she'd surely be put on medication. Maybe she'd had a lucky escape being born when she was.

'Come on, Jill. Don't be so boring. Let's go check out this place.'

I protested at first. 'I'm sure it's lovely. And Max and Cormac walked around it last night. Can't they just tell us about it at dinner?'

'No. That's not the same at all. We should see it for ourselves.' She spoke petulantly, reminding me for a moment of Lauren.

I tried pleading. 'Can't I just read my book for a while?'

'No, you can't. You can read it next week, when you get home and it's raining. You cannot waste a whole day by the pool. Life's too short.'

I smiled. That had been her mantra when we were teenagers. Whenever I wanted to back out of something crazy, she'd fix me with a determined stare and say, 'Life's too short.' Often, in those days, because of the stupid chances she took, I had feared that Linda's life was going to be very short indeed.

She interrupted my musing. 'Come on, Jill. Let's go. The men can mind the kiddies.'

I didn't bother protesting any more. It was too hot, and besides, I knew she'd win in the end. As a token protest, I jumped into the pool and swam one quick length. I dried myself quickly and threw my sundress over my bikini, and we set off for the short walk to the village.

There wasn't much to see. There was a nice, cool church. I went in and lit a candle, praying that Dudley would stay out of my life. Then I remembered Linda's 'Life's too short' and I went back and lit another candle, praying for a nice passionate fling that wouldn't hurt anyone.

We left the church and wandered down a warm, dusty street. There was a war memorial, and a few shops that were closed for long lunches.

I was glad. 'See? There's nothing to see. It's a nice little village. Just like all the other nice little villages we've visited over the past few weeks. Now let's go back to the hotel. I was really enjoying my book.'

I made to head back to the hotel, but Linda took my arm. 'Come on. Don't be such a bore. Let's explore a bit more.'

I sighed. 'OK. Ten minutes more, and then I'm going back.'

Linda led me down a narrow, cobbled street. It was very pretty, with flower-filled hanging baskets decorating the old stone buildings. At the end, the street curved around gently and then opened out onto a leafy square. Four old men, in long trousers with braces and soft white shirts, were intent on a game of *boules*.

Linda was delighted. 'Hey, look. I love that game. I used to play it on the beach with my cousins when we were kids. I haven't played it in years. I wonder if they'll let us join in?'

My heart sank. This was probably a match that had been going on since before the Second World War. I was quite sure there was no place for a pair of bored tourists who were dressed for the beach.

Linda clacked over in her high heels.

'*Bonjour.*'

She smiled brightly at the men. They looked at her in surprise, muttered to one another and returned to their game. Linda was undeterred.

'*Je joue le…er…jou avec vous?*'

Two of the men actually laughed at her, throwing back their heads and showing their bad teeth. Linda recoiled ever so slightly, but she kept smiling. It wasn't that easy to scare her away. One man scratched his bald head and muttered something under his breath. The fourth man said nothing. He caressed his fat belly thoughtfully. He was looking at Linda's long, golden legs, most of which were on display under her very short skirt.

He smiled at her. '*Oui. C'est bon.*'

The other three men looked at him in surprise. One said something I couldn't catch. Then all four threw their heads back and laughed loudly.

There was an old woman sitting on a bench nearby, under a huge plane tree. As soon as the man smiled at Linda, she launched herself from her seat and ran over to him. Under her arm she carried the ugliest dog I'd ever seen. She started flapping at the man with her free arm and screeching hoarsely. I couldn't understand what she was saying, but it wasn't hard to guess. I almost felt sorry for the ugly pooch, whose ears must have been suffering badly. I pulled Linda's arm. 'Come on. She doesn't look very happy. Let's get out of here before World War Three breaks out.'

The man saw me, and slipped deftly away from the old woman. He picked up a *boule* and held it towards Linda. He indicated the jack, which lay about twenty yards away.

'Come on, Linda. Let's go,' I repeated.

She ignored me and smiled at the man. She took the *boule* from him and bent low, revealing even more of her thighs. One of the old men whistled softly. The old woman said something loudly and went into a nearby house, slamming the door behind her. The pots of geraniums on the windowsill shook with the force of the slam. A second later, the dog reappeared from the side of the house and threw himself into a shady spot under the window.

I knew I was beaten. What I really wanted to do was race back to the pool, and my book, but some trace of old loyalty made me feel that I should stay with Linda. So I retired to the relative safety of the now-vacant bench. I pulled my skirt underneath my legs and sat down. I hoped the dog didn't have mange.

Linda was now bending even further down and making a big pantomime of swinging her arm back and forth, much to the enjoyment of the four old men. By now they were clapping Fat Belly on the back. Clearly they were pleased at his decision to allow Linda to play.

Linda took aim and threw her *boule*. It must have been beginner's luck: it flew in a perfect arc and landed, with a small click, right on the sand near the jack. The men clapped and cheered her, and Linda, delighted with the attention, beamed at them and gave a small bow. My heart sank. I could see she wouldn't want to leave any time soon.

The game progressed for a while, though no one seemed to care who actually won. After the first shot, Linda's shots were fairly pathetic, but that didn't seem to matter. Every time she stepped forward to throw, the men edged after her. Then, when the *boule* landed many feet away from the pin, they cheered wildly, as if she'd just thrown the best shot the village had ever seen.

News seemed to be spreading, as more and more old men shuffled along to watch. Some were in their slippers and looked as if they'd just got out of bed. Some looked so old and grey that I was impressed by the fact that they were still mobile. A few women in flower-patterned overalls appeared here and there around the square. They stood with arms tightly folded, whispering crossly amongst themselves. A couple of dark-eyed toddlers leaned out of windows. It was like the set of a movie, and, as usual, Linda was happy to play the starring role.

I had a horrible sense of déjà vu. I'd been there before. As a child, and then as a teenager, I'd seen this kind of thing over and over. Linda's sense of fun and her innate exhibitionism would take over, and she'd lose the run of herself. I knew it would all end in tears, but there was nothing I could do. I, and most of the elderly population of the little village, watched with varying degrees of fascination and horror.

A bottle was produced and passed around amongst the players. Linda drank more than her share. She coughed, and some of the clear liquid splashed onto her face. She wiped her mouth and laughed. One of the men patted her on the back. She seemed to be very pleased with herself. She slipped her feet out of her high-heeled sandals and ran over to me.

'Come on, Jill. Join in. No one will mind. It's such fun, and these guys are so nice.'

I shook my head. 'Thanks, but no. Max and Cormac will be wondering what's happened to us, and Deirdre should be back by now. Why don't you call it a day?'

I knew she'd say no, but before she even got the chance, her new best friends were calling her. 'Linda. Linda. *Viens ici.*'

She ran over and took her shot. This time the boule narrowly missed a parked car, and rolled gently down the street. The old men laughed and gave her another drink, as consolation. A small black-eyed girl in a faded blue dress ran and fetched the *boule*, which she presented to Linda with a small curtsey.

Soon Linda's shots became more and more erratic. She'd never had great tolerance for alcohol, and the combination of the wine she'd had at lunch and whatever was in the bottle began to go to her head. When, at one stage, an old man took a filthy hanky from his pocket and handed it to Linda, and she actually used it to wipe her mouth, I knew she was in big trouble.

After a while, when she bent over to throw, she didn't even try to pull down her skirt, so everyone got a great view of her very skimpy bikini bottom. (And her very curvy bottom.) She laughed loud and often. She chatted animatedly to her new friends. They didn't seem to mind that her French was appalling. They nodded knowingly at everything she said, like she'd just revealed all the mysteries of the universe.

After a while, a small boy was sent for. He was given a few notes, and then he ran off. When he returned, he was carefully carrying another label-free bottle. This was passed around, amidst much laughter and back-slapping, and once again Linda got more than her share.

I made another attempt to get her away. I got up and tried to physically drag her from the scene. I pulled as hard as I could at her arm. 'Come on, Linda. This is crazy. You've lost the run of yourself. Let's get out of here.'

She shook me off rather roughly. 'Leave it, Jill. You go back and be Miss Goody-Two-Shoes if you want. I'm staying here.'

She was bigger and drunker and more determined than me, so I didn't protest further. I went back to my bench and sat down. Even if I couldn't remove her, maybe I could pick up the pieces when, inevitably, everything ended in tears. I wondered if there was any chance that Max or Cormac might appear and rescue me. I kept looking along the road towards the hotel, in hope, but no one appeared.

I figured I'd been there for more than an hour when the real trouble started. Linda bent low to take her shot. She raised herself up and drew back her arm. Just as she released the *boule*, one of her bare feet slipped on a loose cobblestone. She lost her balance, stumbled and tried to right herself. The *boule* flew into the air as she fell to the ground. I could hardly bear to watch. As if in slow motion, the *boule* dropped from the air in a gentle arc. It hit the window of the nearest house, smashing it. It then dropped, suddenly, and hit an ornate pot on the sill.

Unfortunately, the ugly dog had chosen a spot directly under that particular windowsill for his afternoon siesta. The pot teetered tantalisingly for a second or two. Then it gave one final rock and toppled towards the sleeping dog. It hit him right on the head, before smashing on the cobbles in a spray of dry earth, broken terracotta and scarlet geranium petals.

The dog gave a tiny whimper; then his head slipped awkwardly to one side. A small trickle of blood came from his mouth and gathered on the dusty ground. A second later the *boule* dropped to the ground with a loud clatter. It rolled along the footpath and came to rest by the slipper-clad foot of the ferocious-looking woman, who had just stepped out of the house to see what was going on.

Then there was silence. A long, long silence. A silence that oozed and spread out until it had filled every dry and dusty corner of the square.

Linda was still sitting where she had fallen, in the centre of the square. Her new best friends began to edge away from her. Smart men. They knew she wouldn't be staying around for long, but their wives would. There was no question as to where their loyalties should lie.

And still the silence continued. I wondered if I should tiptoe over, grab Linda and make a run for it. I surveyed the square and mentally planned our escape route.

Linda got slowly to her feet. She staggered a little, then regained her balance. She leaned against a tree and observed the crowd. Then she spoke, and only then were the true, awful depths of her drunkenness revealed to me. Her words were slurred beyond belief. 'Oops. Wasn't such good shot, was it? Poor doggie's going to have a bit of a...bit of a headache in the morning. Someone should get him some Pana...Pana... Panadol.'

I don't know much about dogs, but as far as I could see, that poor doggie was actually dead. There would be no more mornings, and no more pain, for him.

I couldn't take any more. For all I knew, half these people could be complete psychos who would relish the chance to band together and kill us both. When I looked closely, a lot of them did look rather strange and brooding. Still, maybe it was just that they were already mourning the dog.

I really didn't want to be the lead story on the RTÉ news that night. I ran over to Linda, took her arm and spoke as firmly as I could.

'Move. Now. We're out of here.'

For once in her life, she did as I asked. She didn't even worry about her shoes, which still lay in the dust. She allowed me to propel her from the square. As I walked, I fumbled in my bag and found a fifty-euro note. I handed it to the fierce-looking woman. She could buy a new pot of geraniums, and maybe a nice cross for the dear departed doggie.

The woman took the money from me, then crumpled it and threw it to the ground. Then she spat in my face. Typical. Linda kills the dog, and I get spat at. What kind of justice was there in that?

I wiped my face with my arm, and we kept walking. It probably could have been worse, but at that moment I couldn't quite figure out how.

Chapter Twenty-Two

When we got back to the hotel, all the others were snoozing by the pool, so I didn't have to explain why I was half-dragging a barefooted and bedraggled Linda along next to me. For once in her life, she looked a complete mess, with her clothes all dirty and torn and her face streaked with dust.

I took her to her room and put her to bed. Not the first time I'd done that. I wondered if it would be the last. Linda would, of course, cheerfully have returned the favour, but the opportunity had never arisen. My good sense always kicked in before I got quite that drunk.

She rolled over on the bed and grunted sleepily. I closed the curtains and left her to sleep off her foolishness.

I went back to my lounger by the pool and picked up the book I'd left there several hours earlier. Cormac opened one eye.

'Where were you all this time?'

'Linda and I went for a walk around the town.'

'That must have been exciting.' He was speaking sarcastically.

'It was, rather.'

'I bet.' He thought I was joking.

I leaned over and whispered to him, 'Honest. It was very exciting indeed. I'll tell you later.'

Just then Max sat up. 'Oh, hi, Jill. Is Linda back?'

I nodded. 'Yeah. We just got here. She was a bit tired, though, so she went to her room to lie down for a while.'

Max lay down again and closed his eyes. He didn't seem to think there was anything strange about Linda retiring to bed in the middle of the day.

Just then, Julie and Lauren appeared from the kiddies' pool. Lauren began one of her whiny little protests. 'Why is my mummy in bed? Is she sick? I want to go up to her. I want to tell her that mean Daddy wouldn't buy me any more Coke and I've only had two cans.'

Poor Linda. Soon her head would start to throb, and the last thing she needed was her whingy little daughter pulling at her and giving her grief. I needed to do my friend a big favour.

'Come here a sec, Lauren.' I spoke as softly as I could, and smiled a sweet smile at her. Luckily she was too young to see just how false my smile was. Luckily she didn't wonder why I was being sweet and nice all of a sudden, after days of ignoring her. She walked towards me, pulling the top of her bikini down over her flat chest. When she was really close, I reached out, took her arm and pulled her gently to me. Then I whispered in her ear.

Her eyes opened wide in horror. Her face turned pale, and her freckles stood out starkly against the white skin. She looked towards her father, who was slumbering peacefully. She opened her mouth. No sound came out. She closed her mouth again. She rubbed her eyes and looked around. I could see she was weighing up her options. Suddenly she made up her mind.

'Come on, Julie. I don't want to go inside any more. Let's go and play in the water again. Bags I have the big blue bucket.'

I grinned to myself. I had enjoyed that little encounter.

Luke was on the sunbed next to me, watching proceedings. He unplugged himself from his music and whispered, 'What did you say to her? She looked like she was going to wet herself.'

I shrugged. 'I just said that, if she went anywhere near her mother's bedroom in the next three hours, I'd break both her arms and both her legs and punch her right between the eyes.'

Luke chuckled softly. 'Way to go, Mum.'

Then he got sense. 'You didn't really say that, did you?'

I shook my head in regret. 'I wanted to, but I was afraid the child-protection people would get to hear about it. Instead I told her I'd smack her bottom so hard she wouldn't be able to sit down for a week.'

Luke smiled. 'Not quite as colourful, but it worked, all right. Will she tell Linda, do you think?'

I thought about it. 'Maybe not. Or, anyway, maybe not until they get home. And it won't matter then. She's an awful little liar at the best of times. Linda will think she made it up. Hopefully she'll get in trouble for telling lies, too.'

Luke giggled. It's a bit sad, how proud I was that I'd impressed him. This was an increasingly difficult feat as he got older. I winked at him, but that was a step too far. He gave me a withering look and plugged himself back into his music.

Later, Cormac and I went to our room to shower and change for dinner. I was feeling rather hot and cross. My head was sore from the sun, and from wine, and I was feeling a bit guilty about what had happened during the *boules* game. I knew that, in the unlikely event of the roles being reversed, Linda wouldn't have let things go so far. If I'd been the one muscling in on the old men's game, she'd have found a way to rescue me before I managed to make a total fool of myself. And besides, after so many years of watching Linda get into trouble, you'd think by now I'd have perfected a way of getting her out of it again.

I gave Cormac a brief account of what had happened. He laughed. 'God, I wish I'd been there. When those old guys looked up her skirt they must have thought they'd died and gone to heaven.'

'More so than if they had looked up my skirt? Are you saying that what's up her skirt is somehow more exciting than what's up mine?' I knew I was spoiling for a row, but I couldn't stop myself.

'No, Jill. You know that's not what I'm saying.' He spoke mildly. So mildly that I got even crosser.

'You can't keep your eyes off her, can you? I've seen how you look at her.'

Cormac towelled his hair roughly. 'Jill, come on. This is pathetic. Stop it.'

I couldn't. 'You're like every other man in the world. Linda appears, and you're like bloody putty in her hands. One flash of that cleavage, and you're helpless. One wiggle of her hips, and you're hooked for life. Don't forget, I've known Linda forever. I've seen how she affects men. When she's around, every other woman, including your wife, seems to become invisible.'

Cormac threw the towel onto the bed. 'OK, Jill, that's enough. What's going on here? What do you want me to say? Linda's very pretty? Well, she is. So what? Looking at her isn't a crime. You look at that shower of actors in white coats on *ER* every Sunday night, and I don't make a big fuss, do I?'

By now my eyes were filling with self-pitying, wine-fuelled tears. 'Well, I only admire those guys from afar. I don't bring them on holidays with me, do I?'

Cormac buttoned his shirt. 'Ha-bloody-ha. That's a laugh, isn't it? Remind me again whose idea this whole holiday was. Oh, yeah. I remember. It was your idea, wasn't it? So stop giving me bloody grief just because I happened to glance sideways at your precious Linda. I'm off to the bar.'

He went out, slamming the door loudly behind him.

Dinner that night was a subdued affair. Linda didn't appear at all. Max said she was still sleeping. Deirdre was her usual quiet self. There was still a sizzling tension between Cormac and me that we could possibly have resolved if we'd had half an hour in private. With Max and Deirdre there, though, we had no opportunity to make up, so we spoke to each other with a horrible, strained politeness.

Lauren was wary around me, and kept close to her father. She and Julie were tired after their day in the sun, so they went to bed without protest as soon as their food was finished. Luke announced that he was going for a walk, and, after he'd patiently listened to all of my warnings to be careful and not to go too far, he set off.

Cormac, Max, Deirdre and I went to the bar for a drink. After the first drink, Deirdre threw her hands up in surrender. 'That's me finished. I'm off to bed. I'm not able for all these late nights.'

The rest of us stayed and had another drink, and another. Finally Cormac got up. 'I'm finished. I'm off to bed.' He looked at me. 'Are you coming up?'

I shook my head. I was still a bit cross with him, though I had no real cause. For his part, he looked pretty cross with me too.

'No. I'm going to finish this one. I'll be up then.'

He shrugged. 'You take your own sweet time. Don't rush on my account.'

I watched as he crossed the lobby. I should have run after him and tried to make up for my earlier bad behaviour. But I was too tired and dispirited. Easier by far to stay downstairs until he was asleep.

Before I could stop him, Max had waved at the waitress for another drink. 'One for the road.'

I shook my head. 'Not for me, thanks.'

'Ah, go on. Sure, a bird never flew on one wing.'

The drink came. I drank it slowly, though I'd had more than enough already. I checked my watch. Cormac would surely be asleep by now. I stood up and tried to stifle a yawn.

'That's me finished. Night. See you in the morning.'

Max gulped the last of his brandy. 'I'm done too.'

We walked to the foot of the stairs together. There was an awkward pause.

'Let's go for a walk.' Max sounded enthusiastic.

I shook my head. 'No. I don't think so. It's late, and I'm tired.'

'Come on, just a quick walk. It's such a beautiful evening. We shouldn't waste it. It's probably raining at home.'

He had the same persuasive powers as his wife. And, besides, he was right. It was a beautiful evening. And we had a day's paddling ahead. It would be better for me to clear my head before going to bed. And anyway, Max was still ogling my younger sister, so I would be perfectly safe.

I shrugged. 'OK. Let's go.'

We went out a small side door. There was a path leading from the hotel to the river. We walked along it without speaking. When we got to the river, the path continued along the bank. Everything was quiet. The moon shone on the water, which rippled occasionally in the soft breeze. The air smelt of summer.

Max chatted about this and that. He was easy company. I'd never really spoken to him much before. Usually, when we were together, he spoke to Cormac and I spoke to Linda. He told me funny stories about his job, and about the guys he played indoor soccer with. I told him about my tennis club and its many eccentric members.

We walked past a small campsite. Loud snoring came from one of the tents. From another there came a series of sighs and moans. We giggled and walked on.

Eventually we came to a small bench on the bank of the river. I sat down and took off one of my shoes. I rubbed my heel, where the skin had been chafed by the leather.

'New shoes,' I explained. 'They've blistered my foot.'

Max sat on the bench beside me. 'Here. Let me. I was a foot doctor in my last life.' He gently pushed my hand aside and began to stroke my foot.

I caught my breath. Was this kinky? Bizarre? Or was he just being helpful? I don't think any man had rubbed my foot before. Certainly my husband of sixteen years had never done so. Still, rubbing my heel, though strange, was hardly a sexual act. And it was in fact very pleasant, sitting there in the dark, feeling Max's warm, slightly rough hand on my skin. I closed my eyes and pulled my cardigan tighter around my shoulders.

Minutes passed. Max removed his hand. 'Better now?'

I nodded. My foot felt cold, missing the warmth of his hand. I wondered if I should pretend that the other foot hurt too. I decided against it.

More minutes passed. A young couple strolled by, wrapped extravagantly around each other. Each had one hand tucked into the other's back pocket. I smiled. 'Young love.'

Max laughed softly. 'Yeah. Takes me back. Wasn't everything so simple when you were young? No kids. No responsibilities.'

I nodded. 'Happy days.'

He spoke again. 'Know what, Jill?'

'What?'

'It's very strange, but the first time I met you, I didn't notice quite how beautiful you are.'

Was that a compliment? In my fuddled state, I wasn't sure.

He continued, 'I must have been blind. How could I not have seen your beauty?'

What could I say to that? I felt distinctly uneasy, sitting in the dark, with my friend's husband telling me I was beautiful. I decided to tell the truth.

'I'm not beautiful, Max. I know that.'

He turned to me and gripped my arms. He put his face close to mine. 'But you are beautiful, Jill. You really are.'

I was fairly sure that he was a cheat. Now I knew that he was a liar as well. He had to be. He said that I was beautiful, but I knew for sure that my devoted mother was the only person in the world who honestly believed this to be true.

Max looked at me with sincerity written all over his handsome face. But I was beginning to realise that I was facing the most insincere man in Western Europe. I mentally ticked off the issues: he was married to Linda; he'd chatted up every pretty young girl we'd met on holidays; and I was fairly sure that, if Deirdre had gone walking with him, she'd have ended up on a similar bench, listening to similar smarmy compliments.

I knew what was coming next, and, as so often in my life, foreknowledge wasn't much use in the face of my inaction.

Max put his cheek next to mine. It was a scarily intimate gesture. His skin was rough and stubbly. I could smell his aftershave and the brandy he'd been drinking earlier.

His voice was soft, insinuating. 'Let's go into the woods.'

'What?' It was a kind of yelp. I had known where he was going, but I hadn't expected him to go there quite so quickly.

201

'Let's go into the woods.'

'Into the woods?' Another yelp. I knew he didn't want to go into the woods to pick mushrooms.

He gave a small laugh and nuzzled my carefully moisturised cheek with his coarse one. 'Come on, Jill. Let's live a little. Let's do something crazy.'

I didn't answer. He was using arguments Linda would have used to persuade me to do something unsuitable.

He gave one more nuzzle. 'Don't be sensible. Life's too short.'

I gulped. It could have been Linda sitting next to me. Except for the small fact that it was her husband, and he was trying to persuade me to have sex with him.

And what on earth was going on here, anyway? I had sixteen years of faithful, happy marriage behind me. I hadn't betrayed Cormac in word or deed for most of that time. Now, in the space of a few weeks, I'd slept with one man and was being propositioned by another. Had I unknowingly drunk some kind of magic potion that made me irresistible to the opposite sex? Had I belatedly become a sex bomb?

Max continued, appealing to my practical nature. 'The ground is dry.'

'But...'

He put one finger on my lips, silencing me. Just as well, because I had no idea what exactly I was going to say. I felt a sudden urge to kiss the finger that was resting lightly on my mouth. I pushed the evil thought away.

'But...' I still couldn't finish the sentence.

'No one need ever know. And no one need get hurt. It'll be our little secret.'

His breath was warm in my ear. He was a handsome, sensual man. If I went into the woods with him, I was fairly sure I'd be

202

well rewarded for my troubles. A few leaves in my hair would be a small price to pay for the pleasure I was sure he knew how to give.

And, besides, I was still really cross with Cormac. I remembered all the times he'd looked a bit too closely at Linda. The evenings he'd whistled in open admiration as she appeared for dinner in ever-tighter dresses. (I wasn't sure if she was doing this deliberately, or if she was just putting on weight as the holiday proceeded.) I remembered all the times Cormac had gallantly helped her into her boat, or out of her boat, or up a steep grassy bank.

Max kissed my ear. My sensible mind was saying no, but my foolish, treacherous body was begging, *Yes, yes. Do it. Go with him.*

And for one very brief moment, I was tempted. For the tiniest second, my guardian angel of sense was caught off guard. She must have been getting old and careless. She'd been sitting firmly on my shoulder since the day I was born, and now, for only the second time ever, she had allowed herself to be distracted. I leaned towards Max and yielded to his caress.

Then, mercifully, my guardian angel got her act together and returned to her post.

I drew apart from Max and edged away from him on the bench.

I wasn't angry at his impertinence. I was almost regretful at saying no. 'I don't think so, Max. It wouldn't be very smart. And I don't want to hurt Linda or Cormac. So, er, thanks, but no, thanks.'

He didn't try to persuade me. He looked almost relieved. He stroked my cheek with the backs of his fingers. 'Would've been nice. But I suppose you're right. Better not.'

I smiled to myself. I wasn't a woman of the world. It looked like I wasn't a serial adulteress after all. The whole thing was so civilised – genteel, almost.

I slipped into my shoes and got to my feet. 'Let's go back. It's late. I need my beauty sleep.'

Max laughed. 'But I told you, you're beautiful already. If you get any more beautiful, I certainly won't be able to resist you.'

'Yeah, right.'

Maybe I should have been cross with him for propositioning me, his wife's friend. Maybe he should have been cross with me for saying no. I had very little experience of this kind of thing, and I suspected that Max had far too much.

We walked home in easy silence, and went to bed with our spouses.

Chapter Twenty-Three

In the morning, I awoke to feel my ear being nibbled. No, not a river-rat who'd mistaken me for his breakfast. It was Cormac, at his seductive best. All of a sudden, I was very glad I'd spurned Max's advances. My life was quite complicated enough already.

Cormac stopped nibbling my ear and whispered into it instead. 'I'm sorry, Jill. I wasn't very sensitive last night.'

I snuggled close to him. 'It's OK. I overreacted. I was just hot and tired and cranky. It wasn't your fault.'

Cormac turned my face to his. 'Seriously, Jill. I didn't make myself clear. It's true, Linda is beautiful. She's the most beautiful woman I've ever seen. She's more beautiful than all those actresses who earn millions for each movie they make. She's so beautiful—'

I held up my hand to stop him. 'This is your apology for being insensitive?'

He laughed. 'God, sorry. Anyway, have I made my point?'

I laughed too. 'Yes, I think I know what you mean. Linda's sort of easy on the eye.'

'Yeah. That's it. But we both know that already. What I'm trying to say is, big deal. You're the one I love.' His voice became husky. 'You're so precious to me. Meeting you is the most wonderful thing that ever happened to me. And marrying you is the smartest thing I've ever done in my whole life. I'm the luckiest man in the world. Please believe me, Jill.'

I closed my eyes. This was the Cormac I had fallen in love with. This was the Cormac I had married. This was the man who made me believe that I was the most special woman in the world. This was the man who had vanished from my life many years earlier, leaving behind a stressed, cranky shadow of his former loving self.

'You are the world to me, my darling Jill.'

He looked like he was going to cry. Maybe if he had known about my night with Dudley, or my almost-night with Max, he would have.

I decided not to think about Dudley. I pushed Max to the back of my mind. There was no room in my marital bed for them right then.

I tried not to worry that the old Cormac was going to vanish again, leaving me with the newer model that I feared I didn't love. I'd take a leaf from Linda's book and live for the moment. Life's too short.

I kissed Cormac's lips. They were warm and dry. I pulled him towards me and inhaled his sleepy scent.

We were late for breakfast.

When we arrived down in the dining room, Max and Linda were already there. Linda looked rather pale, with large black circles beneath her eyes. She smiled at me. I couldn't meet her eyes. I felt guilty, though I had no real cause.

Max grinned at me and pulled out a chair. He didn't look guilty at all, though he had more cause than I did.

We had our breakfast, packed our bags and got ready to reclaim our river for the last time.

Barry and Laetitia were on the riverbank before us. I felt like I hadn't seen them for days. Maybe I hadn't. Or maybe I had been so caught up in the tangled web of my relationships, I just hadn't noticed that they were there.

Barry's black eye was fading to yellowy brown. His left hand was heavily strapped.

'Whatever happened to you? Don't tell me you crashed into another tree,' said Linda, who got to him first.

Laetitia smiled at her. 'No, it wasn't a tree this time.'

Barry gave her a cold, warning look. 'Laetitia...'

She smiled at him. 'Not now, dear. I'm telling a story.' As she spoke, she patted his strapped hand, making him wince. Then she turned back to us. 'You see, I was carrying the boat the wrong way.'

'As usual.' It was almost a growl.

She ignored his interruption. 'So Barry decided to show me how to do it properly. And the boat slipped right out of my grasp, and fell onto his hand. Barry was right: I'm not very good at carrying boats. I'm really very clumsy sometimes.' She smiled a beatific smile and climbed into the boat, and they paddled off.

I was shocked and thrilled. I put my hand over my mouth. 'Oh my God. She did it deliberately.'

Linda giggled. 'And I bet she gave him the black eye, too.'

'She's one scary woman, our Laetitia. I think I'll give her a wide berth from now on.'

'You know, you're right,' laughed Linda. 'She's as bad as he is. I think perhaps those two deserve each other.'

Just then, Dominic and Trevor arrived, their matching Lycra suits glinting brightly in the strong sunshine. Max clapped them on the back.

'Not like you guys to be late. Surely you didn't sleep in? A few glasses too many of the old *vin rouge* last night?'

Trevor looked at Max as if he'd just accused him of mass murder. 'Certainly not. Actually, we've both jogged five miles this morning. And then we had to call our travel agent. We're stopping off in Switzerland on the way home. This canoeing is too tame. We're going to do some white-water rafting.'

In moments, they too were settled in their canoe and set off down the river.

The rest of us lingered on the bank. Julie and Lauren were chasing some half-tame ducks who wouldn't even oblige them by running away properly. Cormac and Max had found themselves a nice seat in the sun and were continuing their endless conversation about football. Luke was sitting on a wall, fiddling with his CD player. He had his head down, but as far as I could see under his horrible fringe, he was unusually pale.

I took a step towards him. 'Luke…'

He didn't answer. Maybe he didn't hear me because of the music playing in his ears.

Deirdre put a hand on my arm. 'You OK, Jill?'

I shrugged. 'I'm fine. Why?'

'Dunno. You look a bit peaky, that's all.' She looked around our little group. 'Actually, everyone looks a bit off colour this morning. What's going on?'

She was right. I could account for several of the pale faces, but thought it best not to. I gave an even bigger shrug. 'We're all just tired, I suppose. Maybe it's time we all went home.'

I realised that this was the truth. There were too many tensions.

Too much going on. We all needed a break from one another.

Unusually, Linda was eager to leave. She dragged her canoe into position. 'Come on, guys. Let's get going. I want out of here before those *boules* guys appear. I'm not getting involved in a rematch.'

Reluctantly, the rest of us got to our feet and prepared to leave. The novelty of paddling had well worn off by now, and it seemed like too much hard work. I was glad it was our last day. For all kinds of reasons.

Soon the canoes were ready to go. 'Will we go together again?' Linda asked me.

I'd have preferred to go with Cormac. After the romance of the morning, maybe we needed to talk. Maybe now was the time to address the serious issues in our marriage.

Linda was insistent. 'Come on, Jill. Let's go.'

I sighed. There would be plenty of time for Cormac and me to discuss our problems when we got home.

'Sure. That's fine.' I climbed into the back of her boat, and we set off.

Before long, Deirdre was ahead of the rest of us. She called back happily, 'Do you mind if I don't wait for you lot? I want to have a good run at this river. I'll see you all later. OK?'

I laughed and waved her off as she vanished around a bend at speed.

Linda too seemed keen to move fast, and soon we'd left the others behind. For a while we concentrated on paddling and didn't speak.

Then Linda began, 'I'm sorry about yesterday afternoon.'

'Don't be,' I protested. 'I feel bad about it too.'

'Why on earth should you feel bad? You didn't make a total fool of yourself. And you didn't take out any of the local wildlife, either.'

'Well, maybe not. But I let things go too far. I should have got you out of there sooner.'

Linda laughed. 'Do you think I'd have gone willingly?'

I raised my paddle to avoid a huge clump of weed. 'Probably not.'

'Well, there you are. I'm bigger than you, and I didn't want to leave. I was having too much fun. I'm just glad you were there to rescue me when things turned nasty, though.'

I shrugged. 'I think I did too little too late.'

She shook her head. 'No. In the end, you saved me. Things could have got very messy if you hadn't been there. Thanks, Jill.'

'That's OK.'

'Really, though. I owe you a lot. You've always helped me. You've got me out of more scrapes than I care to remember. In fact, you've probably got me out of lots of scrapes that I can't remember at all. You've always been a good friend to me.'

Now I felt really dreadful. She wouldn't have said that if she'd seen me thrown shamelessly on that bench the night before, with her husband caressing my foot.

We paddled in silence for a while. I liked the regular splish of our paddles in the water. I liked the way the drops of water falling from Linda's paddle caught the sun and turned to little beads of molten sunlight.

Then Linda spoke again. 'Has Max made a pass at you yet?'

'What?' I was glad Linda was in front and couldn't easily turn back to look at me. I was totally shocked, and I couldn't begin to think how to answer.

It didn't matter, anyway. Once I didn't deny it, Linda knew. 'I take it he has, then. Was it last night, when I was sleeping off the drink? Or did he get to you before then?'

What could I say? She had her back to me and was speaking as calmly as if she were asking me what brand of fabric conditioner

I preferred to use. This kind of conversation was slightly easier when I didn't have to make eye contact, but still, I felt dreadfully uncomfortable. Clearly I'd never be part of the reality-TV generation. I could never face a TV camera and bare my soul to millions of viewers. Speaking to my friend's back was traumatic enough for me.

Linda turned briefly and gave me a quick smile, before the boat rocked dangerously and she had to face forward to stabilise it.

'It's OK. Really. It's not your fault. He tries it on all my friends. I'm used to it. It's not even that big a deal any more.'

The cold, dulled tone of her voice scared me. Linda, who was always so bright and bubbly, sounded like someone who'd swallowed a bottle of tranquillisers and washed them down with gallons of Ovaltine and Rescue Remedy.

'Was he upset when you said no?'

'How do you know I said no?'

She turned and gave me one more quick smile. 'Because if I can't trust you, my oldest and best friend, who on the face of this earth could I trust?'

Now I felt really, really bad. OK, so I'd done nothing, but I had considered it, if only for the tiniest moment. For one small second I had betrayed her in my mind.

'Some of my so-called friends have said yes. Can you imagine that?'

Unfortunately, I could imagine that very well indeed. Max was smarmy and predictable, but he had a certain charm that was difficult to resist.

Linda continued, 'There was this woman whose daughter was in Lauren's class. We used to meet for coffee every Thursday in the Gingerbread House. She used always admire my clothes and my hair. She used to kiss me on the cheek when we parted. I

211

thought we were really close. I thought we were friends. Turned out she was sleeping with Max for months. I used actually like her, fool that I was.'

I was horrified. 'Linda, that's so terrible.'

'I know. Awful thing was, she wasn't the first.'

'So what are you going to do?'

She shrugged. 'Nothing, I suppose. I've made my bed, so I'd better lie on it. While he's lying on everyone else's.'

'But that's so…' I couldn't think of a word to describe what I was trying to say.

Linda shrugged again, hunching her shoulders under the soft, patterned fabric of her T-shirt. 'Don't beat yourself up over it. I don't. Not any more, anyway. I look at it this way. He's a good-looking guy. It's only fair to share him around.'

I suddenly had a horrible thought. If he was sharing himself around so generously, surely he'd have made a pass at Deirdre too. I couldn't watch her every minute of every day. They'd have had plenty of opportunities. And, though she'd said she wouldn't go near him, she wouldn't have stood a chance against his clever ways. If Max wanted her, he would have got her in the end.

The one word slipped out of my mouth. 'Deirdre.'

'Oh, you don't have to worry about Deirdre.'

'But you've seen them together,' I protested. 'He's been flirting with her ever since she arrived. And she's too innocent to resist.'

Linda turned to face me briefly again. 'Trust me on this, Jill. He may have flirted with Deirdre, but he won't have gone further than that, I promise you.'

'How can you be so sure?'

'Max has his rules. He only goes for married women. In his sick male logic, he figures that's less complicated. You have a husband and kids. You wouldn't get seriously involved. He'd be afraid Deirdre might fall for him and make his life too difficult. Single girls are too dangerous.'

I had a sudden thought. 'Bunny-boilers?'

She nodded. 'You got it. My dear Max is cautious, in his own twisted way, so he limits himself to nice, safe, married women. He's always been like that. Ever since the day we met.'

Once again, the detached way she spoke almost broke my heart. I could only begin to imagine what she'd gone through to get to this level of control.

'So why did you marry him? You could have had anyone. You practically had to beat the suitors away from your door.'

She sighed. 'That was it, I suppose. Max was the only one who didn't try too hard. He was the only one who acted as if he didn't care either way. I could go with him or not; it was all the same to him. All the other guys were too easy. Max was the only one who didn't fall at my feet. Max was the challenge. So Max was the one I wanted.'

'Hmm. Seems like a funny kind of logic to me.'

She shrugged. 'Maybe. I didn't think it out. It just kind of happened. Thing is, he wasn't even faithful to me when we were going out together.'

'You still married him, though.'

She gave a wry laugh. 'I made the oldest mistake in the book. I thought I could change him. I thought that, when we were married, everything would be different.'

'And?'

'I was wrong, wasn't I? I don't think Max even knows what fidelity is. I think he was unfaithful on our honeymoon.'

Now I was even more shocked. 'Surely not! What kind of man would be unfaithful on his honeymoon?'

213

'A man like Max, it seems. There was this girl who worked in the bar on the island. A real slutty one – all brown cleavage and white teeth and no brain. She gave him funny looks whenever he came into the bar. I'm fairly sure there was something going on between them.'

This was awful. At least I had waited sixteen years for my first unfaithful act.

I spoke softly. 'You could leave him.'

She gave a long, weary sigh. 'I know I could. But I won't. I don't want to be on my own, and I haven't the energy to start again with someone else. That sounds too much like hard work. And Max and I, we're like two old troopers. Despite all that's happened, there's still something between us. We'll just muddle along. For better or worse.'

I held my paddle in one hand and used the other to stroke Linda's shoulder. It was an awkward gesture, but the best I could manage in the circumstances. She reached her hand back and rested it on mine, and we remained like that, drifting along in the dappled sunshine.

Chapter Twenty-Four

Lunch that day started off as a rather quiet affair. Deirdre didn't show up – I figured she was probably installed in St Julien by the time the rest of us were dragging our boats onto a shingly beach for a well-earned break. As usual, there was no sign of Dominic and Trevor, or of Barry and Laetitia. No doubt they too had finished canoeing and were busy planning next year's holidays.

Unusually, Linda didn't have wine with her lunch. She was quiet and rather subdued – more so than I had seen her before in the twenty-nine years of our acquaintance. Maybe she was sorry she'd been so open with me about her relationship with Max. Maybe putting the whole thing into words made it seem bigger than it had been before.

I had wine with my lunch – not that I particularly wanted it; it was more that, without it, the scene was far too bleak. Just as I was finishing my second glass, my telephone began to ring. At first I tried to ignore it, but after repeated requests from everyone else, I reluctantly took it out of my bag. No number was showing on the screen. So it could be Dudley. Or it could be the lady from the dry-cleaning shop saying that my duvets were ready for collection. It could be anyone at all, and I had no way of telling.

Everyone was watching me as I held the phone in my hand and listened to its plaintive tones. Why hadn't I turned it off? In my panic, it didn't occur to me to do this now.

I spoke brightly. 'Maybe if I ignore it, it'll go away.'

Luke reached over. 'It's doing my head in. I'll answer it, will I?'

I pulled away from him. 'No way. I mean, no, love. Let it ring. It's probably nothing, and I can pick up a message later.'

And if it's from Dudley, at least I won't have to listen to it with an audience of six eager listeners.

Swan Lake seemed to go on forever. I wondered if the other ring-tones were shorter.

Cormac snapped first. He could never bear not to answer the phone. 'For God's sake, Jill. Just make it stop. Answer the bloody thing, or jump on it, or fling it into the river or something.'

The last option sounded the most attractive to me, but perhaps that would have been a bit extreme, especially since I'd just upgraded my phone, and it was a particularly knacky little one that managed to impress even Luke.

I pressed the green button lightly and held the phone to my ear. 'Hello?'

'Jill, is that you?'

A man's voice. I raised my eyes. Everyone had put down their glasses and their knives and forks. They were all looking at me expectantly. What were they like? They should get out more.

'Jill?' The line was bad, and I still couldn't quite place the voice. I wondered if it was too late to throw the phone into the river. Should I pretend it was a wrong number?

'Jill?' This time the voice was so loud, it must have been audible to the others. Too late for pretence.

'Yes. This is Jill. Who's speaking, please?' Brisk and business-like, exactly the opposite of the way I felt.

'Oh, hi, Jill. This is Johnny.'

I was so relieved I didn't answer.

'You know, from Cormac's shop.'

I gave a brittle laugh. 'Johnny. How are you?'

At the mention of Johnny's name, the company picked up their utensils and resumed their meal. Everyone, that is, except for Cormac. He almost jumped to attention. He leaned over and held out his hand. 'Here, give it to me. Let me talk to him.'

I was happy to oblige. I handed him the phone, returned to my meal and listened to Cormac's side of the conversation. It didn't sound very good. There were lots of 'oh, no's, and more than one 'blast that effing shower', and one particularly ugly adjective that caused Julie and Lauren to giggle loudly.

Finally, Cormac clicked off the phone and laid it on the table beside me.

I touched his arm. 'Bad news?' It was kind of stating the obvious.

Cormac's face was serious. 'Very bad, I'm afraid. Very bad indeed. You know the Roche order?'

How could I not know the Roche order? He'd been going on about it for weeks. It had consumed his every moment. Because of the Roche order, Cormac had missed who knew how many family dinners, and Julie's school play, and Luke's guitar-playing debut at his school's open day.

I nodded.

'Well, it's going down the tubes. Some eejit in Dublin's messed up, and the Roches are threatening to go elsewhere with their business.'

'But if it's not your fault—'

'Fault?' he snapped. 'This is business. Fault doesn't matter. When the deal has gone west, no one cares whose fault it was.'

Max leaned over. He put one arm on Cormac's shoulder. His voice was calm, reasoned. 'Can the deal be retrieved?'

Cormac shrugged. 'Probably not. But maybe, just maybe, I can make a few calls when I get home tomorrow. Get some serious damage limitation going. Maybe something can be salvaged.'

Max grinned. 'That's sorted, then, isn't it? Now, do we need another bottle of wine?'

Cormac shook his head. 'Not for me. I need a clear head to work out the details.'

He took a pen from his pocket and began to scribble names and figures on a corner of the paper tablecloth. His face had recovered the tight, stressed look it had at home. The calm man who'd been in bed with me that morning was gone. I should have taken a picture of him while I had the chance.

Linda looked up from her meal, which I noticed she had hardly touched. She was still pale, and her smile wasn't as bright as usual. 'There's nothing you can do now, is there? So why don't you try to forget it for the moment, and we can try to enjoy the afternoon?'

'Fat chance.' This was Luke. 'One phone call and he forgets the rest of us. Don't you know that business is my dad's god? He can't forget it. And he's such an eejit, he actually thinks he owns the business.'

Julie piped up. 'But Daddy does own it. It says his name over the door. I've seen it lots of times.'

Luke gave a bitter little laugh, far too mature for his tender years. 'Don't kid yourself, little sis. Dad's got it all wrong, as usual. It's the business that owns him.'

'Luke…' It was my best warning voice. Not good enough, though.

'Stay out of this, Mum.'

I raised my hands in a gesture of peace.

Cormac wasn't impressed, though. 'Don't you speak to your mother like that.'

Luke looked at him coolly, with the one eye that wasn't obscured by his ridiculous fringe. 'What's it to you? You don't love her. You don't love us.'

My hands were beginning to shake. I was used to rows between Cormac and Luke, but this wasn't the usual spat. This was bitter and personal, and all the more horrible because it was being played out in public.

Julie got up. 'Come on, Lauren. I don't like fights. Let's get out of here. Let's go sit under this nice tree.'

I had to admire her maturity. The girls walked away, and I wondered if I should join them. Linda and Max were looking embarrassed. Luke was staring defiantly at his father, who looked as if he'd like to strangle his only son.

I spoke softly. 'Luke, don't say that. Your father does love us. All of us.' I wasn't sure if this was true, but it seemed important to say it anyway.

Luke gave another sneering laugh. 'Ha. You believe that, do you? You mean he's kidded you too? God, how blind can you be? Dad loves his business. He loves his stupid files and his folders and his catalogues and his targets. That's what he loves. He loves things, not people.'

Cormac went to get up. Max touched him on the shoulder. It was a light touch, but enough to make Cormac sit down again. As if to compensate, he thumped the table. The cutlery jumped in the air, and Linda just saved her wine glass. I flinched but said nothing.

219

'You ungrateful child,' Cormac hissed at Luke. 'You selfish, ungrateful child! Who do you think paid for this holiday? Who do you think bought those outrageously expensive runners you wear on your feet? Who put a roof over your head and food on your plate? Who? Bloody who?'

Luke kept his cool stare going. He shrugged expansively. 'You do, great provider. But what good is that? You're never there for us. When you come home, you don't even talk. All you do is run figures through your head while we talk to you.'

This was, in fact, a fair comment. I hadn't thought Luke had noticed it, though.

Luke's face was reddening. He was beginning to look a bit afraid, as if he realised he had gone too far. Still, though, he didn't pull back. 'You don't even know us. Let's try a little test. What's Julie's teacher's name?'

Cormac fell into the trap. 'I know that. It's Mrs Philpott.'

Luke laughed. 'Ha. Even I know that's not right. That was about four years ago. Junior infants, I think. Now, let's try an easier one this time. What's the name of my band? No, maybe that's too hard. How about this? Who's my best friend?'

Now Cormac did stand up. 'You brazen little pup. You're not too big to—'

Linda stood too. 'Guys. Calm down. You're losing the run of yourselves.'

Cormac spoke coldly. 'This is family stuff, Linda. Back off.'

She shrugged. 'Suits me. Come on, Max, let's leave them to it.'

Max got up. He looked at me. I shrugged. Best for them to leave us. I'd stay and try to keep the men in my family from killing each other. Linda leaned over and whispered in my ear, 'We'll just be over there. Call if you need us.'

I nodded. This was pathetic. It was like a cheap movie, with all the action centre stage, and the reinforcements hiding under the nearest tree, waiting for their big moment.

I looked from Luke to Cormac and back again. Their faces were tense, wary. I wondered who I should appeal to. Who would be most likely to listen to me? Luke was drumming his fingers on the table. Cormac was shredding a beer-mat.

Unable to decide, I addressed them both. 'Come on, guys. Why don't you discuss this later, when you're both calmer?'

Cormac said nothing. It looked as if he just might be considering it.

Luke rallied again. 'I'd love to talk about it later, Mum. But no doubt Dad will be too busy.'

This time Cormac really lost it. He jumped to his feet, leaned across the table and grabbed Luke by the shoulders. 'You little...'

I could see Max jumping to his feet also, ready to intervene. Luke looked at his father calmly. Cormac, who was not generally a violent man, released his grip.

Luke pulled free. He whispered, 'Mr Big Businessman. Too busy even to hit me. You go back to your figures. We'll be just fine without you.'

I tried again. I put a hand on his arm. 'Luke, please...'

He brushed me aside roughly. 'You stay out of it, Mum. You're no better than he is. You're—'

And then, finally, Cormac lost all control. He kept his hands by his sides, with his fists tightly clenched, and he spoke in a cold, sharp voice. 'Now you listen to me, you ungrateful young scut. How dare you push your mother aside? How dare you mock me? How dare you belittle everything I have worked for? Let me give you some news. You are just a waste of space. With your super-cool friends, your pathetic, ugly hair, your filthy, ragged clothes, and your stupid, stupid guitar.'

221

At the mention of the guitar, Luke recoiled slightly. I took a deep breath. It was OK for Cormac to mock Luke's friends, or his appearance, but mocking his guitar was a step too far.

Cormac saw the reaction and kept going. 'You actually think you can play it, don't you? You think you're bloody Rory Gallagher reborn. No one dares to tell you the truth, so why don't you let me be the first? You're crap. You can't even keep in tune. You're a complete waste of space, and I'm ashamed of you.'

Luke gave me a despairing look. Then he stamped down towards the water. He sat down and began to pull up large clumps of grass, which he threw far across the river.

Cormac almost slumped across the table. I put an arm around him and watched as my son decimated the riverbank. Would things ever be right between those two?

Julie sidled over. She cuddled up against Cormac. 'It's OK, Daddy. Mummy and I still love you.' I smiled at her. She was at least half right.

Cormac absently patted her head. I wondered if he was thinking about how to mend fences with Luke.

Or maybe he was deciding on new rescue strategies for the Roche deal.

Chapter Twenty-Five

Later, when we went back on the river, Linda's family decided to travel together. They probably figured they would be safer that way.

Luke was already in his canoe, and I prepared to join him. I could see that he was hurt and upset. 'No, Mum,' he said. 'Why don't you go with Dad?'

'But, Luke, love, we should talk. Your dad didn't mean all that stuff. He lost his temper, that's all.'

'Mum, I said no. I'm going with Julie. Right?' There was something strange about the way he looked at me. His row had been with Cormac, so why did he seem to be so cross with me too?

Julie skipped over. She didn't seem to realise just how serious things were. 'Shove up, Lukey. I'm coming in.'

Luke smiled at her. I was relieved to see that he didn't hate his entire family. Julie climbed in, and they pushed off. Maybe it was for the best. Maybe Julie could calm her brother with her endless innocent prattle, and I could work on their father. So I climbed into Cormac's canoe, and we followed them.

Cormac paddled like his life depended on it. His shoulders were hunched over, and I could see veins in his neck twitching. Luke had been completely out of order, I knew that, but Cormac had overreacted. He was the parent. He was meant to be able to soak up the abuse. Instead he had humiliated his son in public. It wasn't right, but this wasn't quite the time to point that out.

Maybe I could change the subject by telling Cormac about Max's pass at me the night before?

Probably not a good idea. Cormac was mad enough already. And Max was bigger than him, and looked like he'd be better able to handle himself in a fight.

So I said nothing for a while. Even though Cormac was paddling so furiously, we didn't catch up with Luke and Julie. No doubt Luke was paddling equally hard. The men in my family had a lot of aggression to work off.

We skimmed along, faster than I had moved all week. We passed numerous groups of canoeists – happy families and friends, laughing and chatting and enjoying the sunshine. I caught drifts of disjointed conversation as I sat in fearful silence, watching Cormac's rigid back and the angry way he stabbed at the water. I resisted the temptation to slip into the cool green water and swim away from all the turmoil.

After ten minutes or so, I figured Cormac would have worked off at least some of his anger. I decided to be brave.

'Cormac?'

'What?' His reply was sharp, not exactly the response of a man who wanted to be drawn into a conversation about his feelings.

'Do you want to talk?'

He turned briefly to face me. He even tried a smile. It didn't really succeed, but I appreciated the effort. 'Thanks, Jill. But no. I just need to think.'

'You're sure?'

He nodded. 'Sure, I'm sure. We'll talk later, OK?'

'OK.' It wasn't OK, but I knew it was the best offer I was going to get.

There wasn't much point in me paddling – Cormac was doing more than enough work for both of us. So I tried to make myself comfortable in the back of the canoe. This wasn't easy, but I did my best. The gentle rocking of the boat was soothing, and when I closed my eyes and let the sun warm my face, I could almost imagine I was somewhere else.

Dudley and I went boating once. It was near the end of our relationship, but of course I didn't know that then. I was sure it was just the beginning. I was sure it was just one of thousands of blissful days that we would go on to share. In one unimaginably foolish moment, I thought I was storing away golden memories that I would one day share with our grandchildren. And the thought of being old didn't frighten me, because I would have Dudley with me to make everything all right.

We'd hitchhiked to West Cork. We had no particular destination in mind, and when the last driver who picked us up said he was going to Mill Cove, that sounded fine by us.

We jumped out of the car, and the driver shook his head at us as we engaged in a long, passionate embrace. He was still tutting as he got into a small fishing-boat and headed out to sea.

Dudley and I sat on the pier, with our young brown legs dangling over the edge, and tossed pebbles into the still, dark water. It was early evening, and the sky was just turning pink. I sighed.

'Wouldn't it be nice to have a boat? Wouldn't it be nice to be able to drift away from here, to a secret place, just for the two of us?'

Dudley grinned and bowed ostentatiously. 'Your wish is my command.'

He took my hand and pulled me over to where a few punts were stacked behind a low wall. Together we dragged one down to the water. I felt briefly guilty, but Dudley kissed my fears away. 'We'll put it back.' He kissed me again. 'In the morning.'

I thought I'd die, I was so happy.

We rowed across the bay towards a small, shingly cove. I felt like a fairy princess, being rowed to her happy fate. It didn't matter that the boat was leaking slightly and smelled of rotten fish.

We hit the shore with a sudden bump. We rolled up our jeans and jumped out. Dudley pulled the boat clear of the water. We sat on a rock and watched the sun go down. I laid my head on his shoulder, and he stroked my hair and whispered endearments.

Later, we ate soggy sandwiches, and black bananas, and chocolate-covered digestive biscuits that had melted and stuck together. We licked chocolate from each other's lips. We drank warm beer as if it were the sweetest nectar. We laid our sleeping-bags on the shingle, and we made love in the almost-darkness.

Dudley dozed off with his arms around me. I looked at the stars and dreamed of the future. I was due back at college in a few weeks, to do my teaching diploma. Dudley would be there too, finishing off his business degree. But I'd be sensible. I wouldn't abandon my friends. I wouldn't be one of those clingy, possessive girlfriends. I'd still have fun. I'd still go to parties and discos. But I wouldn't be prowling, like the other girls, because I'd have Dudley. It was going to be the most perfect year of my life, and for-ever afterwards, I was going to give thanks that I had broken my wrist and had to miss the trip to Copenhagen with Linda.

We woke early. I was half frozen. The dew had soaked through our sleeping-bags. My feet were wet and almost numb. We jumped up and down on the pebbly shore. We rowed quickly back to the other side and replaced the punt, exactly as we had found it.

Then we walked the mile into Rosscarbery. We persuaded a nice B&B lady to give us breakfast – a big pile of fried food, with mountains of toast and gallons of strong black tea. She refused our offered money, laughing. 'Wisha, 'tis only a few rashers and eggs. And, God help us, you look like you need them.'

She smiled and patted my hand, and I almost loved her, because she had become part of my special day.

Cormac poked me gently with his paddle, and I opened my eyes. He was smiling, and he seemed slightly less tense. Maybe he had been working off his demons, while I reclined behind him and worked on a few of my own.

'At least you could pretend to do some of the work.'

I sat up and helped him to paddle, and not long afterwards we drew into St Julien.

Peter was waiting for us. He wore the hunted look he seemed to reserve for our party. I almost felt sorry for him. He caught our rope and tied our canoe to the small jetty. We climbed out. I was stiff and sore, and rather glad that we had no more canoe-ing to do. This was the end of the line.

Cormac got us each a glass of water, and we sat on the river-bank and waited for the others to notice that we had arrived. Luke and Julie were first, scrambling down the grassy bank towards us. When Luke saw us, he turned around and scrambled back up again. I could feel Cormac tense beside me. I put a hand on his. 'Leave him for a while. He's got a lot of cooling off to do.'

And a lot of apologising, and a lot of forgiving.

Julie wasn't happy. She stamped along the grass towards us.

'I'm never canoeing with him again in my whole life. He's so boring. All he did was listen to his music and give out that I wasn't going fast enough. And when we bumped into trees he said it was all my fault. It's not fair.'

She sat next to me, and I cuddled her.

'Never mind. He's just being a teenager. You'll be like that in a few years' time.'

'Yuck.' She made a face.

Just then Linda, Max and Lauren arrived from the small coffee shop just along the shore. Linda looked at me pointedly. 'Everything OK?'

I looked pointedly back at her. 'Sure. Let's talk later.'

She nodded.

Max gave a huge sigh as he sat down behind us. Clearly he had decided to do an ostrich act, and pretend he had forgotten that he had witnessed the apparent collapse of my family only a few hours earlier. 'Now, wasn't that fun? What's on for next year? Cycling? Roller-blading? Mountain-climbing?'

Lauren gave a big wail. 'No, Daddy. I get too tired. Next year let's just stay in one place.'

I smiled at her. 'For once, Lauren, I'm with you.'

Peter came over and interrupted her. He described how to get to the campsite, a few minutes' walk away.

Cormac got to his feet. 'Better get going, then. We need to get started on digging the toilet hole.'

Lauren looked as if she was going to get sick. 'What's that?'

I smiled at her and spoke in a manner that I hoped wasn't a bit reassuring. 'We have to dig a big hole in the woods, and we use that as a toilet.'

Lauren's face crumpled, and the wail began. 'Muuummy! I don't want to wee in a hole. Can we go where there's a real toilet? It's disgusting. Don't make me wee in a hole.'

Everyone laughed. I didn't particularly fancy using a hole in the woods as a toilet, but it would almost have been worth it, just for the pleasure of seeing how it would upset Lauren.

We strolled the short distance, with everyone busy joining in with the pretence that everything was OK. Every now and then, I turned around, and was relieved to see that Luke was slouching along behind us. Once or twice I smiled at him encouragingly, but each time he avoided my eyes. I decided that perhaps he had some more cooling down to do before he'd be ready to talk.

Unfortunately, the campsite had all modern conveniences, including sparkling clean toilets and showers. It was camping lite: our tents were already erected, and there were even inflatable mattresses, already inflated, lest our tired and pampered bodies become too well acquainted with French soil.

Everyone showered and changed, and then, with a heavy heart and a serious dose of trepidation, I joined the others as they headed into the small town for the last night of our holidays.

Chapter Twenty-Six

The evening started out calmly enough – considering the events of lunchtime. But then, maybe that's the way these things happen. After World War One, it must have seemed initially that World War Two was going to be a quiet, understated kind of affair.

Luke and Cormac were sullenly ignoring each other, but there was no sign of an imminent return to hostilities. I didn't interfere – maybe a frosty silence between the two was as good as it was going to get.

Deirdre was all bright and bubbly, so I hadn't the heart to rain on her parade by telling her about the big lunchtime row. Linda and her family seemed closer than usual. Maybe it helped them to see that our family was just as dysfunctional as theirs.

Peter had recommended a restaurant, telling us it was one of the best in France. Of course we were reluctant to believe him, fearing this was the ultimate act of revenge – sending us to a place that came with a guarantee of food poisoning. When we got there, though, Barry and Laetitia were there already, and we had no reason to believe that Peter had it in for them as well.

We sat near them, and were distracted and entertained by Barry's efforts to let the wine waiter know that he was a wine expert.

'I don't want the Gigondas if it's not 1999. 1998 just wasn't the same at all. And I want it served at precisely seventeen degrees. Anything less and the vanilla aroma simply doesn't get through.'

Just when the waiter was really impressed, Laetitia butted in. 'Don't worry. He's never actually tasted any of those wines he's going on about – he's just read about them on the internet. You can bring him any old plonk. He won't know the difference.'

Barry gave her an evil look, and she smiled sweetly back at him.

The food was superb – simple, fresh French food at its best, washed down with bottle after bottle of simple French wine. Max ordered the wine, loudly mocking Barry. 'Waiter, bring us your best wine. It simply has to be red, and in the biggest bottle your cellar can provide. And if it's not frozen, or boiling, it'll do fine.'

And so we muddled our way through the meal. We talked about the weather, and the food, and exchanged stories of canoeing mishaps and near-misses. We chatted and laughed with varying degrees of conviction, and pretended that the holiday had been a success, and that we would surely have a similar holiday next year.

After the meal, we wandered back to the campsite and sat on the ground in the soft darkness. It was a pleasant scene, with tents scattered around amongst the trees. Two young Americans were strumming guitars and singing softly.

Lauren and Julie, excited by the prospect of sleeping under canvas, decided that they were actually tired, and retired to their tents without even being asked.

Luke plugged himself into his music and sat with eyes closed, leaning against a tree. Every now and then his head swayed in time with a melody no one else could hear. He looked young, and lost. Once or twice I thought of going to sit with him, but something stopped me. He didn't seem ready to talk, and I wasn't sure I could find the right words anyway. Surely it was best to wait until morning, when we'd all had time to sleep on the issues.

After a while, we saw Barry and Laetitia going into their tent, and shortly afterwards we were treated to the sound of their lovemaking. There was a long series of moans and groans, and then the unmistakable sound of fabric tearing. They were separated from us by ten yards, and a millimetre or two of canvas. How could they think we couldn't hear them?

Linda giggled. 'I bet they know we're listening.'

I gasped. 'Never.'

Max grinned. 'Linda's right. I bet they're getting a thrill from knowing we're here. They must be secret exhibitionists.'

Just then, there was a high-pitched squeal from their tent. I wasn't sure if it came from Barry's or Laetitia's lips. We all laughed in guilty horror and poorly disguised interest.

Cormac shook his head and wiped tears of laughter from his eyes. 'This is the best entertainment I've had in years. I hope Laetitia makes a few wrong moves, and we get to hear Barry instructing her on how to do it right.'

Linda shook her head. 'That ain't going to happen, Cormac. Trust me. Laetitia's poor-me act is exactly that – an act. She is very definitely in charge of that relationship.'

I gave a sudden laugh. 'Get ready, guys – things could get very kinky in there. Brace yourselves for the clanking of chains and the cracking of whips. I've a feeling those two are only warming up.'

Deirdre stood up. She didn't seem to find the situation as funny as the rest of us did. 'I'm off to bed. See you all in the morning.'

I could have kicked myself. How insensitive could we be? How could the smug married couples have forgotten that Deirdre was on her own? Our relationships might not be perfect, but when the time came to retire to our tents, we would at least have someone warm to cuddle up against. If we chose, we could even get involved in a little companionable moaning and groaning of our own. And if we completely lost the run of ourselves, we could even make babies together. And Deirdre could do none of those things.

After a while Dominic and Trevor appeared, looking rather unfamiliar without their Lycra outfits. Now they were clad in matching chinos, smart button-down shirts and shiny new deck-shoes.

'Bankers on holiday,' whispered Cormac.

'No. Wankers on holiday,' giggled Linda.

I laughed out loud. Maybe things were going to be OK after all. Linda was back on form, and, even better, Cormac seemed relaxed, and he'd gone at least an hour without mentioning work, or the Roche deal, or damage bloody limitation.

Dominic and Trevor came over to where we were sitting. They shook our hands and said goodbye, explaining that they would be leaving at first light, ready for the next part of their trip. They retired to their tent, and not long afterwards the sound of loud snoring mingled with the strumming of the Americans' guitars. Mercifully, the Barry-and-Laetitia love-fest had come to its noisy conclusion some time earlier, so all was quiet from that end of the woods.

Luke followed on to the tent he was sharing with Julie, muttering that sitting outside a tent with a shower of dinosaurs wasn't exactly his idea of a fun holiday and next year he was going surfing in Lahinch with his friends instead.

I sighed. I'd miss him, but maybe it was for the best. Maybe the days of happy family holidays were well and truly behind us.

Just when I was thinking it might be nice to turn in, Linda went to check on Lauren. She returned waving a bottle of red wine in the air.

'Where did you get that?' I asked.

'In a street market the other day. I knew it would come in handy. Anyone got an opener?'

Max did have an opener, and I managed to produce a few plastic cups from the back of my tent. As I tried rather awkwardly to balance the cups on the rough grass, Max stood up. 'You know, I'd much prefer a beer. What do you think, Cormac?'

Cormac hesitated. He looked at his watch. 'I don't know, Max. It's late. And I've a big day ahead tomorrow. There's the journey, and I've got to hit the ground running when I get back. The Roche deal is at stake.'

I sighed. Who had I been kidding when I thought that Cormac had briefly forgotten the Roche deal? It was always present, somewhere in the depths of his stressed-out brain. And when the Roche deal was over, I knew there'd be another deal ready to take its place, ready to come between Cormac and his family, between Cormac and what I thought of as real life.

And all of a sudden I realised that was the way he liked it. He liked the cut and thrust and the daily risk-taking of his business life. Luke was right. It had become part of him, and nothing we could say would change it.

Max was still standing with his arms folded. 'Well, Cormac. What's it to be?'

Cormac checked his watch again. 'I...'

'For God's sake, Cormac. It's only a drink. Just go,' interrupted Linda. 'Forget your stupid deals and go and have a drink. Time enough for worrying tomorrow.'

That decided him. 'Well, all right, so. But just one. I need a clear head in the morning.'

They set off. Linda giggled as they went. 'Don't worry, we won't see those two for hours. Max will see it as his mission to get Cormac so drunk he won't know the Roche deal from a game of tiddlywinks.'

She held the bottle of wine in the air. 'Now, Madam, would you like red, or lots of red?'

I pretended to think. 'Lots of red, I think. It's been a very long day.'

I was uncomfortable from sitting on the hard ground, so while Linda was opening the wine, I went into my tent and dragged out my inflated mattress. Then I used my and Cormac's sleeping-bags and made myself a cosy little nest. Linda copied me, and soon we were as comfortable as it is possible to be in the great outdoors. We propped the wine on the ground between us and took turns to swig out of the bottle, a habit we'd perfected very early on in our relationship.

For a while we bitched about Peter, and then we speculated as to the state of health of the poor dog who'd been struck by the flying terracotta pot.

('Do you suppose he's dead?'

'Yup.'

'Pity.')

Then it was time for more serious topics.

I started. 'I'm sorry about today. You know, the row at lunchtime.'

'Don't apologise. It was hardly your fault.'

'Maybe not. But I feel bad anyway.'

She touched me lightly on the arm. 'Do you want to talk about it?'

I considered for a moment. Did I want to talk about the limitations of my relationship with Cormac? Did I want to try to explain how his work ruled our lives? Did I want to put into words how unloved and unappreciated I sometimes felt? And would any of it make any sense if I didn't mention Dudley too?

I smiled at Linda. 'Thanks, but it's all a bit raw yet.'

She smiled back. 'OK.'

We didn't say any more for a while. The odd slurping noise, as we swigged our wine, was mingled with occasional snores from the surrounding tents.

Linda spoke next. 'I've had a really wonderful holiday.'

'Yeah, me too.' In some limited ways, it was true.

She took a long drink from the bottle. 'You know, Jill, I've really missed you.'

She handed me the bottle, and I drank. 'What do you mean?'

'You've left me behind. Ever since you moved to Limerick, you've made yourself a whole new life. You've got a whole new circle of friends.'

'Do I?' I had to think about that for a moment.

'Yes, you do. I hear you talking about Rita. She sounds lovely. And you're friends with all your neighbours, and the people from the tennis club, and parents from Julie's school.'

'But surely you must have plenty of friends too?'

She shook her head. 'Actually, I don't.'

Linda had always had heaps of friends, and I couldn't figure how that could have changed. I protested, 'But you must have.'

She shook her head again. 'Really, Jill. Believe me. I don't have any friends at all.' Her voice was sad, but almost matter-of-fact.

This made no sense at all to me. 'But why? How? You were always the most popular girl I knew. Whatever happened? How could someone like you not have friends?'

Linda thought for a moment, and then she gave a brave, rather forced smile. 'Well, it's not that complicated, really. First you have to eliminate all the women who've slept with my husband. That's not conducive to a good friendship, I find.'

'Oh, Linda.'

'Then most of the ones who haven't slept with my husband think I'm sleeping with their husbands, so they're not likely to want to be my bosom buddies either. It's hard to blame them, I suppose.'

'Oh, Linda.' I knew I was repeating myself, but I couldn't think of anything else to say. She didn't seem to mind.

'So you can see why I'm still hankering after the old days, when you and I were best friends. When we were at school together, and then college. When we used to share our apple drops and our Kola Kubes and our lecture notes. When we used to see each other every single day, and still we never ran out of things to talk about.'

I smiled. The very mention of Kola Kubes took me right back. 'We did have some good times, didn't we?'

'You know, Jill, I've never told you this before, but...' She stopped.

'But what?'

'No, I can't say it. It's going to sound a bit too strange, now that we're supposed to be all grown up.'

I hit her lightly on the arm. 'You can't half-tell me something. Be brave. Say the words. I can take it.'

'It's just that...I mean...' She took a deep breath and rushed out the words. 'I've always been a bit jealous of you.'

I was so surprised that I put the wine bottle down without taking my drink. Where was she coming from with this? Was she winding me up? Was this some kind of twisted revenge because Max had chatted me up?

She didn't say any more. I drank twice from the bottle, and still she didn't speak. I decided it was a wind-up.

'*You* jealous of *me*? Yeah, right. I nearly believed you there for a second.'

Suddenly she sat up straight, gathered her sleeping-bag around her shoulders and looked at me closely. 'I'm not joking, Jill.'

I still couldn't see where she was coming from. I sat up too. I couldn't argue properly from a semi-reclining position. 'OK. Let's get this clear. You're prettier than me. You're smarter than me. You're funnier than me. You always got the cool guys. And yet *you* were jealous of *me*?'

'Yeah. I was.' She spoke softly, almost as if she was afraid to admit it.

'So what exactly were you jealous of? My interestingly small mouth? The particularly mousy shade of my hair? The way I never had to strain my brain trying to decide between a string of suitors? My distinctly average exam results? Come on, Linda. Spit it all out, share your jealous feelings with me.'

I felt cross and bitter, and I was sure it came across in my voice. I didn't care.

Why was she teasing me so? Was all this because of Max? That hadn't been my fault. And, besides, I had said no to him. Perhaps I shouldn't have. Maybe Linda didn't deserve my loyalty. Maybe I should have been like all the others and taken her husband's generous offer of an energetic bout of commitment-free passion.

'You really don't know?' It was almost a whisper.

'No, I bloody don't, and since the specialist subject seems to be jealousy, how about this? I was jealous of you. Ever since we were tiny. Ever since that first day when you sidled into my life and offered me madeleines. Everything I did, you did better, with knobs on. Every moment of my life, I wished I could be more like you and less like me. I wanted your looks, your brains, your courage, your sense of fun. Everything. I wanted the whole package. Warts and all.'

I could hear the pitch of my voice rising. I had twenty-nine years of jealousy to express, and the words came tumbling out. I didn't try to stop them. 'In the unlikely event of you ever having anything as common as warts, I'd have bloody well wanted them too.'

I swigged from the wine bottle and slammed it onto the ground. I was angry now.

'You know what my greatest dream was?' I didn't wait for her answer. 'I dreamed that I'd go to sleep, and wake up as you. I dreamed that I would vanish forever. My pale, mousy self would be no more. That's what I wanted. I wanted to be you.'

'I never knew.' Linda spoke so quietly, I had to strain to pick up her words. 'Honestly, Jill, I never knew.'

'For a supposedly smart girl, you weren't very perceptive, then, were you?' I could hear the bitter twist of my words.

Linda kept her voice even. 'You see, so what if I was pretty and smart? I took all that for granted. It was just part of me. Nothing special. Nothing to get excited about.'

I grunted my disagreement with that statement, but Linda ignored me and continued. 'And all the time I envied you.'

'But why?' My anger was gone now. It had slipped away when I wasn't paying attention. I was just puzzled.

'Because I thought you had everything. Your parents were so lovely, and mine were always drinking and fighting and giving me grief over nothing. They were never happy, and I was just a weapon they used to hurt each other.'

It was true that her parents had been rather volatile, but I'd always thought that seemed kind of like fun. Next to them, my parents had appeared dull and boring.

Linda continued, 'And you had Deirdre, and I had no one. I envied you so much, going to bed in the same room as her. I used to lie in my room at night, thinking how nice it would be to have a sister, to be able to chat about nothing before going to sleep.'

I smiled to myself. My strongest memories of bedtime with Deirdre were of lengthy rows about whose socks were filling the room with rich, malodorous fumes, or whose turn it was to get up and turn off the light.

'But it wasn't just your family,' Linda went on. 'It was you too. You were always in control. You were cool and calm, while I spent my time running around looking for attention. You could do stuff.'

I laughed despite myself. 'Stuff? What kind of stuff?'

'You know. You were capable. You could change tyres, and fix plugs – that kind of stuff.'

I laughed again. 'You were jealous of me because I could change tyres? That's a bit pathetic, don't you think? Why didn't you just envy that handsome, lanky mechanic down in Donovan's garage?'

She gave a sly giggle. 'Jamie? I went out with him once. We went back to the garage when it was closed, and we —'

What was she like? I held my hand up. 'Enough already. Anyway, you never needed to do tyres and plugs and that kind of stuff. All you had to do was smile and bat your long lashes, and some poor man would rush over and do it for you.'

Linda grinned. 'Yeah, you're right. I could be guilty of that.

But it's not quite as satisfying, is it? I always end up feeling rather cheap. It's not a great feeling, believe me.'

'Hey, I have to believe you. I'll just never know for myself.'

Linda sighed and lay down again. 'I know I'm not getting this across very well. It sounds stupid. But...' She stopped, and for a horrible moment I thought she was going to cry. Then she took a deep breath and continued. 'And now you have your family. Cormac and the children. They're so great.'

'Hello? Where were you today?'

She waved her hand. 'OK, so they had a bit of a row. Big deal! Stuff like that happens. Luke's a good kid.'

'Yeah, he is. But...'

'And Julie's a little darling. You should be very proud of her.'

'I am. But Lauren—'

She raised her hand to stop me. 'Now, don't get me wrong, I love Lauren to bits, but I'm not stupid. I've spoiled her rotten, and it shows. She's an obnoxious little pest sometimes, and it's all my fault.'

She was getting upset, and I felt I had to help her out. 'My life's not perfect, you know. Far from it, actually. Cormac and I...'

'Oh, I know. Cormac works too hard, and he's stressed out all the time. It's not perfect, but it could be a lot worse, you know.'

'I'm sure Max isn't a bad guy. He's funny, and good-looking and kind.'

She sighed. 'Yes, he is all those things. Unfortunately, as you know, he's also a serial adulterer. At least when Cormac isn't at home, you know he's flicking through computer catalogues or working on his tax return. When Max's late, I know he's working on his seduction technique, or flicking his fingers through some young blonde's hair.'

What could I say to that? Nothing, it seemed.

'Max doesn't know how to be faithful. He just doesn't see the point. And I still love him, despite that. I think he even still loves me, underneath it all. We're all tied up in each other, for better or worse. Maybe we're like Barry and Laetitia. Maybe we deserve each other.'

We lapsed into silence again. The Americans had stopped singing and were plucking stray melodies from their guitars. I lay back and looked at the sky, and tried to work out all that Linda had said. This time, I was the first to speak. 'You know what's funny?'

'What?' She sounded as if she was about to drift off to sleep.

'Max wouldn't have looked twice at me if I'd met him while we were in college.'

'You don't know that.'

'Yes, I do. And, what's more, you wouldn't have looked twice at Cormac.'

She didn't argue.

I hadn't thought a whole lot about this before, but now it seemed suddenly clear. 'You see, it was a game. And we all played by the rules. The good-looking guys got the pretty girls, and the rest of us matched off as best we could. But there was a twist that none of us were smart enough to predict.'

Linda was fully awake now, and listening closely. 'What was that?'

'Well, we lesser mortals were always half jealous. We wanted the handsome guys too. But so many of those were arrogant and horrible, underneath their clear skin and strong jaws and crinkly eyes. And none of us thought then that the guy we'd marry might need to be kind and considerate and loving. What good are looks when the baby's screaming, and your husband is burying his handsome face in the duvet and pretending not to hear? Does it matter if he's got the cutest butt in the Western world, if he doesn't even know where the vacuum cleaner is kept? I'd have gone for those guys too, but luckily I didn't get the choice. They didn't want me.'

I stopped, then decided I might as well continue. 'Well, there was one notable exception. I did get the handsome guy once. Just once.'

'Who was that?'

'Don't you remember Dudley?'

'Dudley?'

'Yes, Dudley. Dudley Adamson. The first love of my life.'

'Oh. Dudley. American Dudley? Now I remember him. He was really cute, wasn't he? We...' She stopped. 'Hey, hang on a minute. What do you mean, the love of your life?'

I closed my eyes and breathed deeply for a few seconds, in an effort to calm myself. How could she not have known that Dudley was the first love of my life?

While I rehearsed all kinds of replies to her question, she spoke again. 'Oh, yeah. I forgot – you and he had a little thing going that summer when I was in Copenhagen, didn't you?'

Now I couldn't hold myself back. 'We had a little thing going? God, how could you have been so insensitive? I adored him. I thought I'd die when it was finished with him. He was the only guy besides Cormac that I ever felt anything for.'

I was getting excited, and the pitch of my voice was rising dangerously. Linda leaned over and took my hand.

'Hey, Jill. I'm sorry. I never knew he meant that much to you. You never said.'

My voice was quiet. 'I didn't know how.'

Suddenly she slapped her free hand to her head. 'Oh, no. I went out with him a few times, didn't I?'

I nodded slowly. 'Yes. You did go out with him a few times. Four times, to be precise. Once to the pictures. He took you to

243

see a James Bond movie, and you hated it so much you ate a whole box of chocolates. Once he took you to a disco, and afterwards you snogged at length in a laneway off Patrick Street. You even showed me the place the next day. And twice you went to a pub. On the second date, he bought you a bunch of baby pink carnations. You brought me into your house and showed them to me. You even made me smell them. You brought "rubbing my nose in it" to new heights.'

'Oh, Jill.' It was a whisper. I ignored it.

'You told me all about you and Dudley. Every last detail. And then you finished with him because he was too serious.'

Linda held my hand tightly. 'What happened between you two, anyway? I only met you with him once, when I got back from Denmark. Then you said it was over. I thought it was just a casual thing. You never told me it was so serious. Honestly, Jill. You never said a word.'

It was so many years ago, but still, I felt a rogue tear trickle down my cheek. I wiped it away with the back of my hand. 'I thought you'd know. I was so upset. I couldn't eat, or sleep. I couldn't understand why you didn't see it.'

Her forehead puckered as she tried to think herself back nineteen years. 'That's right. You were in really bad form after I got back that summer. I even asked you why. Actually, I remember now. You'd hurt your hand, hadn't you? You said you were just fed up because of not going away that summer.'

I spoke bitterly. 'And you believed me.'

'Why wouldn't I? I wasn't expecting you to lie to me. We were friends. And why didn't you tell me the truth, anyway?'

I didn't answer.

She continued, 'And what did happen between you and Dudley? What went wrong? Why did you finish up with each other?'

'We didn't "finish up with each other", as you so delicately put it. He finished up with me. There's kind of a difference, don't you think?'

'But why?'

I spoke softly. 'Remember that very first night when you got back, and we all went for pints?'

She nodded. 'Yes, I remember. I was really excited, because I hadn't seen you for months. There was a big crowd of us. We went to the Long Valley.'

'So you do remember that night?'

'Yes, I do. I do now. That was the first time I met Dudley. And it was the only time I ever saw you two together.'

I pulled my hand away from hers. 'Well, the minute you joined us, that was that. You danced into the pub, all tanned and beautiful and funny, and the rest, as they say, is history. Dudley was so taken by you, he almost climbed onto your lap and made love to you there in the pub.'

'Are you sure? I don't remember that.'

I gave another bitter laugh. I was getting good at them. 'Maybe it wasn't your fault. Maybe you were so used to that kind of thing that you didn't even notice. Trust me, though. I noticed. I noticed everything. Dudley didn't take his eyes off you the whole night long. It was as if I had vanished. He barely spoke to me for the whole evening. And I knew. Even then, I knew.'

'Jill...'

I put my hand up to stop her. This had to be said. 'And next day Dudley came to me laden down with all the old lines – "too serious too soon...it was fun while it lasted...we can still be friends..." You've heard them all before. Well, actually, now that I think of it, maybe you haven't, but every other girl in the world has. And I begged him not to leave me. I begged him not to go.

245

Like that was going to make him change his mind. He was kind enough not to mention you, but he didn't have to. I knew anyway. I might have been a fool back then, but even I could see what had happened. And then, after a decent few weeks had passed, he asked you out. I don't know how he held out for so long. You even asked me if I minded. I said no. I said he was just another guy, and that he meant nothing to me. Nothing at all.'

'But why didn't you tell me the truth? I wouldn't have gone out with him if I'd known. You know that.'

'That's true. You were always fair. But what was the point? If you had refused him, it's not like he'd have come running to me looking for all his old clichés back. I knew that too.'

Linda sighed. 'He never meant anything to me.'

'I know. That made it even worse. You had the only guy I'd ever wanted, and you didn't even want him. You ditched him as soon as you could.'

Linda put her arms around me and whispered, 'Jill, I'm so sorry. If only I had known. I never would have done it. I never would have hurt you. Please forgive me.'

I pulled away from her. 'There's more. Remember we'd planned to do our H.Dip. together? We were going to be the most enlightened and wonderful teachers Cork had ever seen? One day statues would be erected in Patrick Street to the two great educators we were going to become.'

'Yes. I remember that. And then, at the last minute, you said you didn't want to be a teacher. It was too boring. Too predictable. I thought you were mad. I tried to make you change your mind. But you were unusually determined.'

Another twisted smile. 'Yeah, so determined I was even able to resist you.'

I was glad to see that Linda flinched slightly at these words. I felt rather pleased with myself, in a sick kind of way. Perhaps, somewhere deep inside, I had been planning this showdown for years. It hurt, but I was almost enjoying myself. It was as if I was finally getting my moment of glory.

I continued. 'Well, get this. I still really, really wanted to be a teacher. That hadn't changed at all. I only abandoned the great teaching plan because I couldn't bear the thought of being in college with you and Dudley. I thought that looking at you strolling around the campus arm in arm would break my heart. How pathetic was that? I abandoned my career plans because I got dumped. And then, to add insult to injury, you dumped him a few weeks later. He went back to America shortly afterwards. So I'd ditched my glorious career for nothing. My whole life changed because of a three-week fling of yours.'

Now Linda was crying. 'I'm sorry. I'm sorry.' She repeated the words over and over.

I interrupted her. My anger had suddenly evaporated, and I was feeling the first stirrings of regret for my harsh words. I couldn't take them back, but maybe I could soften them somehow. 'Anyway, you did me a favour in the end. I took that job in Limerick instead of going back to college, and I met Cormac and I lived happily ever after.'

Linda wiped her eyes and looked at me closely. 'Are you happy, Jill?'

I wiped away the last of my tears and smiled at her. 'Almost.' Then I returned her question. 'Are you happy, Linda?'

She thought about it for a moment. 'What's happiness?'

She hadn't answered my question, but I thought I knew what she meant anyway.

Chapter Twenty-Seven

A few hours later, Linda and I had talked through our very different slants on our joint past. We were emotionally drained, but I knew everything was OK. For the first time in a very long time, I was glad to be her friend.

By now, we were lying on our backs, looking up at the trees and the dark sky.

'Any wine left?'

This must have been the tenth time she'd asked.

'No, Linda. We finished it an hour ago. Remember?'

'Just checking.'

I had to laugh. I stood up. 'Come on. Surely it's after our bedtime. It's almost—'

Just then, I was interrupted by the strains of 'Show Me the Way to Go Home' drifting through the trees.

Linda giggled. 'Sounds like our menfolk are back.'

Cormac and Max came into the camp, full of drink and bluster. They were arm in arm, but it was difficult to see who was supporting whom. They stumbled in our direction and stood before us, swaying and grinning like people who had kept drinking for hours after they had already consumed enough. They looked very pleased with themselves. Max disentangled himself, considerately propping Cormac against a tree. 'Listen to this, girls. Cormac has a party trick to show you – haven't you, Cormac?'

Cormac nodded obediently, and Max continued, 'OK, Cormac, tell us all about the Roche deal.'

Cormac grinned broadly, showing all the expensive dental work he'd had done that year.

Max gave a big, theatrical sigh. 'Never work with children, animals or people with drink taken. Now let's try again. You have to answer me, remember?'

Cormac nodded.

Max spoke slowly and carefully. 'Now, Cormac, tell us about the Roche deal.'

Cormac grinned again and shouted at the top of his voice, 'Fuck the Roche deal!'

Then the two men collapsed into a laughing heap. Eventually Max sat up.

'See, Jill? Look what I did for you. You gave me a stressed-out workaholic, and I brought you back a…a…'

'…a drunk?' I finished helpfully.

Max shoved out his bottom lip in a pathetic imitation of a hurt look. I had to laugh, even though I knew that the stressed-out workaholic would be back in the morning, not improved by the addition of a monumental hangover.

The men stumbled towards the toilet block, cursing loudly as they tripped over assorted guy-ropes and gas cookers and bicycles. There was a chorus of multilingual complaint, which prompted even more curses from Cormac and Max. Then we all crawled into our tents and settled down on our inflated mattresses for our night under canvas.

I lay down and closed my eyes. There was a brief battle between my busy thoughts, trying to keep me awake, and the alcohol I'd consumed, trying to send me to sleep. The alcohol won, and I went to sleep almost immediately.

It was still dark when I woke to the sound of fumbling at the zip of the tent. I was disoriented, and at first I couldn't figure out what the noise was. I couldn't quite fit it into my vivid dream of fights and reconciliations. Then I heard Julie's voice. 'Mum. It's me. Let me in.'

I sat up and bottom-shuffled in my sleeping-bag towards the entrance of the tent. On the way, I sat on Cormac's arm by mistake. He groaned and muttered something about selling the business and going to live in Hawaii. I pushed him to one side as best I could, and continued my journey. Either it was a very big tent, or I was a very poor bottom-shuffler. At last I could feel the thicker, rougher canvas of the tent's front door. I fumbled for a moment with the zip. I wondered why it wasn't made to glow in the dark – which would have made life much easier for campers. But then, maybe campers, by their nature, don't want easy lives – if they did, they would surely hang out in five-star hotels instead of draughty canvas shacks.

Eventually, after I'd broken at least two fingernails, the zip slid open with a satisfying whizzy sound. Julie crawled into the tent and wriggled until she was inside my sleeping-bag with me. It was nice, as her bare legs were lovely and warm, and I was rather chilly. I stroked her hair and allowed her soft breath to warm my neck. We were quiet for a while, except for Cormac's loud snoring and his occasional aggrieved mutterings about stockbooks and box files.

Then Julie wriggled her body in distaste. 'Yuck. Smells of rudies in here.'

I laughed and hugged her closer.

I was just drifting back to sleep when she spoke again. 'Mum,' she whispered. 'Where's Luke?'

Chapter Twenty-Eight

I crawled into the tent where Luke and Julie had been sleeping. It was tiny, so it didn't take long to establish the fact that Luke wasn't inside it. It was empty, except for two crumpled-up sleeping-bags and the dirty clothes Julie had been wearing that day.

I crawled outside again. I checked the area around the tent, in the vain hope that perhaps Luke had somehow managed to wriggle out in his sleep, but there was no sign of him.

I slipped quickly into silent panic mode, shaking my head in an effort to clear the last traces of alcohol from my consciousness. I'd consumed a lot of wine, and I knew I had been pleasantly woozy at one stage, but I was fairly sure I'd checked on Luke and Julie before going to bed. I was almost certain that they'd both been slumbering gently when I had finally settled myself in the next-door tent.

I ran the few steps back to my own tent. I put my head inside and called Cormac, who responded with a lot of gobbledegook about a soccer match and a crooked referee. I crawled into the tent and shook him by the shoulders, deliberately hurting him. He sat up and rubbed his eyes. 'Hey, that hurt. What's wrong?'

'Luke's missing.'

Cormac was out of the tent before he was fully awake. He stood there in the moonlight, looking rather absurd in his boxer shorts, one white sock and a soccer jersey. He scratched his head. 'Maybe he's just gone to the toilet.'

Of course. How could I have been so foolish? I was always jumping to the worst, the most horrific conclusions. Clearly Luke had woken up and gone to the toilet.

Only he hadn't.

We ran over and checked all the toilets, and the showers too, for good measure. This was exceedingly optimistic, as Luke wasn't overly fond of showers even in the daytime. What were the chances of him taking a shower in the early hours of the morning? All we found were a few lurking lizards and an elderly French gentleman, who clearly had rather nasty digestive problems.

We came back to our tent, and we stood together in the middle of the French wood and wondered just how serious this was. Julie appeared at my side and slipped her hand into mine. 'Don't worry, Mum. We'll find him. We'll get him back.'

And then I really began to worry. Underneath his carefully nurtured cool image, Luke was a sensible boy. He wouldn't just wander off in the middle of the night. It wasn't his style.

But he'd been so quiet over the past day or two. Was there something wrong with him that I hadn't noticed? We had always been close, but the past few days had been very strange. And then there had been that awful row with Cormac. Those two always seemed to be at each other's throat, but this was different. This was worse than any row I'd witnessed before. This was deep and personal and hurtful. And I had meant to talk to Luke about it, but I just hadn't found the time. I could have punched myself in the face. I'd found time for a heart-to-heart with Linda over things that had happened almost twenty years earlier, yet I hadn't managed to spare a moment for my own son.

I ran over to Linda and Max's tent and called them. Cormac woke Deirdre. Soon all three were standing outside in the warm night air with us.

It was very strange. I was really, seriously worried, but didn't know if such worry was justified. Would Luke just wander back from a moonlight stroll, laughing at us for our concern? Or had something dreadful happened to him while I was sleeping off my drinking excesses?

Max came over to me. He held both my arms and looked me straight in the eye. 'Jill, just answer yes or no. Is this out of character for Luke?'

I nodded. 'Yes.'

'Well, then, we need to get organised and find him.'

I was so grateful to Max for taking charge that I could hardly speak.

He spoke briskly, with authority. 'Right, everyone put some shoes on, and get a phone if you have one, and then we'll get started.'

We all did as we were told, reaching into our tents and pulling on whatever footwear we found.

Max spoke again. 'OK, everyone ready? No point everyone rushing around madly. Jill, you walk towards the village; take the path, and don't leave it – we don't want to lose anyone else. Linda, you stay here with the girls, and have your phone ready so you can let us know if he comes back. Cormac, you go down the river that way, and I'll go the other way. Deirdre, you come with me. No chance anyone has a torch, I suppose?'

'I have.' It was Dominic, who'd just poked his head out of his tent. 'But what do you want a torch for, at this time of the night?'

Max explained, and seconds later both Dominic and Trevor were out of the tent and ready to help, each clutching a strong, bright-beamed torch. I could have hugged them, and I mentally apologised for mocking all their techno-geek equipment.

The other five searchers arranged themselves into groups and headed off along the riverbank in opposite directions, while I set off for the village. I was cold and scared. I sincerely hoped that this was all a dreadful misunderstanding, and that I'd soon be apologising to everyone for wasting their time and disturbing their sleep.

I walked along the quiet path, calling Luke's name every now and then. I got to the village quickly – far too quickly, as I had no idea what to do when I got there. It was absolutely deserted. Its two streetlights cast a lonely glow on the dusty street. I had no idea how to begin looking for a fourteen-year-old boy in such a place. There were no convenient amusement arcades or bars or clubs. A small, thin cat slipped past my feet, but otherwise it seemed as if the entire population of the village was healthily slumbering. There was no one to ask. No one to help me.

The silence was broken by the first notes of *Swan Lake*. My mobile phone. My hand shook. I flicked impatiently at the green button. It was Linda. 'Come back, Jill. Come back.'

'Oh, thank God. Is he there? Is he all right? Where was he?' My voice was shaking, as I willed her to say everything was OK. She didn't.

'Just come back, Jill. Please. Hurry.'

I ran all the way back, stumbling in the flimsy sandals I'd pulled on in a hurry. When I got back, Linda was standing by my tent. Next to her were Max and Trevor. Max was holding a boy's runner.

I felt a cold chill through my body. 'Where did you get that?'

'Is it Luke's?'

I couldn't answer. 'Where did you get it?'

Max hesitated for a second. 'It was down by the river. Next to the water. Come on, Jill, concentrate. Work with me. Is it Luke's?'

I had no idea. It was big enough, and dirty enough, to have belonged to Luke. All runners looked pretty much the same to me. All I did was hand over an outrageous amount of cash every few months, and Luke would arrive home with a bright new white pair, which only days later would look just as bad as the ones they'd been bought to replace.

Julie was by my side again. 'It is Luke's, Mummy. Remember, he got them just before the holidays, the day I got my sandals. I know he got the ones with the purple tick on them. I told him purple was a girl's colour, but he got them anyway. They were very expensive.'

I reached out and took the shoe from Max. Even at arm's length I got the strong odour of adolescent male feet. I gave a small sob. I immediately thought the worst. I wondered how I'd ever again manage to enter Luke's room, with its smell of dirty runners and hair gel and the kind of body spray that comes in sleek black aerosol cans. What would I do with his things? His awful leather coat? His CDs? His guitar?

Max put one arm around me. 'There could be a simple explanation for this. He might have lost his shoe earlier today. It might not even be his. Don't panic, Jill. Not yet.'

Deirdre came and stood beside me. She didn't say anything, but I recognised the tense, fearful look on her face. It made me feel even worse.

Linda put her fleecy jacket over my shoulders and carefully buttoned it at my neck, as if I were a child. She hugged me. 'It's going to be all right, Jill,' she whispered. 'I know it. Luke's a sensible boy. He wouldn't do anything stupid. He's going to be OK.'

I sobbed and clung to her. And for a second I thought of our conversation that evening, when she'd asked me if I was happy. How could I have been so arrogant and presumptuous? How could I not have been happy, when I had been blessed with such riches?

Linda took me by the arm and sat me outside our tent. Someone brought a sleeping-bag and wrapped it around me. Like everything was going to be OK as long as the hysterical mother was kept warm.

Julie came and curled up in my arms. Lauren was still sleeping. Linda looked at Max and Trevor. 'What are you waiting for, guys? Let's go. Jill, you stay here, in case Luke comes back. And keep your phone on.'

I knew she was trying to protect me. I knew she was afraid of what they might find down by the river. She went off with Deirdre and the men, back along the river, flashing the torch across the surface of the water and calling. I clung to Julie, and waited.

Some time later, there was a rustling in a nearby tent. I jumped up and ran over, hardly daring to hope that it might be Luke. Maybe he'd got up during the night, and wandered back to the wrong tent by mistake.

It wasn't him, of course; it was Barry, on the way to the toilet. He was surprised to see me. He looked at his high-tech glow-in-the-dark watch-*cum*-compass. 'It's very late, Jill. Why are you still up?'

I told him, and he was immediately concerned. He woke Laetitia, who crawled out of the tent magnificently clad in a long white lace nightie and high-heeled shoes, which would have greatly amused me in different circumstances.

She came over to me and patted my shoulder. 'You poor thing, you must be so worried. But I'm sure he'll be OK.'

Barry joined us. 'I'm sure he will, but I read about this kind of thing on the internet lately. The ages twelve to eighteen are the worst for accidents amongst boys. How old is he, exactly?'

I knew he didn't mean to be insensitive. Laetitia gave him a poke in the ribs, which had no effect. He continued, 'It seems that, at that age, their sense of adventure is heightened while their sense of fear is at its lowest. Statistically, ouch!'

Laetitia had viciously driven one of her high heels into his bare foot. He hopped on his good foot and rubbed the other, while giving his wife evil looks, which she ignored. She turned to me. 'Come on, love. Come and sit by our tent. I'll light the gas and make us a cup of tea. Barry, you go and help to look.'

Barry was still rubbing his sore toe. 'Where should I look?'

I didn't know. I had no idea what was best to do. Panic had muddled my brain. Then Laetitia had an idea. 'Peter lives in the village. We saw him going into a house yesterday evening, remember, Barry? The one just off the square. Why don't you call him? He said he's there for emergencies. He knows the area. He'll know what we should do.'

I didn't know if that was a good thing to do or not. I clung to Julie and tried to think straight. I couldn't manage it.

Barry put on some shoes and a pair of shorts and set off for Peter's house. I obediently sat down on Barry's all-purpose super-comfortable camping chair while Laetitia fussed over me. I could hear the voices of the others calling Luke's name. I couldn't tell if they were getting closer or further away. All I could tell was that they were calling and calling, but getting no answer.

Laetitia spoke soothingly as she lit the gas stove and prepared to make tea. I've no idea what she said, but her gentle words and her calm air kept the wild, screaming edges of my panic at bay.

Julie was curled up in a sleeping-bag at my feet. After a while she sat up and said, 'Yuck, Mummy. That's soooo gross.'

'What? What's gross?'

She pointed at my arms. 'That is. That's gross.'

I looked down. I never would have thought that the day would come when I would be sitting in a French campsite in the middle of the night, cradling a damp, dirty, smelly running shoe. I considered putting it down, but I found I couldn't. Would this turn out to be my last link with my son? If I put it down, would it be like abandoning him?

Julie made a face and resumed her idle pulling at the grass.

Before long, Cormac came back to check if Luke had appeared. He looked pale and tense. When he saw Luke wasn't there, he kissed me briefly, absently, and set off on his search again.

When did the awful moment arrive when you knew you could no longer rely on the help of friendly, concerned bystanders? When did it move beyond the exaggerated horrors that plague parents, and take years off their lives, but turn out all right in the end? When was the right time to say 'this is really serious'? I wondered aloud if we should try to contact the police.

'Maybe not yet,' said Laetitia. 'Let's just wait and see what Peter says. He's lived here for years, you know. He knows the area almost as well as the locals do. He knows the dangers. He'll know what's best to do.'

I didn't argue. I didn't know how.

The tea was made, and went cold in my hand, and still there was no sign of Luke. Laetitia had almost run out of soothing prattle and was repeating herself, on an endless loop of comfort, and still he wasn't back.

Max, Linda, Deirdre and Dominic came back. Linda came over and sat beside me. Her legs were all scratched and muddy. The strap of her sandal was torn and hung limply across her ankle. 'We went as far as we could. I'm sorry, Jill, there's no sign of him.'

Deirdre smiled a weak smile at me and held my hand. Her face was streaked with tears.

Max and Dominic stood a bit away from me and whispered to each other. I could see by their grim faces that they feared the worst.

A few minutes later, Cormac and Trevor came back. Cormac looked ten years older than he had when he'd come rolling back from the pub, only hours before. He came over to me. 'It's bad, Jill. I'm really worried. This is so unlike Luke. And it's all my fault. I shouldn't have spoken to him the way I did. I was angry, but I shouldn't have spoken like that. It wasn't right. He's just a boy.'

I hugged him. This was no time for blame. 'It's not your fault, Cormac. Let's just get him back. Then we can talk.'

He nodded. 'OK. But this is too big for us. I think it's time we got the police.'

When Cormac, the eternal optimist, was so worried, I knew it was time to be very worried indeed. I clung to him and sobbed. He stroked my head, and I could hear him gulping back his own tears. Were these the precious last moments before we actually knew the worst? Were these the last moments when we still dared to hope?

Just then I heard Peter's voice from the direction of the village. It was the sweetest, most wonderful sound I'd ever heard in my life. 'It's all right. We have him. He's safe.'

I ran towards the voice, along the path to the village. I met them just at the edge of the campsite: Peter, clad in an absurd paisley silk dressing-gown; Barry, still in his T-shirt and shorts; and Luke.

I ran towards them. I threw myself at Luke and hugged him. I cried and kissed his face. He didn't even resist. Cormac and Julie ran over and joined in the embrace, while everyone else stood around and smiled at one another, like the survivors in a disaster movie.

After a few moments, Cormac disentangled himself. 'What's that? Something's sticking into my ribs.'

It was the old runner, which I was still holding to my chest. I looked at Luke's feet. Each was neatly encased in a runner with a purple tick on the side. These runners, incidentally, were significantly cleaner than the one I had clutched to my breast.

Embracing your lost son's runner is one thing. Clinging to someone else's son's smelly shoe is rather different. I threw the filthy thing to the ground. 'Yuck.'

Julie kicked the shoe away. 'Double-mega-smelly yuck with knobs on.'

Everyone laughed, glad of the excuse.

When we finally finished our hug-fest, Peter explained what had happened. 'In the afternoon, I saw this chappie with a group of young French people. And later on, I saw those same French people pitching their tent in a field at the other side of the village. So, when Barry here told me the boy was missing, I decided they might know something. So we set off and found their camp, and lo and behold, wasn't this young chappie sound asleep in the middle of it?'

I looked at Luke. Whatever could have possessed him to go off like that? Everyone had spent the evening telling me how good and sensible he was, and now he'd done this stupid, irresponsible thing. He must have known we'd be worried sick.

He kept his head down and didn't meet our eyes. 'I'm sorry, Mum, Dad,' he said. 'I woke up and couldn't get back to sleep. So I decided to go for a walk. And I met those guys I'd been hanging out with earlier, and I stayed with them for a while. I must have fallen asleep. I'm sorry.'

That wasn't really enough of an explanation for me. After all, I'd spent most of the past hour mentally planning his funeral. But Luke looked tired and rather shocked, and it wasn't fair to demand lengthy explanations, especially in front of all these people. I put my arm around him again.

'It's OK. We'll talk more tomorrow.'

He nodded gratefully, and let me hug him.

Just then Laetitia appeared, resplendent in her white lace, like a ghost from a distant past. 'The kettle's boiled again. I think everyone needs a nice cup of tea. Earl Grey, anyone?'

As we made our way back to her tent, Lauren appeared, with her hair all sweaty and tousled. 'Muuuummy. Where are you? Why is everyone up? If there's a party on, can I have some Coke?'

Chapter Twenty-Nine

In the morning, there was a strange, calm air about the campsite. Everyone moved more slowly, more easily, almost as if rushing would have been unseemly after the drama of the evening before. Dominic and Trevor even delayed their départure, saying that they could catch any train that day, and that there was no need to rush. They lingered, slowly packing up their gear and chatting with everyone else. Linda went to the *boulangerie* and came back with a huge bag of croissants and *pains aux raisins*. Laetitia boiled her kettle over and over again, and made strong coffee for everyone. Peter arrived earlier than necessary and joined us as we sat around in the sunshine. He was still a pompous ass, but, since he was the one who had found Luke last night, I was almost in love with the man. All of a sudden, his eyes didn't seem quite so small, or his voice quite so snooty. I could forgive him anything, because he was the one who had put an end to my worst fears.

We all sat around the campsite and reminisced about the trip. Everyone had a story about a night when they'd drunk too much, or eaten too much, or simply not slept enough. There was a lot of nervous, forced hilarity. There was a lot of talk about blistered hands and sore bottoms and wet feet. No one mentioned the events of the night before.

Eventually, after Laetitia had provided us with enough caffeine to keep us awake for several weeks, the group began to break up. Dominic and Trevor were the first to move, explaining that they had to catch a train. Then Deirdre appeared, already packed and ready to get on the bus. I was surprised. It wasn't like her to get the arrangements wrong. 'We're not going on this trip,' I told her. 'Peter's going to the station first, and then coming back to take us to the airport. We don't leave for ages.'

She hugged me and smiled. 'There's been a small change of plan. I'm not going to the airport. I'm going to the station. I'm going white-water rafting with Dominic and Trevor.'

Now she had me totally flummoxed. 'But...' Of all the questions running around my head, I didn't know which to ask. 'When...?'

'We've just arranged it this morning. It was easy. Dominic and Trevor asked me if I'd like to join them, and I said yes. So they phoned the travel company and booked me a place.'

'But you hardly know them.'

She shrugged. 'What's to know? I don't think they're axe murderers, and anything else I can discover as I go along.'

I grinned at her. 'You old devil. And tell me, is this just about white-water rafting, or is there something more serious going on?'

Deirdre smiled her open, innocent smile. 'At the moment, it's just about the white-water rafting, I promise. But we're going for ten days, and, sure, anything could happen. Couldn't it?'

I looked at Dominic and Trevor. Had they any idea of the designs I was sure my sister had on their genes? Should they be warned?

Still, they were grown men. Surely they could look after themselves.

I hoped their tight Lycra shorts hadn't done them any permanent damage.

Barry and Laetitia decided to leave as well, so Peter wouldn't have to make an extra trip to the station. They piled their luggage into the minibus, and we said our goodbyes. I felt like I was now linked to this unusual bunch of people, because of the part they'd played in my recent drama.

Barry went to check that he'd packed his laptop, and Laetitia came over to Linda and me. We shook hands rather awkwardly, and then hugged. Linda whispered to her, 'You shouldn't let Barry bully you the way he does.'

I shook my head at her. Watching Laetitia being bullied wasn't much fun, but it was hardly our business. Laetitia saw my look. 'It's OK. I don't mind you mentioning it. I know he sounds like a bully, but I just let all that wash over me. You can only be bullied if you allow it to happen. And I don't. You see, my first husband was a dreadful wimp. He did everything I said. Nearly made me sick, it did. Barry and I are very happy together. Underneath it all.'

Hmm. Strange logic. But if she was happy, who were we to argue?

Dominic and Trevor pumped our hands energetically by way of farewell. Just when I thought my shoulder was about to be permanently dislocated, they stopped. I tried to be discreet as I felt my arm, checking for muscular damage. We all exchanged addresses. An exercise in futility and a total waste of paper, of course, but etiquette seemed to demand it.

I hugged Deirdre one more time, and she jumped into the minibus. We waved goodbye, and I almost felt sorry to see them go. We then had an hour to wait until Peter returned to bring us to the airport.

I turned to Luke. 'How about you and me go for a walk?'

'Nah. No, thanks. I'm a bit tired.'

'Luke.'

He tossed his fringe out of his eyes and looked at me. Only then did he see that it wasn't really a request.

He shrugged. 'OK, then. Let's get this over with.'

Cormac looked up from packing his bag. 'Whatever your mother says goes for me too, OK, son?'

Luke nodded.

We walked down to the river, and along the path that Cormac had searched so frantically the night before. Luke spoke first. Maybe he had been paying attention, after all, when Cormac was going on about damage limitation.

'I'm sorry, Mum. I shouldn't have gone off like that. It was stupid. I know you must have been awfully worried.'

I nodded. 'You know what, Luke? Until you have your own children, you will have no appreciation of exactly how worried we were. You can't even begin to imagine how we felt. Or what we thought. Believe me, on occasions like this, parents always think of the worst things first. When children go missing, innocent explanations are very slow to materialise.'

He looked at me again. 'I know, Mum. I'm really, really sorry.'

We walked on for another while. I had a lot to say to Luke. Sadly, I wasn't really sure what exactly I should be saying, much less how I was actually going to say it.

The poor boy even tried to help me along. 'I suppose I'm grounded forever?'

I didn't answer. I couldn't answer.

'It's OK. I don't mind. I deserve it. I won't even give you grief.'

He wouldn't, either. I knew he'd take his punishment without a murmur of complaint.

I turned to look at him. He was at that awkward stage of adolescence when, to put it bluntly, he was no beauty. His skin was blotchy and bumpy. His hair, though washed the day before, was lank and greasy. He'd always had huge brown eyes – one of his best features. One was bloodshot, with a big black ring, almost a bruise, under it. The other was covered by the asymmetrical fringe I hated with a passion. A fine, downy stubble grew like a rash around his upper lip. His teeth would one day be perfect, but for now they were clad in long strips of shiny metal. He'd just had a growth spurt that made his movements seem awkward and stilted. He was wearing revolting baggy denims, the fabric of which would surely have been sufficient to make ten normal pairs of jeans. Over these he had a black T-shirt, with a picture of barbed wire down the front and a large, blood-dripping logo – 'Death'.

I wondered if I could ever love anyone as much as I loved him.

I took the liberty of putting my arm on his shoulder. I had to take advantage of the situation, after all.

'Just tell me, Luke. Why did you go off like that? You've never done anything like that before. You knew how worried we'd be. Why did you do it?'

'I don't know. I just did.' His one visible eye didn't meet mine. I knew he wasn't telling the truth.

'Luke.' My tone made him look up. He even flicked back his fringe, and I got a rare glimpse of both eyes at once. It was like when you're trying to tune the DVD recorder and you get one clear flash, one moment when the picture is visible, before it vanishes once more into a black-and-white fuzz. Luke moved his head slightly, and his fringe dropped back into place.

'What?'

'The least you can do is tell me the truth.'

I knew he was struggling. We came to a bench and I sat down. He stood beside me, his hands plunged deep into his pockets. All of a sudden I felt dreadfully inadequate. My son had something to tell me, and I had no idea what it was. I'd always felt that the essence of good parenting was being clued in, knowing what was going on. The manuals I half-read always wittered on about keeping the lines of communication open. Somehow, I'd lost track of Luke. The lines of communication between us were very definitely down.

Was this all because of the row with Cormac, and the endless niggling that went on between them? Or was it something else? I ran the possibilities through my mind. Was Luke jealous of Julie? Was he being bullied? Was he a bully? Was it school? Was it sex? Drink? Drugs? Sex?

'Come on, Mum,' he said. 'Let's keep walking. It's easier to talk that way.'

I obediently got up and walked along beside him. He walked quickly, without speaking. I had a funny feeling that, if he had had a choice, he'd have kept walking until the Dordogne flowed into the Atlantic. He could make himself a boat out of the yards of denim in his jeans, and sail off out of my life forever.

'Come on, Luke. Spit it out. It can't be that bad.' In my heart I feared it was very bad indeed.

'Mum, I have to say something.' He stopped again.

I felt like shaking him.

'But promise you won't be mad.' Oh, dear. Very, very bad.

I smiled in what I hoped was a reassuring manner. Considering my state of mind, I may have missed the exact look I was striving for. In fact, I probably looked like a total raving lunatic. I felt like jumping up and down and screaming. I tried to speak lightly. 'I'll make no rash promises, but I'll do my best. How about that?'

'OK.' He kept walking and said no more. The parenting manuals said it was important to talk to your teenagers, but what was I supposed to do when he wouldn't talk to me? Wrestle him to the ground and beat the words out of him? Unfortunately, he was a good six inches taller than me, and not likely to submit lightly to such an assault.

I looked at my watch. Was he deliberately running down the clock? Did he think he'd be saved by my morbid fear of missing planes? Did he hope we'd have to turn back without ever having got to the point? Was he going to avoid being on his own with me for the rest of his life?

Finally, he took a deep breath. 'Mum...' He stopped again. A tree blocked our path, and we had to walk around it. I looked at its gnarled bark and wondered if punching it would make me feel better. Probably not.

'Mum...' I held my breath. 'Are you having an affair?'

What? Where had that come from? I had thought all this was about Luke. When had it become about me? And how on earth could I answer him? I'd only been with Dudley once, so it was really more a fling than an affair, but this probably wasn't a good time for a talk on semantics. Anyway, at the back of my mind, I was still kind of hoping that what was between us would develop into an affair, so perhaps it didn't matter anyway.

But how did Luke know about Dudley?

What had I done, that my teenaged son was using adult words like 'affair'?

And what if he told Cormac?

'Mum, answer me.' Luke sounded scared and almost defiant.

I played for time. 'What exactly do you mean, Luke?'

He shook his head in frustration. 'I mean what I said. Are you having an affair?'

This was awful. 'I...'

I stopped. Maybe it was time to get back so we wouldn't miss the plane.

Now he was really cross. 'You're always going on and on about honesty, so why don't you practise what you preach, for a change? Just tell me, Mum. Are you and Max having an affair?'

Whew. Me and Max? At least I could answer that one truthfully without having to shock my impressionable teenager.

I tried to act casual, like the concerned parent with a child who's been the victim of a huge misunderstanding. I couldn't let Luke know that he'd chanced upon the right stick – he'd just managed to catch hold of the wrong end of it.

I smiled what I hoped was the right kind of smile – not patronising, but not showing the slightest trace of guilt, either. 'No, Luke, Max and I are not having an affair. But why do you ask me that?'

He spoke falteringly. His self-righteous outrage was fading. 'You see, I saw you with Max the other night. I'd gone for a walk, remember? And I saw you between the trees, on a bench by the river.'

'But that was—'

He ignored my interruption. 'You were all, like, cuddled up together. He was rubbing your foot. At first I was going to go over. I thought you'd fallen and hurt yourself. I even started to walk towards you. I said your name, but you didn't hear me. I was just going to call you again, but then I heard the way he was talking to you. So I turned around and went back the other way.'

'Oh, Luke. It wasn't as it seemed. It—'

'I tried to forget it. I tried to pretend I had imagined it. I nearly even convinced myself. And then, last night, I was in my tent, and

I couldn't sleep, and you and Linda were having this long, serious talk. I couldn't hear what you were saying, but it sounded like you were fighting. I was sure it was about Max. And I didn't know what to do. I didn't know if I should tell Dad, or what. I didn't know if that would make things better or worse. And I tried and I tried, but I still couldn't get to sleep. I thought I was going to suffocate inside the tent. I had to get away. I knew those French guys were camping in the village. So I went there. I kind of wanted to scare you, too. That was part of it. But I fell asleep. I didn't mean that. Anyway, Mum, tell me the truth. Don't try to bluff me. Are you having an affair with Max?'

The poor boy. He looked far too young to be asking such serious questions. And surely the notion of me having sex with my lawful wedded husband was abhorrent enough to him? How could the poor child be expected to deal with the notion of me romping in naked abandon with another man?

I stopped. He took a few paces ahead; then he turned back to face me.

'Tell me, Mum.'

'Luke. Believe me. I'm not having an affair with Max. I promise you that.'

I could see relief spreading over his young features. Then he looked worried again. 'But what were you doing? I saw you, remember. Dad and Linda weren't there. It was just the two of you. It didn't look like you were discussing the soccer results.'

I sighed. How could I tell him the truth? It was too sordid for such young ears. Could a boy of fourteen even understand the notion of a man in his forties being a serial adulterer? Could he get his head around the idea of anyone in their forties actually being sexually active, let alone desirable? What would he think if he ever knew about me and Dudley?

271

'Luke, it's hard to explain. We'd both had a lot of wine. But nothing happened between us. I hurt my foot and he was rubbing it. It was a bit inappropriate – a bit stupid, even – but nothing more. Can you believe that?'

I could see he wanted very much to believe it. He took a small coin out of his pocket and examined it closely. Was he going to toss it to see if he trusted me or not? Was my fate as a mother to be decided by the random spinning of a five-cent piece?

He tossed the coin into the river. It made a 'plink' sound and disappeared in a small splash. He looked up and smiled at me. 'Yes, Mum. I believe it. And I'm sorry. I shouldn't have asked.'

I put my arm around him. All the trauma was nearly worth it, for the luxury of being able to touch my son again. I hugged him and stroked his lank hair. And, as I did so, I knew I wouldn't see Dudley again. It just wasn't worth it. I had too much to lose. I wasn't going to toy with my family's happiness – or my own – any more. I'd find a way to work through my differences with Cormac. If we made the effort, I knew we could be happy again.

And I'd put Dudley where he belonged – in my past.

Luke was subtly trying to wriggle free of my gasp. I released him. I could happily have held him for an hour, but that would have been asking a bit much, even of a good boy like him. And besides, if I did, we'd miss our plane.

'Don't fret in silence about stuff you don't understand, Luke. Always ask. Don't worry, and don't run off and frighten us all half to death. Always ask what's going on. And I'll always be as honest as I possibly can. OK?'

He smiled. 'OK.'

There was still one more thing. 'Luke, you know this thing with you and your dad?'

He stiffened slightly. 'Yeah?'

'He loves you, you know. He loves all of us. He's just let himself be sucked into the business. It's my fault too. I should have done something sooner. When we get back, we'll sort something out. We can make things better. Can you just, er...'

He grinned. 'Back off for a while?'

I nodded. 'Yeah, that's it.'

'Sure thing. Leave it to me. I'll be the perfect, submissive son...for at least a week. And, Mum – tell me the worst. How long am I grounded for?'

I had to think. What business had I grounding him? Surely I should be grounded for my own bad behaviour? One adulterous act, and weeks of lecherous thoughts – what kind of a grounding did that deserve?

And this thing of Luke running off...that was hardly a grounding situation, but still, something had to be seen to be done. We didn't want to be starting any dangerous precedents here.

I grinned at him. 'Actually, you're not grounded at all.' He grinned back at me, before I continued. 'But...'

His grin faded.

'You have to be really, really nice to Lauren for the rest of the day.'

He groaned and pretended to clutch his chest in agony. 'No. Not that. Anything but that. It's too hard. Don't make me.'

We both laughed, and turned back towards the campsite.

It was time to go home.

Chapter Thirty

We stood in the car park of Cork airport. It didn't seem like very long since we had been there before. Still, a lot of water had flowed under the bridge in the past fourteen days (so to speak). Our cars were parked near each other, almost as if they'd been looking out for each other while we were gone. Max and Cormac were busy loading the suitcases into the boots and discussing the latest Premier League transfer news. Lauren and Julie, the best of friends now that they had to part, were swapping e-mail addresses and planning long weekends in each other's house. Luke, still on his best behaviour, offered to go to the pay machine with the car-park tickets. Linda and I leaned on her car and smiled at each other. There had been times on the holiday when I would cheerfully have throttled her, but now the prospect of leaving her was strangely daunting.

'It's been great,' I said. This was partly true. There had been some great moments, and perhaps the less wonderful moments would turn out to be valuable in their own way. In some respects, it had been quite a voyage of discovery.

Linda laughed. 'You mean it was great, considering.'

I shrugged. 'Yeah, whatever. It was great, considering.'

We were quiet for a moment. There was a lot I wanted to ask her, and a lot I wanted to tell her. Very little of this was suitable for a car-park conversation. We needed to run off to a trendy wine bar, get sozzled and have a sentimental heart-to-heart. There was no chance of this happening, of course. I wondered when we would next get the chance to spend time together.

I moved a little way from the others, and Linda followed. 'Is everything OK with you and Max?' I asked. 'You looked like you were having a serious talk on the plane.'

She shrugged. 'Yeah. We were. He's promised to be faithful from now on.'

'Hey, that's fantastic news.' I was genuinely pleased for her. I reached out and gave her a brief hug.

She pulled away gently, and shook her head. 'I wouldn't get too excited if I were you. He does that every year after our holidays. Must be the sun or something. Or maybe it's the wine.'

I put my hand on her shoulder. 'Maybe this time he really means it.'

She gave a funny smile. 'He means it every year. That's the awful thing. He really thinks he knows how to be faithful. And he'll try for a while. By Christmas, though, he'll be back to his old tricks. Maybe even sooner, if the right girl comes along. He'll smile his sweet smile, and all his empty promises to me will vanish like petals in the wind.'

I squeezed her shoulder. I didn't know what to say.

She smiled at me again. 'It's OK. I told you before. I know what I'm dealing with. I know I have to live with it, or leave him. So I live with it. That's not going to change. It's not so bad. We'll keep on muddling along. I might even take a toy-boy for myself sometime.'

She tossed her head and laughed. It was the Linda I'd always loved, defiant and confident, no matter what.

We hugged, and I was shocked to feel a small tear trickle down my face. When we let go, Linda too was surreptitiously rubbing her eyes. If our young selves could have witnessed the scene, we would have screamed with laughter and derision.

Max and Cormac had finished packing up the cars. Max came over and tapped his watch. 'What are you two like? You've had fourteen days to talk. What could there be left to say?'

Linda grinned at him. 'You'll never know, my darling. And what you don't know can't hurt you.'

He pulled her to him, and they embraced. They both looked happy. Maybe they'd be all right after all.

When eventually Linda and Max disentangled themselves, we all climbed into our cars. We wound down the windows, called our last goodbyes and set off.

We followed the others down the broad sweep of the airport hill, and waved madly as they took the last exit on the round-about and headed for home. We continued on to the Limerick road.

Cormac wriggled as he settled himself in his seat. 'Well, all's well that ends well. Now, anyone know the exact dates of next year's World Cup finals? We'd better book early, or all the best places will be gone.'

From the back seat there was a loud chorus of moans and groans and muttered threats to call Childline. I smiled to myself. It was good to be back.

Chapter Thirty-One

Next day, Cormac got up early for work, already back into his old routine. Before he left, he brought me up a cup of tea. I sat up and drank it while he cleaned his teeth. He came back into the bedroom. 'What are your plans for the day?'

I shrugged. 'Not much. Unpack. Wash. Iron. I might give Rita a shout and see how she got on in Kilkee.'

He sat on the bed beside me. 'You know, Jill, I loved being with you for the past two weeks.'

I sipped my tea. It was too milky, and almost cold, but the generosity of the gesture made up for this. 'Yes, it was nice, wasn't it?'

He took my hand, and I spilled some of the tea onto the duvet cover. Another job for my list. *Change duvet cover.*

Cormac didn't seem to notice. He was looking at me closely. He seemed sort of nervous. 'You know, Jill, before we left, in those last few weeks before the holidays, I was worried about you.'

'Why?' I wasn't sure I wanted an answer to that particular

question, but I felt I had to ask it anyway. Some things are required in this sort of conversation.

'I don't know. You were kind of preoccupied. Distant. You weren't yourself at all.'

I spoke as lightly as I could. 'Well, you know me. I always get a bit worked up before the holidays.'

He shook his head. 'No. It wasn't that. This was something different. You know' – he gave a small laugh – 'for a while I was even thinking there might be someone else.'

I sipped my cold tea again, glad I had something to do. I couldn't meet his eyes. 'That's ridiculous.'

Ridiculous, but true.

He smiled. 'I know. Anyway, I feel like you're back now, and that's what matters.'

I sipped more tea. Time to change the subject. 'Are you all set for the Roche deal?'

He laughed. 'Max was right. Fuck the Roche deal.'

'But you worked so hard for it. It means a lot to you.'

He shook his head. 'That night when Luke was missing, I realised what means a lot to me. If anything had happened to him, regrets would have haunted me for the rest of my life – all the things I never did with him, all the nights I came home after he was in bed, all his dreadful band practices I deliberately missed. I thought that providing a good home would compensate for all that. I thought material goods could make up for all those lapses on my part.'

'You have given us a lovely home. We all appreciate that.'

He shrugged. 'Big deal. That's not enough. It took that fright with Luke to show me that. You've been such a good mother, I let myself forget that Luke and Julie need a father too.'

'But...'

He ignored me. 'Anyway, things are going to change around here.'

'How?'

'I did a lot of thinking last night. Linda was right, you know.'

I had to laugh. 'Well, I never thought the day would come when you'd say that Linda was right. Whatever did she say or do that impressed you so much?'

He laughed too. 'Now don't get me wrong, I still think she's totally cracked and far too adventurous for her own good – but I'm prepared to concede to her on one point.'

I smiled. 'I can't wait to hear this.'

'Well, it's that phrase of hers. The one she uses about a hundred times a day.'

I grinned. '"Sorry about this, Lauren's just a bit tired"? Or "I'm thirsty, whose round is it"?'

Cormac laughed out loud. 'Now you mention it, I heard a lot of those over the past few weeks, but that's not what I meant. I meant the other one – you know, "Life's too short..."'

'You're right. She does say that a lot.'

Unfortunately, that was the phrase that had led me into phoning Dudley from France. And it was that kind of thinking that had made me have that fling with him in the first place. That kind of thinking could be very dangerous indeed.

Cormac continued, 'Anyway, what I've decided is that life's too short to spend twelve hours a day working.'

I felt the first glimmer of hope. 'So what are you going to do?'

'You know Johnny in the shop has been muttering about retiring for years? Well, I've decided to make him an offer he can't refuse.'

'And that will help how, exactly?'

'I'm going to get someone new in. Someone younger. Someone with a bit of go in him. Someone who can really take charge when I'm not there. And as soon as he's settled in, I can spend more time with you and the kiddies.'

I laughed. 'Is that a threat or a promise?'

He laughed too. 'It's very much a promise.'

'I promise to keep you to it.'

He smiled. 'That's a deal. And be sure to remind me of Luke's next concert. I want to be there.'

'You'll hate it, you know.'

'I know. But that's not really the point, is it?'

He leaned over and kissed me. 'I love you, Jill.'

I put my arms around him. 'I love you too, Cormac.'

He went off, closing the bedroom door behind him. I put my cup on the bedside table and snuggled back under the covers. Maybe everything was going to be all right.

Telling Cormac about Dudley would be a bad idea, I knew that. It would just have to be my little secret. The only secret in my otherwise relatively blameless life.

Chapter Thirty-Two

After a short, indulgent snooze, I went downstairs. Luke and Julie, who were still on school holidays, lingered in their beds. I didn't mind. They were tired after travelling, and I was quite happy to potter around the house for a while on my own.

I emptied all the suitcases, and rescued the few things that hadn't been used and were still clean. Then I sorted the mountain of dirty clothes and loaded the washing machine.

Just then the phone rang.

'Hi, Sis.'

When had she started that stupid habit of calling me 'Sis'? And when was she going to stop? 'Hi, Deirdre. Is something wrong?'

'No. Nothing's wrong. Just checking that you got home safely. Can't your favourite sister do that?'

'I'm sorry. Of course you can. We're all fine. Ten more washing-machine loads and it will be as if we never left home at all. But how are you? Any news?'

She laughed. 'Well, everything's fine here, too. We've had our orientation meeting, and we've signed our lives away, but we don't go rafting until tomorrow. They're giving us twenty-four hours to contemplate our doom. They're probably hoping that half of us will get cold feet and head off home.'

'You know that's not what I'm asking. Have you any real news? How are Dominic and Trevor doing? Is there anything happening?'

She laughed again. 'Well, Dominic has to be eliminated. Turns out he's a priest, which might make things rather too complicated.'

I laughed too. 'I think you're right. I think your situation might well be complicated enough without involving the clergy.'

'But Trevor...' She hesitated.

'But Trevor what?'

'Well, we had a lovely night last night. Dominic went home early, and Trevor and I went out for dinner together. He's a widower. His wife died ten years ago. They didn't have any children.'

I thought of the over-enthusiastic, gauche man with the bad dress sense. Could he really be the man of my sister's dreams?

Deirdre continued, 'He's really nice when you get to talk to him. You know, kind of gentle, and shy. He's...well, he's lovely.'

I had to laugh. She sounded all dreamy, not at all the logical sister I knew and loved. 'He sounds just perfect. You go for it, Deirdre.'

'You know, Sis, I think I will.' Her deep chuckle made me laugh out loud.

I wondered if it was too soon to start knitting baby clothes.

I was just emptying the first load of clean clothes into a basket when Rita arrived at the front door. I was delighted to see her. We hugged briefly, and I ran to put on the kettle before she could tell me she wanted to do something energetic like going for a walk. The canoeing had been enough exercise to last me for months.

Rita sat at the kitchen table. 'So?'

I feigned innocence. 'So what?'

She laughed. 'Come on. You can't bluff me. I know you too well. You went off on holidays all stressed and worried, but now you look tanned and happy, so it can't have been so bad. Just tell me.'

I put a cup of coffee in front of her and joined her at the table. I produced the last of the fancy biscuits Luke had bought for me in the duty-free the day before, and we ate them from the packet.

'It was fine. More than fine, actually. We had a great time.'

She sighed. 'Pity. I'm very happy for you, but it doesn't make for a very interesting story, does it?'

I grinned at her. 'Well, there were a few isolated incidents.'

Her face lit up. 'Great. Let's hear it. Tell Auntie Rita everything.'

So I took a deep breath, sat back in my chair and told her almost everything.

She was suitably shocked and sympathetic when I told her about the fright Luke had given us on the last night. She was pleased when I told her of Cormac's plans to work shorter hours. I told her about Deirdre's sudden arrival in France, but decided to skip the bit about her trying to get pregnant – I hadn't quite got my head around that one myself yet. Then I lightened the tone of the conversation by telling her about some of Linda's escapades – the *boules* incident, Peter's unplanned swim.

Rita was impressed. 'Hey, I've got to meet this girl. You can't go on keeping us apart. She sounds like great crack.'

I nodded. 'Oh, she is. There's never a dull moment when Linda's around. But anyway, there's more.'

Rita leaned forward. 'Great. I'm all ears.'

So I told her about the long chat Linda and I had had about our different versions of our shared past. And I told her about the incident with Max.

Her eyes opened in mock horror. 'Oh, no. Adultery on the Dordogne.' She was smiling, but something about her reaction made me glad I'd never told her about my little fling with Dudley. Rita was too honest to be comfortable with that kind of knowledge.

I raised my hand to stop her. 'Hey, don't get carried away. It was only attempted adultery. I refused his advances.'

'Yeah, but were you tempted at all?'

I shrugged. 'Nah. Not so's you'd notice.'

I told her how Linda knew about Max's serial infidelity, and we discussed that for a while.

Then Rita said, 'Oh, I forgot to tell you. My painter's an awful old gossip. Every time he arrives at our house, he has a new story about Dudley and Miranda. He said he was there last week on his own, and he answered the phone. It was Brown Thomas, saying that Miranda was now on the waiting list for the latest Prada handbag, and that she should be getting it by Christmas.'

I laughed out loud. 'So you're saying she was on a waiting list to go on a waiting list to buy a handbag that probably costs as much as a small car?'

Then I felt really bad. After all, her husband had slept with me and with God knew who else. Who was I to mock her because she sought some comfort in shopping?

Rita leaned forward and lowered her voice. 'There's more. It seems like poor old Miranda won't be here at Christmas to pick up her handbag.'

Now she had my interest. 'But why?'

Rita lowered her voice even further. 'Now, this is real gossip, and I shouldn't even be telling you.'

I smiled. 'So why are you telling me?'

She hesitated. 'Well…because of that night in the South Court. I know there was more going on there than I could see. So maybe it's best that you see this guy's feet of clay. In case you have any lingering, you know, feelings for him.'

I didn't answer, so she continued. 'Anyway, this is all from my painter, but he's usually reliable, so I'd say it's true. He was working in the garage one day last week, and Miranda and Dudley were in the back garden. They were having a huge row.'

My heart sank. Could she have found out about me? 'Did he say what they were rowing about?'

'Of course. That's the interesting part. It seems some big-shots were over from Japan, doing business with Dudley's firm. And Dudley tried it on with one of the wives. She was having none of it, and she told her husband. There was a huge scandal. Senior management got involved. Sounds to me like it wasn't the first time. So now he's not taking over the Limerick plant after all. He's been sidestepped and sent to some small town in the Midwest of America.'

'And Miranda?' I felt sorry for this woman I'd never met – even though I, too, had been part of her betrayal.

'The painter says she's going with him. The dream house is on the market already. Seems like poor old Miranda's taking "for better and for worse" a bit too seriously. She probably had the "love is forgiving" reading at her wedding, and she's taking it to heart.'

I put my head down. So I hadn't been special to Dudley. I hadn't been the missed opportunity from his past, the love of his life whom he had let slip from his grasp in a moment of youthful folly. I had just been a convenient distraction, a silly, bored woman seduced by his good looks and his easy charm. Would I really have been prepared to throw my marriage away for a shallow man like him?

All of a sudden, my fling with Dudley seemed like a silly mistake, and with this thought came a flash of inspiration. I knew that I'd actually got over him a very long time ago. What I hadn't got over was the fact that he had left me for Linda. That was what had hurt so badly for all those years. I had a funny feeling that, if Dudley had left me for someone else, he'd have remained where he belonged – firmly in my past.

Rita tapped my hand lightly. 'Hello? Are you still there?'

I looked up. 'Sorry, my mind just wandered a bit.'

She suddenly looked concerned. 'Hey. Maybe I shouldn't have told you about Dudley. He doesn't still mean something to you, does he?'

I looked her in the eye. 'Don't worry, Rita. Dudley Adamson means nothing to me. Nothing at all.'

I made fresh coffee, and we had more biscuits. We laughed for a while over Rita's trip to Kilkee, and then she got up to leave. 'I'd love to linger, but I've got to get back to Fiona. She's been behaving herself of late, but I still need to keep a close eye on her.'

I walked to the front door with her. 'Tennis as usual in the morning?'

She nodded. 'Sure. I've missed our game. Oh, and don't forget: book club is on Thursday night.'

I made a face. 'I had forgotten. *Girl with a Pearl Earring*, isn't it?'

She nodded. 'Did you like it?'

'Like it? I haven't even opened it. My holidays were kind of busy. I only read one book. What's it about? Could I bluff them, do you think?'

Rita smiled. 'Don't worry. I'll distract them by telling them about you and Max. They'll forget all about the book, I promise you.'

I laughed. 'You're a true friend, but no, thanks. I think I'll just read the book. I've got a few days.'

'Whatever.'

I waved goodbye and closed the front door behind her. I could hear the sound of Julie splashing and singing in the shower, and the first strains of music were leaking under Luke's door. I went back into the kitchen and sat at the table. I ate the last biscuit and crumpled up the packet. It was lovely to see Rita, and to settle back into my life again.

Moving to Limerick, and leaving Linda behind, had been the best thing I'd ever done. But I was older, and wiser, and more mature now. Now I could cope.

I leaned over, picked up the phone and dialled.

'Linda, it's me, Jill. How are things?'

'Hey, Jill. It's so great to hear from you. What's happening?'

I smiled. The warmth of her voice was wonderful to experience. I could picture her, jigging around in her hallway, wearing some skimpy, unsuitable outfit, grinning happily.

'Oh, you know – nothing happening, really. I'm just settling back in at home, wrestling with the washing machine. How many loads have you done?'

She gave a long sigh. 'Oh, Jill. What are you like? Why are you talking about laundry? Life's too short to spend sunny days like this washing.'

I smiled. 'So what are you doing, then, on this fine sunny day?'

'Well, I was just doing my nails, and then Lauren and I are going to feed the ducks in the park, and after that Max and I are going for lunch in that lovely new restaurant in Bridge Street. I might do the washing tomorrow. If I get around to it.'

I felt a funny, unfamiliar pang. I was missing her. I spoke quickly. 'I'd love to see you. How about we do lunch next week? There's a lovely little café in Buttevant. We'll meet early, and get back in time to pick the girls up from school. How about it? Does Friday suit?'

Her voice was warm. 'Fantastic, Jill. That's so fantastic. I can't wait to see you again.'

We chatted for a few minutes and hung up. I smiled to myself, picked up the basket I'd abandoned earlier, and went to hang out the washing.

With her wild red hair, hippy clothes and high Nelly bicycle,
Claire is known as a loveable eccentric. Neighbours and friends
in her Cork suburb regard her as 'colourful' and 'interesting',
avoiding words like 'downright odd'.

But Claire feels a fraud. The illusion of suburban bliss is just that
- an illusion. And one that papers over the cracks of the past.
Fifteen years before, she had been a carefree student backpacking
around the Greek islands, looking for no more than the hottest
clubs and a bit of romance. But something changed that, shatter-
ing her innocence forever. Now all those years later, the dreams
have returned, and Claire finds she has to go back to Mykonos to
lay the ghosts of the past to rest - even if that means sacrificing
her marriage.

There, it will take the warmth of the sun, the easy pace of life
and the love of a wonderful man to help her.